Praise for
Desperate Hoodwives

"A can't-miss new series . . ."

—*Essence* magazine

"Let's just say this sassy, sexy, streetwise story could kick some butt over on Wisteria Lane." (Listed as REQUIRED READING)

—*New York Post*

"The authors hold back little in this cautionary tale dripping with sex, vice, and yearning."

—*Publishers Weekly*

"A wonderfully written story with colorful characters that will keep you flipping the pages—I loved it."

—K'wan, *Essence* bestselling author

"Move over Wisteria Lane. Drama and scandal have permanently moved to Bentley Manor. *Desperate Hoodwives* is a wonderfully written novel that is sassy, smart, and unadulterated!"

—Danielle Santiago, *Essence* bestselling author

"A sexy tale that will keep you gasping as you turn the pages . . ."

—Miasha, *Essence* bestselling author

Praise for
Shameless Hoodwives

"*Shameless Hoodwives* by Meesha Mink and De'Nesha Diamond is listed as one of the magazine's TOP 10 Summer Sizzlers!!!"

—*Essence* magazine

"Diamond and Mink deliver a compelling hood tale that is a true page-turner."

—RAWSISTAZ

"This is the ghetto Wisteria Lane, called Bentley Manor, and anything can and will happen here."

—Coast 2 Coast Readers

"Invigorating plots magnify the intensity of each scene that creates a breathless anticipation as you delve further and further into the sordid lives of the people that occupy this notorious neighborhood."

—Urban Reviews

Praise for
The Hood Life

"A great page-turner! It's easy to get lost in this novel. The story is so vivid . . . it will keep you on the edge of your seat the whole ride of this book about four men in their story of struggle in Urban America."

—Savvy Book Club

"A scandalous tale of four men who found themselves always at the wrong end of the track. They ultimately got what they deserved. This book was definitely a page-turner."

—Q.U.E.E.N.S. Book Club of Mississippi

Also by Meesha Mink

The Hood Life
Shameless Hoodwives
Desperate Hoodwives

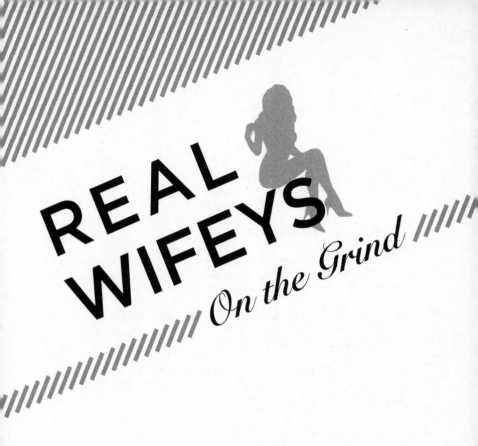

REAL WIFEYS

On the Grind

MEESHA MINK

A Touchstone Book
Published by Simon & Schuster
New York London Toronto Sydney

Touchstone
A Division of Simon & Schuster, Inc.
1230 Avenue of the Americas
New York, NY 10020

Designed by Akasha Archer

Manufactured in the United States of America

ISBN 978-1-61129-269-5

To the Hoodwives fans, I thank you all times a million.

Prologue

It's the key to life
Money, power, and respect
Whatchu' need in life.

—Lox and Lil' Kim, "Money, Power & Respect"

I'm young but far from dumb.

My ass done been broke, busted, and disgusted damn near all of my twenty-two years. Hunger pains, bummy clothes, and moving from one shithole to the next *used* to be my best friend until my mama left me and I lived with my grandma, Mama Bit. My life with Mama Bit was much better but it still was filled with strugglin'. Fuck that and fuck *it*. I been done had enough of that dumb shit for real.

People see me and they judge me. She wearing this or that. She is this or that. She thinks she this or that. I used to care. They don't know shit about where I been and hate on where I'm going.

I learned early and often that this thing called life—especially up in the hood—is all about getting your shit straight by any means necessary. You do what you gotta do. Some of the shit is right and a lot of it is wrong. Yes, I like nice things. I'm the first bitch to admit that I ain't never had shit, so I ain't used to shit . . . and now I'm all about getting shit. The only thing my mama and daddy gave me was my good looks and not shit else.

Sighing, I locked my eyes on my reflection in the mirror hanging on the back of my bedroom door. I'm fine as hell—not being conceited or stuck-up or none of the big-head shit. I'm just being real. I'm fine.

But it's not enough.

It's never been enough.

Before my eyes, the image of me at five showed up in the mirror. Skinny. Crust around my eyes and my mouth. Jeans too high and too tight. My hair looking like a dirty cotton ball with blonde tips. My skin bright enough to make people hate me for no damn reason.

Sometimes I still heard the laughter when kids teased my ass in school.

Sometimes I still felt the shame of a crackhead mama and an invisible white daddy.

I turned away from the mirror and my past. I can't let none of that shit get at me. It's in the past. I ain't going back. But trust and believe I've already seen and fucking survived my worst days. Life was better. More was coming for me.

I know this because a bitch like me *ain't* accepting anything less.

Money

1

And we can pop bottles all night
Baby you could have whatever you like. . . .

—T.I., "Whatever You Like"

"Whaddup, Goldie?"

I smiled and waved at the security guard in his navy rent-a-cop uniform as I strolled into On Your Back—one of my favorite clothing stores in downtown Newark. I completely ignored that hungry-ass "please let me fuck you" look in his eyes. He had a better chance of winning the lottery than of getting anywhere near *my* pussy. *That's* the realest talk ever.

Armina, one of the store's three personal shoppers and the owner's daughter, was at my side quicker than a crack-head could outrun the police. "Hello, Miss Goldie. Looking for anything in particular?" she asked, that unmistakable East Coast accent present.

"Just felt like shopping," I told her as I removed the plush faux silver fox I wore over a matching silk turtleneck and fit-ted dark denims.

"Hurts to be you, Boo," Armina teased lightly as she took the coat from me. "We just got in a new shipment that I *know* you're going to love."

I didn't do shit but smile as she led me to one of three small rooms at the rear of the store. On Your Back was definitely trying to take shopping to the next level for those dropping at least a grand or better. Butter-soft leather club chairs, flat-screen TV, and polished hardwood floors awaited. I didn't have shit to do but accept my crystal flute of champagne she poured for me, slide my ass in the chair, and turn the TV to BET or some shit. I waited for Armina to bring back items she hoped I'd want to purchase.

Not bad for a twenty-two-year-old chick like me without job the first. Oh, I gets mine.

Just watch me work.

There was a double knock to the door and I swiveled in the chair just as the door swung open. "Whaddup?" I asked, eyeing Damion "Dyme" Gunners, the six-foot-nine owner of On Your Back.

He smiled, flashing his white teeth, as he closed and locked the door. "You . . . as always," he told me, unzipping his tailored Gucci slacks as he walked over to me with his dick growing hard as a motherfucka in his strong hand.

"Now *that's* what's up," I whispered to him before swirling my tongue around his thick smooth tip. I could smell the faint scent of his cologne in the soft hairs surrounding that rock-hard motherfucka as I pulled all of him into my mouth.

The feel of his dick throbbing against my tongue as I deep-throated him made me squirm in my damn chair. Dyme was every bit of forty-five—silver hair and all—but his face was still fine, his body was still hard, his dick game ain't no joke, and this motherfucka knew how to make me cum a hundred different fucking ways. So what he's twenty-three years older than me. Humph, that's just twenty-three years of this motherfucka getting his dick and money game right to take care of me.

"Suck that dick," he whispered down to me, bringing his hand up to twist in my doobie-wrapped, mid-back-length auburn hair with goldish blond streaks.

I squeezed his thick dick tight as hell with my hand as I pulled it from my mouth and leaned back to look up at him with much attitude. "Do you tell *that* bitch to suck your dick?" I asked his ass nasty as hell. "What I tell you 'bout that, huh?"

"Man, come on Goldie," he said to me, begging and shit while he tried to steer his dick—still covered with my IMAN lip gloss—back near my mouth.

I let his dick go so hard that that motherfucka bobbed up and down like a diving board. "Sit down," I ordered him, as I stood up and stepped aside to let him do as I said.

I dropped my hundred-dollar silk panties and jeans before I climbed on his lap and onto that dick that was standing up like a fucking soldier. Inch by inch that dick filled me up real good and got my pussy slurping like a wet-ass kiss.

"Damn, Goldie," he swore, his hands digging so deep into my ass that I knew he was gone leave prints and shit. Fuck it. When it's on, its motherfuckin' on.

"Pussy good?" I asked him, before I leaned down and sucked his whole mouth into mine as I started twirling my hips and making my pussy slide up and down on him.

He slapped my ass hard as hell. And I liked it. *We* liked it.

He knew what I liked and I knew what he wanted. We oughta. I been fucking this nigga since I was sixteen. Six fucking years. Matter fact, On Your Back was all my idea, including these personal-shopper rooms. Oh, he's married, but fuck that old bitch. Trust and believe it's *all* about me.

Niggas in the street respect Dyme. He never sold drugs, his money was always legit, but young heads looked up to him. Five businesses, several cars, a few houses, and a bad bitch like me locking this pussy down for him and only him. Dyme was the shit for real and he didn't take no shit either.

But see this pussy right here done had this grown-ass nigga with street cred in my arms crying quite a few times after I fucked the hell out of him. Our sex was *crazy*. Our love was crazier.

"You gone spend the night tonight?" I asked him, licking the sweat from his upper lip as I rode that dick hard enough to make me lose my breath.

"Goldie—"

I bit my bottom lip and fucked him harder. "Yes or no?" I asked him in between pants.

"Goldie—"

I put my hand over his mouth tight as hell and rode him angry and horny as hell just long enough until I was cumming all over that dick. As soon as I busted my nut I hopped off that dick and left the air to blow him. I don't like to be told no—straight out or otherwise. Shit, I got me. Fuck it.

Dyme held up his hands, his diamond jewelry 'bout bright as the sun. "Oh you gone leave me hanging?" he asked, his dick standing up like a big-ass chocolate-dipped banana.

I reached in my oversized gray patent leather purse for my packet of moist towelettes—fuck walking around sex funky 'til I get my ass back to the house. After I cleaned up a bit and got back in my clothes, I still didn't say shit as I held out my hand to him and wiggled my manicured fingertips like only something heavy would stop them.

Like clockwork this nigga went right in them pockets and

peeled me off some cash. "You want the rest of this pussy and that nut that got your balls big as hell, then you come lay next to me tonight and get it, Dyme. And I'm not playing. Why I had to spend another Christmas and another damn New Year's Eve by myself? Why I always gotta sleep alone? Let that ugly, hairy, big-titty bitch know how it feel to hug pillows all fucking night. Fuck the dumb shit, for real."

"Goldie, baby—"

I turned and counted my money. "Go on and sneak out like you snuck your ass up in here, Dyme."

I heard his clothes rustling behind me. I tried to swallow my disappointment. Straight up, this old dude mean the world to me. I put my whole life on hold for this man. Shit, I even dropped out of high school to lay up and fuck him all day while the wife thought he was running his businesses. I done had two abortions because he wanted me to. He was my first and only dick. I never tripped and dipped on him. Never. I kept all this pussy for him. Shit, I don't know who the *real* dumb bitch was: me or her?

Me and this nigga right here been through it all.

I felt him walk up behind me, but I gave him nothing but my back.

"Man, Goldie, stop tripping," Dyme said to me, sounding aggravated as he wrapped his arm around my waist and tried to pull me closer to him.

And the feel of his hand was warm through my clothes. I tingled where he touched me. My heart was racing like all of him was new to me. And when he bent down to press a kiss to my cheek, I can't even lie that I didn't tilt my face up to him.

"You know I love you, Goldie," he whispered in my ear.

I cut my eyes up to look at him, right in those eyes of his with those long lashes that usually fucks me right up each and every damn time. "Then I'll see you tonight, Dyme," I told him, holding strong. *Man, fuck that.*

He pressed his lips down on mine real quick before he turned and eased the door open to peek out.

The devil was right up in my ear telling me to push his ass out the door and make a big scene for his daughter and employees to see . . . but I didn't do it. I turned so I didn't see this nigga I loved to death slip out the door. I know he made his way to his office at the end of the hall. *Might be calling his wife with the sweet scent of my pussy still on his dick.*

I shook off the tears that filled my honey-colored eyes. I shoved the pain in my heart back down. This shit ain't nothing new . . . but even after six fucking years it hurt like a motherfucka. A no-good motherfucka. A no-good double-dipping motherfucka.

By the time Armina knocked and rolled a clothing rack with about five outfits into the room, I had my shit back together. The smell of our sex was covered by several spritzes from the square bottle of Gucci Rush from my bag. My hair brushed back into place. My lip gloss replaced on my mouth.

"I don't know what your budget is today but I pulled you the best we have in the store right now," Armina said, looking every bit like Dyme.

I circled the rack, touching this and that. "How much for all of it?" I asked, fingering a fly-ass charcoal silk ruffled blouse.

Armina didn't flinch. "About three grand," she answered, straight on point.

I dug out the stash her daddy gave me and counted off thirty one-hundred-dollar bills. “I’ll take it all and keep the change,” I told her, reaching for my glass of champagne to toast her for her taste and secretly toast her father for paying for it all.

By the time I was done with my shopping, the winter sun of January was beginning to set. My ankles and ass hurt from walking in these heels all day. Shit, I was more than happy to ease back into my hardtop convertible 2005 Lexus SC 430—a gift from Dyme for my eighteenth birthday. It was an older luxury vehicle, but the custom cherry-red paint and tricked-out interior—gold with red leather details—made up for it. That day I was so happy it felt like I didn’t ever go without Dyme’s dick in me: ass, mouth, or pussy.

He made sure it was maintained well and I ate the miles up wherever I had to go. Fuck taxis *and* New Jersey Transit. I loved my car and what I loved the most was the fact that this bitch was all mine. In my own name and all. Of course, Dyme thought he was slick and shit but I knew he ain’t had no choice but to put the car in my name or his wife might snoop out a whip that ain’t parked in their garage. Like I always tell him, I’m young but far from dumb.

That’s why it’s time for him to take me up out of my two-bedroom apartment in King Court (short for Martin Luther King Court Housing Projects) and put me in my own house . . . *our* own house. Not that I hated living in King Court. Shee-it, most times it was fun as hell. Shit *stayed* popping off in that motherfucka. But a bitch like me deserved that big pretty-ass brick five-bedroom motherfucka where they lived—*and* the big-dick motherfucka who lived in it and paid the bills for it.

Releasing a sigh filled with a lot of the bullshit Dyme had put me through, I drove my Lexus off the snow-filled streets outside King Court and onto one of the parking spots lined up outside the buildings. I made sure to activate my alarm. I wasn't tryna to have Lil Mook and the rest of his crew joyriding and fucking drifting in my shit. Them little motherfuckas could steal a car in ten seconds or less. Then have the nerve to videotape they shit and put it up on YouTube. Hella bold.

Grabbing my garment bags from the trunk, I paused for a sec to peep King Court. The damn brick seemed to go on for days with all the low-rise buildings planted around this concrete jungle. The windows looked crazy as hell with all the different-colored curtains or sheets hanging at them. Even though it was winter and cold as shit, snow-covered air-conditioning units stuck out waiting to chill those wanting to beat the summer heat when it came through. The last of the dirty snow was pushed up in piles looking so different from the inches of still white snow that fell on the ground earlier that morning. Stray dogs and cats strolled through like they ass paid rent. Graffiti on the brick walls. Glass broken on the streets. The aluminum fence surrounding this motherfucka making it look more like prison than it already did. People bundled up in their winter coats and hats chilling outside like it wasn't cold as fuck.

I can't front and say I ain't had a good-ass time up in this bitch. Home fucking sweet home. I'm gone miss this brick bitch when I move into my own shit.

"Goldie!"

I stopped and looked up to see my best friend Yummy's

crazy ass hanging out the window. Her shoulder-length weave was dyed bright pink this week, so her ass was always hard to miss. Her name ought to be Rainbow Bright from all them crazy colors she be wearing in her hair. "He-e-ey," I hollered back up to her.

"Come up real quick."

My eyes dropped back down to the front door of her building. It had STAY OUT spray painted on it and I already knew that motherfucka was locked tight. I hated fucking around with Yummy's building. Baseem and his crew of dopeboys had her building on lock—bold as a motherfucka. They was on some real *New Jack City*–type shit.

"I'll be back," I lied, knowing damn well my plan was to take my ass home and set the scene for Dyme spending the night.

"Good afternoon, my Nubian Queen—"

I whirled around and clutched my purse and my bags tighter to me thinking I was 'bout to get jacked for my shit. Stickup kids didn't give a fuck—especially this close to the holidays. A big six-foot raggedy Shaq-looking motherfucka was standing there.

"My car broke down and I just need bus fare to go to a job interview—"

"Negro, please," I told him, holding my hand up before I dug a crumpled dollar bill out my back pocket. "Save me the sad song. Here."

After that I ain't had shit for him but my back when I turned and walked away. Everybody got some sad-ass song to sing or fucking sadder story to tell to get money. Man, just ask for the dollar and bounce, save me the damn entertainment.

A cold wind whipped through the middle of the buildings

and I felt it to my damn bones. My little outfit was cute for shopping but it didn't have nothing on the cold. I was glad to rush into my building. The faint scent of ammonia failing to cover up the stench of piss never smelled better to me.

I was unlocking my door when the door to the apartment on the corner opened. I looked up as Mr. Wilson strolled his tall and slender ass out into the hall. Like always he was dressed to kill in a suit, smelling good, eyebrows arched, and his hair permed and slicked back. He was gay as the day was long and I loved the old fag to death even though he loved liquor way too much. You could see the effects in his eyes and in the redness of his bottom lip and the way his belly was round even though he was skinny as shit.

"Hey, Mr. Wilson," I called down the hall. "You sharp as a tack."

He snapped his slender fingers. "Everalways, baby. Everalways."

I couldn't do shit but shake my head and laugh as he continued down the hall like he was on a New York fashion week runway.

I focused back on getting into my apartment and preparing for my night with Dyme. Oh, I knew he was coming. I laid it on the line and I wasn't taking no damn shorts.

It was eleven when I finally gave up on Dyme showing up and midnight when he called with some excuse about being out of town on business. I felt dumb as hell sitting around my apartment in nothing but a damn thong and some fuck-me pumps all damn night. I smoked all the Purple Haze I could take before that shit had me throwing on one of my black

Juicy Couture tracksuits, tall fur boots, and my short hooded sable. I grabbed my cell phone and keys. I dialed and walked at the same time. "Yummy, you dressed?" I asked my best friend when she answered her phone, as the metal door to my apartment slammed close behind me.

"Hell, yeah. Whaddup?"

"Meet me downstairs."

And *that* bitch hung up right then and there.

I barely noticed the dope fiend giving some young dude a nasty wet blow job in the hallway as I jogged down the pissy stairwell and out the building into the freezing-ass winter night. By the time I crossed the courtyard and climbed into my Lexus, Yummy was striding out her building at the front of the complex. She had on her bright pink quilted bomber jacket and thick gray sweatpants. Most of her bright hair was under a print fitted cap that framed her pretty china-doll-looking redbone face.

She hopped right on in the passenger seat and the scent of her Bath & Body Works mango mandarin blended with my Gucci Rush perfume and the cherry-scented trees hanging from the rearview mirror. "What's poppin'?" she asked, her Newark accent so thoroughly in place. "I thought you and Dyme was hookin' up tonight?"

I sucked air between my teeth and pulled out into the night traffic. "So did I. That nigga didn't show. When I talked to him earlier he said he had business to take care of out of town but he was coming."

Hurt feelings made me lay down on the pedal and the street lights flashed by as I drove like I was trying to win a race.

Yummy turned the digital radio to Hot 97 and one of

Jazmine Sullivan's old jams, "Bust Your Windows," filled the car. "Man, that's fucked up but damn, all that shit Dyme lace you with, I wouldn't even give a fuck, Goldie," she said in her squeaky little Rosie Perez–sounding voice as she lit a Newport cigarette.

I laid on the horn as a bunch of girls started play-fighting in the middle of the busy-ass street. "Humph," I said as they scattered while I whizzed past them.

"Wrote my initials with a crowbar—"

"Humph," I said again at Jasmine's words. I knew exactly how the fuck she felt.

"Where we going any damn way?" Yummy asked, as she pulled her cell phone from her coat pocket with her free hand and flipped it open.

"To show Dyme I ain't the one to fuck with."

Yummy lowered the window and let the butt of her cigarette fly out. "You know I got your back but I can't get locked up again. I still got to go to court for beating that bitch ass downtown last week."

"I bust the windows out your car . . ."

During the entire drive I thought of all the good things Dyme had done for me and to me. Good things. I didn't have no money problems. I didn't have to boost clothes, sell ass, or do none of that crazy shit to pay my bills. He handled that and well. But don't lie to me and don't try to fucking play me. Not me. I ain't fucking having that shit.

He better not be there . . .

He better not be there . . .

That's all I kept thinking as I drove. I was hoping, wishing, and daring all at the same damn time.

"Lying motherfucka," I swore as soon as I slammed on the

brakes, stopping my car in the middle of the street . . . right outside Dyme and his wife's house.

His silver Jaguar was home and parked pretty as hell on the street behind her Black Benz. If the Jag was there, he was there too.

Like I said, just keep it funky with me. "No, Goldie, I'm not spending the night. It is what it is." Straight up, I'd prefer that over a motherfuckin' lie like I'm dumb as hell.

I popped the trunk and hopped right out the car to grab the tire iron.

"No, Goldie. Don't," Yummy hollered, scrambling out the car behind me.

"Fuck that. I'm sick of his shit!" I felt the fire of my anger fuel my ass.

Swing, batter batter swing! Derek Jeter's arm ain't got *shit* on mine.

CRASH!

Yummy's eyes damn near popped out of her head as I turned and walked back to my car. With trembling hands I tossed the tire iron back in the trunk and fought hard to breathe through my mouth as I used all of my anger to slam it shut.

WHAM!

"Daaaamn, Goldie," Yummy said as she hurried back into the passenger seat.

I gave the damage I caused one last glance before rushing to hop back in the driver's seat. As I squealed off into the night, tears blazed trails down my cheeks.

"I'm glad I did it 'cause you had to learn . . ."

2

I know, I got a lot of things I need to explain

But baby you know the name and love is about pain.

—Ja Rule, "Always on Time"

2004

"Tryna make a dollar out of fifteen cents."

I heard that once in some rap song but it suited just how I felt about my clothing situation. I stayed trying to stretch four decent pair of jeans and some shirts that was steady crawling up my arms with every wash.

Fail. Matter of fact . . . big motherfuckin' fail.

Sighing, I reached in my small and narrow closet to grab a pair of jeans and a Baby Phat tee that looked as second- and third-hand as it was. I wanted more. I needed more. Still, I never grumbled or complained to my grandmother and legal guardian, Mama Bit. My mama left. My daddy never made an appearance and left behind nothing but the tell-tell signs of being the seed of some faceless white man all and up through the gold tips of my hair and the honey color of my eyes. Mama Bit raised me and did the best she could. I learned a long time ago not to fuck with the hand that feeds you . . . especially when Disappearing Mama and Invisible Daddy didn't give two shits.

Closing my closet door, I turned, and if I reached out I could touch the wall of my room. It was that small. Just enough room for that closet, a twin bed, and a window. A heavy flowered curtain instead of a door. No nightstand with a lamp. No dresser to fold and put away my clothes. No frilly, girly decorations. But it was clean and neat and all mine for nearly all of the sixteen years of my life . . . so I loved that motherfucka.

The apartment was above greasy-ass Leroy's Down Home Diner and was lacking a whole lotta shit. The building was built back when Newark was predominantly white. The 1900s or some shit. Humph, it looked like it too.

People talk about the projects ain't shit but you ain't seen a real shithole until you run up in some old-ass building with a landlord who couldn't care the fuck less.

A little mouse 'bout black as the streets raced from under my bed but I didn't even trip. No matter how clean we kept our crib, living over a diner in a run-down building meant plenty houseguests who ain't had shit on the rent.

I was running late so I rushed into my underclothes and outfit before I plopped down on the bed. The bedsprings sang like a church choir at the sudden weight—even though I was barely a hundred pounds, and most of that was in my hips, butt, and thighs.

Mama Bit said my mama had that same won't-bring-you-nothing-but-trouble-and-a-wet-behind kind of shape. Not that any little boy could get anywhere close to me to wet my ass. Mama Bit kept me in check and under watch.

I snatched on my one pair of decent sneakers—a low-end

pair of Reeboks that was all black to make sure it matched all my clothes. Poor Folks' Fashion Tricks 101.

Mama Bit was already downstairs working as a cook in the diner and I knew she had her eyes on the clock listening for my feet on the stairs. She didn't have to wait much longer as I left the apartment and used my key to lock the door. The scent of the diner food was strong as hell as I raced down the stairs and out the door to the street.

There was no one roaming on the streets but a few people on they way to work and fiends searching for one of those all-night dopeboys to sell 'em a bag.

I took a deep breath of that winter air as I turned and looked through the smudged glass window of the restaurant. Sure 'nough Mama Bit was already looking dead at me from her spot by that hot-ass grill. I waved and kept it moving before she could wave me inside. My ass was skipping out on a lecture. There was always a lecture. Always some life lesson. Always warnings. Always.

I loved Mama Bit, but I wasn't even in the mood for none of that ish today. Nada.

My stomach was straight growling when I was halfway down the block to the bus stop, and my ass was regretting not stopping in to eat.

My steps paused when I neared the bus stop on the corner of Sixteenth Avenue and Eighteenth Street. Normally there was a bunch of people waiting on the corner for the bus. I knew I had missed a bus. But that wasn't my main problem. Only three teenage girls stood there and I had to fight the urge to go to the diner and fake being sick to Mama Bit.

"Here comes that light-bright bitch. Ugh, she makes me sick."

I heard them bully bitches talking shit about me before I got to the bus stop. Every damn day these hoes gave me a hard time—and it got worse when there was no adults around. Every motherfuckin' day. I ain't even know these chicks' name but I recognized them from around the hood. They were older than me. Bigger than me.

The fat chick squeezed into a bright pink and gold Baby Phat outfit. The tall trick with the funny-colored eyes, long nose, and an outfit that I knew cost more than everything in my closet. And the other thick one with gold rings on all her fingers.

I just thanked God they didn't go to my high school.

Like always, I tried to ignore them even as my heart was beating like a motherfucka in my chest. I stood a ways down from the bus stop and pretended to look at something—anything—but these bully bitches.

"Look at them run-down shoes. Them shits look gray she done wash 'em so much."

They all laughed.

"If I see that faded-ass shirt one more fucking time," another one said, sounding just as mean and angry at me as always.

"Think she cute, old half-white ass. Fucking mutt."

I bit my lip to keep from crying.

I squeezed my hands into fists to keep them from shaking.

I just wanted them to leave me alone.

"I oughta box that bitch in her face. I can't stand her bony, lightbulb-bright ass."

I felt ashamed because I was afraid of them.

I just wished I could disappear . . .

"With them fucking no-name jeans. She better start tricking like her hoe ass Mama—"

I turned around and glared at them bully bitches. My chest heaved.

"Oooh, she mad, y'all. She mad."

The chubby one walked over to me, looking like some pudgy-face Porky Pig in a wig. "And? What you gone do?" she asked, reaching up to nudge my face with her finger.

The other two walked up and the three of them surrounded me. Yelling shit in my face and pushing my ass around in the middle of them like a ball. All I could think was, What the fuck did I do to deserve this?

"Goldie, you sure you don't want to hit this?"

My eyes focused and the red light we were sitting at became clearer. It's funny how the past can fuck you up right in your present. But you had to look back sometimes to get a clearer view of just where the fuck you was going. That same hurt caused an ache in my chest that I tried to bury deep.

Ever since them chicks damn near jumped my ass at that bus stop, I stopped catching the number 1 bus and instead walked three blocks over and caught the number 25 downtown to my connecting number 13. Punk-ass move? Yeah, but who wanted to get jumped? To prove what?

I hated that I let them jealous bitches handle me any kind of way.

"Goldie?"

I turned and looked at Yummy, her eyes squinted against the thick silvery haze of the smoke wafting up from the blunt she held.

The scent of kush was heavy as hell in my car. "Yummy, you know I don't smoke in my car," I told her as I lowered the windows, letting the cold air in and some of the weed scent out.

Yummy sucked her teeth. "Girl, *Dyme* didn't want you smoking in the car . . . and I know you ain't stressing that shit right 'bout now?"

I cut my honey-colored eyes over at her before I took the blunt she offered, careful not to let the lit end burn the acrylic tips of my nails as I took a big toke and let it fill my lungs. I needed to chill the fuck out. I needed to forget a childhood I couldn't change. My shit was nowhere near as bad as other kids'—molestation, rape, physical and verbal abuse—but it was enough to leave me wide open for any man to come through and give me motherfuckin' esteem.

The light shifted from red to green and I handed Yummy the blunt before accelerating forward. She changed the station on the radio and the sounds of some banger filled the car. Really, I needed to be alone to think about what I did, why I did it, and what was coming after it.

I ain't had the easiest life. I try not to complain about it, try to keep it moving . . . still I can't forget it. Ever. It's the foundation of the house I've become.

Shit like what I been through sticks with you and affects everything you fucking do and the way you view everyone you meet.

Poverty.

Humiliation.

Shame.

People hating me and hating on me because my daddy was a white man. For some fucked-up reason it made girls before and after them bully bitches take so much fucking pleasure in pointing out shit like my freckles or my Wal-Mart jeans, my no-name sneakers, the huge braids my granny put in my head until I was old enough to do my own shit, or the thick white stockings she made me wear with my skirts. To keep from being picked on I would keep my ass quiet as hell . . . just hoping, wishing, praying for one school day where I didn't get teased and shit. Just one day where motherfuckas didn't make me sit in the mirror and wonder why me. Just one day.

Humph. Picture that shit. Never happened.

And maybe that's why the first time I laid eyes on Dyme, his smile fucked me all up on the inside . . .

2004

Nina Sky's "Move Ya Body" was playing on somebody's car radio as I walked up Broad and Market. I was singing along as I turned down a side street and slowed down at a small clothing store. There was a headless silver dummy with a bad-ass pink Apple Bottoms velour tracksuit like the ones all the girls be wearing. Like the ones I wanted so bad. I could just picture that fly motherfucka on my back.

"That would look good on you."

My body got stiff from the deep voice. My eyes focused in the glass and I saw past my own image to this tall-ass dude behind me.

"I ain't got shit for you to stick me up for," I told him, sounding nervous as hell this nigga was 'bout to run my pockets.

He laughed and shit.

My eyes glanced up and the down the street. I was grateful as hell that plenty of folks was out and about.

"I'm not no stickup kid. I'm a grown-ass man that owns this store," he said. "Shee-it. How I know you not 'bout to boost that outfit?"

I shifted my eyes up to look at him in the glass. He smiled, his eyes on my reflection. Watching me close and shit. He was fine. Hella fine.

Tall. Caramel skin. Dark hair. Goatee. Deep-ass dimples.

He smelled real good and looked even better in this butter-soft leather coat, with a crisp button-up shirt and dark jeans.

I turned and moved to walk past him. "Excuse me."

He stepped in my path. "I could hook you up with a good price on that suit."

It was my turn to laugh. "I was just window-shopping because I ain't even got the dollars to buy the dream," I said, tilting my head back to look up at him.

His eyes touched my body. From the side ponytail of my blondish-brown hair to the tips of my sneakers. He ain't miss shit in between. Not the fit of my T-shirt or the snugness of my jeans. Nothing. "A female like you should have a man to buy her all her dreams."

I looked away from him, even while my heart was beating so fuckin' loud I thought my ass was about to pass out. Nigga had game. There was no denying that. "I don't have a boyfriend," I answered, knowing I should walk away.

Knowing the way this man was looking at me was wrong.

"Fine-ass thick thing like you don't have a boyfriend?" he asked, sticking a toothpick in the corner of his mouth.

I shook my head no.

"A little boy wouldn't know what to do with all of that anyway."

I didn't say shit but my inside turned straight to mush.

"Stay right here," he said, moving past me to walk into the store.

I kicked some pebbles in the street, looking down at my feet. A verse from Mya's song floated in my head: "Should I stay? Should I go? I don't know."

I didn't get a chance to decide.

"Here you go," he said, handing me a brown paper shopping bag.

I frowned even as I took the bag. Mama Bit telling me, "Give it back, Kaeyla. Give it right back, right now," echoed, but I ignored it.

"You look about a size seven. Right?" he asked, shoving his hands into the pockets of his coat.

I nodded as I opened the shopping bag and looked down into it. There was the outfit I spotted in the window, a matching long-sleeve tee, and the cutest gold flats. True baller move. Damn it, he was really trying to do the man thing.

"Yo, Dyme, you got a phone call," another man called from the store.

"Give it back, Kaeyla. Give it right back, right now."

"I gotta get this but I'll see you around . . . Goldie." He tugged at my ponytail before he turned and walked back inside the store.

"My name's not Goldie," I called behind him, but the bell over the door jingled as it closed.

I clutched the bag tighter like he was gone walk back out and snatch that shit from me. No way. Not when I was already planning to wear that shit to school tomorrow. With one last look at the store, I turned and walked back up toward Broad Street feeling like I had won the lottery.

I never had nothing so nice to wear in my life.

Never.

As I neared the corner, passing by a couple of preaching Black Israelites with a portable microphone and speaker, I dug my hand into the bag just wanting to touch it. I pulled out a business card that was snuggled in the folds of the clothes.

On the front was the name of the store. Urban Fashions, and his name, Damion "Dyme" Gunners. On the back, a handwritten phone number and a note: "Come by the store tomorrow and let me see you in it."

My heart pounded.

"Give it back, Kaeyla. Give it right back, right now."

I knew what taking them clothes meant.

I knew what calling the number meant.

I knew what coming by the store meant.

A hell-fine man who owned his own clothing store? Stupid wasn't written nowhere on me.

Hell yeah I was gonna rock that hell out of that outfit.

I was going to call him.

Right after school, I was going to stroll my ass right on back to that store.

"Sorry, Mama Bit," I whispered aloud.

Fuck the dumb shit. For real.

I felt like an entirely new chick in my outfit. I did my hair different. I walked different. I felt different.

And I liked it. I couldn't wait to get through school and get my ass downtown to that store. I was so ready to see Dyme and to see his reaction to his gift on me. I was so excited on the bus ride downtown like I was going to see Mary J. live in concert or some shit. Hell, I been excited since last night.

In my bedroom I laid under the covers on my little bed and held the card Dyme gave me. I had used the tip of my finger to trace over the words he wrote. I raised the card to my nose and inhaled, hoping to catch a whiff of his scent. Just holding it in my hands made my whole body tingle. Made my heart pump faster. Made me feel happier. I couldn't stop smiling like a damn fool.

I wished I could call him last night but the only phone we had was in Mama Bit's bedroom and I wasn't even tryin' to get caught on the phone with a grown-ass man. Mama Bit woulda tore my ass up and called the police on him. No joke. Major drama.

"Maybe he'll give me more clothes," I whispered to myself as the crowded bus came to a stop and I made my way to the front of the bus to get off, careful not to scuff my new flats.

I had just walked up Broad Street and was about to turn the corner down the side street to Dyme's store.

"Hey!"

I stopped. With the heavy bustle of people and loud buses and cars blaring their radios, I could just barely make out a voice.

"Hey, Goldie!"

"Goldie? Me?"

I looked up the street at Dyme standing next to a parked dark green Ford Expedition. He closed the car door and came walking up the street looking hella fine in all black. My heart felt like it was in my damn throat as I hitched my book bag higher up on my shoulder and made my way to him. I waited for him in front of the store, noticing it was locked with a Closed sign hanging on the door.

He eyed me from head to toe as he stepped up on the sidewalk. "I knew that outfit would look good on you," he said, taking me all in.

The way he was eyeing me again I knew he meant that shit. I smiled and tilted my head to the side, trying not to show that my stomach was flip-flopping like crazy. This nigga had me gone. "Thank you," I said, feeling good as hell.

He reached in his pocket and pulled out his keys, turning to unlock the door to the shop. "Come on in."

"My grandmama told me not to go places with strangers," I said, my Newark accent real heavy while I flirted. Hard. "I don't know you . . . yet."

He laughed and nodded his head, wiping his hand over his mouth. "True . . . true. So can I get to know you, Goldie?"

My eyes locked with his. "Why? Why me?" I asked, surprised that I felt so bold.

He frowned like he was all confused by my question and then he said, "Why not you?"

I dropped my head and licked the gloss from my lips as I twirled my side ponytail around my finger.

"Come on. I got a surprise for you," he said, before walking inside and holding the door open for me to walk in behind him.

And I stepped right the fuck on in. I knew it was risky. I knew I was taking a chance with this stranger. I knew that I knew better. But I got in. "How can you have a surprise for me? You ain't know I was coming back."

He side-eyed me. "I knew," he said, all cocky and shit as he locked the door to the store.

Click.

That *shit made me nervous as hell but I didn't get a chance for what-ifs.*

He took my book bag from my shoulder and then slid his large hand in mine to pull me behind him toward the back of the store. I shivered and felt all warm between my thighs from his touch. My nipples got so hard they ached. I'd had crushes on boys before, but the way Dyme was making me feel was all new to me. All new and all *good.*

In his office he dropped my book bag and let my hand go. He nodded his head toward the clothes laid out on the leather sofa against the wall. All colors. All patterns. All materials. All designers.

Dyme smiled. "Try them on," he said, reaching for the vibrating cell phone in his belt.

All mine?

My eyes got big as shit as I walked over to the sofa. I counted ten full outfits. Oh, a bitch was about to be laid for sure.

"Oh shit. Oh shit. Oh shit," I kept saying.

I turned around and Dyme was standing right behind me. I had to tilt my head back to look up at him. His hands came down on my shoulders, rubbing them.

"You like 'em?" he asked, bending down.

I nodded, all nervous and shit.

"You like me?" he asked, his head coming down closer to mine.

I nodded again, feeling breathless like I was drowning or some shit.

"Good," he whispered against my mouth, just before his tongue traced my bottom lip.

It felt like electricity shot through my body. This wasn't shit like no kiss I ever had before, especially when his tongue slipped inside my mouth. His hands started undressing me and I knew when I walked out that store that I wasn't gonna be a little girl no more . . .

* * *

That led to the beginning of me and Dyme. And the end of life as I knew it. He laced me with plenty money, plenty clothes, my own cell phone, and a life filled with secrets. The fact that he was so much older didn't mean a motherfuckin' thing to me except I had to keep my mouth shut to keep him from getting in trouble, just the way he told me.

Dyme taught me how to shop. Dress. Fuck. Roll a blunt. Smoke weed. Drink. Party. And lie like a motherfucka.

I had to explain all the newness and I lied and told Mama Bit I had a job. She believed me and that freed up plenty of time after school for me to enjoy being the lady of a real top-notch baller. From then on it was on and popping.

Knowing that nigga had my back made me cocky, bold, and confident. My fashion game was on point. I kept my doobie fresh once a week at this Dominican spot. My nails airbrushed to perfection. My closet overflowing.

I was the shit. *We* were the shit.

Life was good as hell.

We couldn't get enough of each other . . .

2005

"This beats the hell out of sitting up in school all fucking day," I said aloud to myself with a stretch of my body against the silk sheets of Dyme's king-sized bed as I took a deep drag of the blunt and then tilted my head up to blow smoke rings to the ceiling. This was my first time at his apartment and I was straight loving it.

We used to meet after school to lay up in a suite at the Hilton, but that shit wasn't cutting it anymore. We was sick of not being able to see each other until after school. So when Dyme told me to skip school this morning, I did. Fuck it. All I knew was that motherfucka had me gone and I didn't give a fuck 'bout nothing else.

I cut my eyes up to the mirrors on the ceiling, lifting my arms above my head as I stretched the naked body Dyme loved so much. Every bronzed-honey inch of me.

Who needed school and to hang around duck-ass kids all day when I was getting all the education I needed from the School of Hard Dick?

Rolling off the bed I left his bedroom that was bigger than half me and Mama Bit's apartment. Dyme was paid. A lotta people thought he sold dope but that was a bunch of bullshit. He came into a bunch of loot at twenty when his parents died in a car wreck. He used the money to open up businesses that made him even more money. Boss-ass three-bedroom condo. A black-on-black Denali and a Benz SL500. Custom motorcycles. Diamond jewelry. Designer clothes. The good life. Dyme was all about the hustle and the hustle paid off well for him.

And now it was paying off well for me. I was that *bitch.* His *bitch. Fuck it.*

Of course there was a lot more he wanted to do for me that had to wait until I was older. And I couldn't wait. Trips out of town. Moving in together. My own car.

The best was yet to come.

I was just about to stroll my ass around the corner into the kitchen when Dyme stepped his fine ass into the hall in front of me. I could tell by the look on his face that something was up.

"I need you to do something for me," he said, moving past me to walk back into the bedroom.

Frowning, I turned to follow him, but he was already walking out the room with all my shit in his hands.

What the fuck?

"Dyme. What's up?" I asked, even as he pushed my shit in my hands and then pushed me toward a closet in the living room.

"Just trust me and stay in here 'til I come get you. Don't come out for shit," he said.

I got scared. Was this one of those "my man 'bout to get taken out" scenes in all those street-lit books I loved to read? "I'm not getting in no fuckin' closet or nothing else 'til you tell me what the fuck going on!" I said, standing my ground as I dropped my clothes to the hardwood floor and stood there booty-butt-naked with my arms crossed over my titties.

"Look, Goldie, I'm married and my wife's on the way up," Dyme said, wiping his hand over his goatee and mouth as he looked down at me.

My heart dropped right along with my bottom lip. I'd rather have faced bullets than hear this shit.

"She don't mean shit to me. I'm getting a divorce but I gotta play my position right or she'll get half of our shit." Dyme bent his tall figure down to scoop up the clothes and then open the closet door.

Our shit. Ours. *Why did that shit matter to me when this motherfucka just cracked my world?*

Keys rattled on the other side of the door. "I know this some grown-people shit, but I need you to grow up right now. Get in there and wait 'til I let you out. Do this for me, Goldie. Do this for us."

The key turned in the lock and Dyme gave me a quick kiss

to my lips before he pushed me inside and closed the door in my face.

I stood there holding my clothes, scared as shit to move and make a noise. I would do this for him. He would explain. He would make it all better. Dyme always took care of me and looked out for me. He wouldn't stop now. He was doin' this shit for us. For our *shit.*

But the shit was still fucked up.

The front door closed and soon I heard heels on the hardwood floors. I hated that I wondered what she looked like. Fine as me? I doubted it or I wouldn't ever have caught Dyme's eye.

I could barely make out their conversation. Their voices were muffled. There were more footsteps. And then silence.

The closet was a nice size but filled up with coats. I could feel the softness of furs against my naked body and shit. The warmth of the closet was making the scent of me and Dyme's sex rise from my pussy and between my thighs.

Suddenly the closet door opened and Dyme grabbed my arm and hustled my naked ass out of the closet and then out the front door to the hall. He pushed keys into my hand. "Go to the Benz and wait for me."

Dyme stepped back in the apartment and closed the door, leaving me ass-naked in the hall while he was lamping in his apartment with his wife, with my dried pussy juices on his dick.

Fighting the urge to kick the door and put his ass on blast, I walked down the hall to the elevator. As soon as I stepped in and the doors closed behind me, I dropped my clothes to the floor and started to get dressed.

The elevator slid to a stop.

Ding.

I was just pulling my lime green lace bikini up when the doors slid open. I looked up. An old white couple stood there with their eyes big as shit. I was too mad and hurt by Dyme to even give a fuck.

I paused in scooping up my bra. "Y'all getting the fuck on or what?" I asked with plenty of attitude.

The woman turned and caught the man eyeing my titties. Just before the door closed she slapped the shit out of him. . . .

I was mad at Dyme, but I had to laugh at that *shit.*

Six years. No sign of a divorce. Just a new house for him and his wife that I heard about on the streets. Just a hair salon he bought for that bitch. Just her staying firmly locked as Mrs. Gunners while my ass was steady playing my position as wifey in second place. Steady accepting them fucking lies. Steady putting up with his shit.

Abortions that he sweet-talked me into. My first at just sixteen. My second only a year later.

Getting cussed out like a criminal or cut the fuck off financially when he got in one of his jealous "somebody trying to fuck my pussy" moods. And over dumb shit, like I can stop a motherfuckin' dude from speaking to me.

Promises he couldn't keep.

Nothing but fucking cries, lies, and alibis.

My cell phone lit up and vibrated on the console.

Yummy picked it up and looked at it. "Ooooh, bitch, it's Dyme," she said, handing it to me.

I snatched it out her hand and flipped it open while I steered the night streets.

"Goldie, I know motherfuckin' well you didn't bring your ass to my house—"

"No, Dyme, I know motherfuckin' well your ass ain't lie to me while you laid up with Mrs. Gunners," I yelled into the phone as I sat up in the seat. "I'm sick of your lying ass."

"All the shit I do for your ungrateful ass and you gone pull some shit like this," he yelled.

"Man, fuck you and your big-back bitch of a wife."

Yummy laughed her ass off at that as she lounged in the passenger seat still blazing. "That bitch do look like a Tazmanian devil and shit."

"Goldie—"

Tears filled my eyes as I looked through the windshield at the street life laid out before me. "No more, Dyme. I'm done. Stay the fuck away from me. Only thing I ever did was fucking love you and I'm done. It's a done da-da. And I mean it. Leave me the fuck alone."

I snapped the phone closed and flung it toward the backseat as I pushed my foot down on the accelerator.

"Girl, you and Dyme been getting down way too long for him just to leave you alone like that," Yummy told me, passing the blunt before she fucked with the radio stations.

I ain't say shit 'cause there wasn't shit to say. I just sped up until it felt like we were flying across the ice-slicked streets.

Yummy slammed her hands on the dashboard as I quickly came up on a double-parked car and had to hop in the left lane quick as hell to avoid crashing into it. "Slow your ass down, Goldie. Fuck that."

God—and nothing but God—got me and Yummy's ass across town safely so far. Between my anger and my tears we were lucky I didn't flip that bitch. Blessed that I didn't wreck and kill us.

"Pull over and let me drive," Yummy offered.

I shifted my eyes over to her at the sound of nerves all up and through her voice. My hands gripped the wheel tighter as I sped up the ice-slicked street.

My cell phone vibrated from the backseat. That nigga was blowing my shit up . . . just like he always did when I threatened to leave his ass alone.

"Lying, old-ass, uncircumcised-dick no-good motherfucka," I spat, that pain and oh-so-fucking-familiar feeling of disappointment surrounding me.

Yummy squealed. "GOLDIE, WATCH OUT!!!"

This lady and a small child stepped from behind a car into the street.

"Shit!" I swore, slamming on the brakes.

The tail end of my Lexus swung out sharply as the woman and child scurried across the street to safety.

"Damn, bitch, learn how to drive!" the woman yelled.

That made me want to zoom forward and truly run her ass over.

"I know Dyme is a . . . a lying, old-ass, uncircumcised-dick no-good motherfucka, but how 'bout we keep from being two dead motherfuckas. You feel me?" Yummy snapped with a mix of anger and fear.

I closed my eyes and released a heavy-ass breath. I couldn't let Dyme hurting me push me to do something stupid. Fuck that. My ass would wind up dead and that nigga would be looking for the next piece of side-ass.

And that's all I was to him.

The truth of that shit hurt like a motherfucka.

3

Do you get pillow talk? (No)

Held at night? (No)

If you don't make his breakfast then you's a sideline ho.

—Monica, "Sideline Ho"

I didn't sleep all night. Between Dyme blowing up my cell, the cops raiding somebody's damn apartment in the complex early this morning, one of the neighbor's dogs barking all fucking night, and reminiscing on the last six years of my life, I just tossed and fucking turned. Alicia Keyes wasn't lying, because it was hard as hell trying to sleep with a broken heart.

I glanced over at the huge round wooden clock on the wall across from my bed. It was just after eight. I normally didn't even get out of my fucking bed 'til noon. Kicking off the covers, I climbed out of my king-sized bed that really was too big for this little-ass bedroom. I couldn't even fit nightstands on either side of the bed.

But Dyme wanted a king-sized bed to lay up in . . . when he was here.

And what Dyme wanted from Goldie, Dyme got. Like the tat on the deep dip of my lower back. His name in cursive script surrounded by a huge scroll design.

"Let motherfuckas know who that pussy belong to," he said that day, as we rode to Brooklyn to the tattoo parlor. How many times that nigga done fucked me from behind and then pulled out just to nut all over that tat?

That was just one of six tattoos on my body, and the one on my back was my all-time favorite . . . until whenever Dyme pissed me the fuck off.

Yeah, I had a nigga's name tatted on me big as hell, but at least I didn't get "5 Star Chick" tatted across my neck like Yummy's wilding-out ass. That bitch was straight crazy for that shit. Following up a rap song? Never that.

My tats were all to emphasize something on my body that I loved. The panther on my thigh. The dripping cherries on my titties. The rose on my ankle. The small row of black stars on my collarbone. And my own name on the back of my neck. All shit I could cover up if I wanted to—most times I didn't. Fuck it. It took time for me to learn to love my body, and once I did, I loved it to the fullest.

Damn, Mama Bit was mad as hell when I visited her apartment and she saw Dyme's name on my back when I bent over to pick up something. She raised much hell that day.

"He too old for you, don't care that you young as hell and dumb as hell for dropping out of school, he pay your bills to keep you on your back . . . and now that Viagra-popping jackass gone brand you like a fucking mule? Where all the sense God and me gave you. Huh, Kaeyla? Where it at?"

My eyes shifted to the glass-framed picture of her on the edge of my cluttered dresser. Once I was eighteen, I got a two-bedroom apartment in King Court. One of my friends back then had got an apartment easy as hell and I followed her lead using Dyme's store for my job, his cell phone as the contact number, and the bold-ass lie that I had a roommate to get the extra bedroom. Dyme was pissed at first that I made them moves and decisions by myself until he saw how cheap my rent was. Who the fuck gone complain about a hundred dollars a month for rent? Plus I figured I wasn't gone be there long because soon I was moving right into the house and position of Mrs. Gunners. Okay?

I was more than happy to get out of that cramped little bedroom and into my own shit even though I knew Mama Bit was disappointed as hell. But I was legal, feeling grown, and fucked-up in love with this nigga old enough to be my daddy.

I never could make her understand that I loved that motherfucka, but trust and believe I understood that she hated him.

Mama Bit gone on to heaven three years ago. Her death just made me cling to Dyme even more. He really became all the fuck I knew or wanted to know.

There was more—a lot more—of my secrets that she could see from heaven. Things I never told her. Shit that would make her hate him even more. Shit that probably had her straight spinning in her grave. The weed smoking and drinking. The arguing. Dyme's wife. The abortions.

Standing by the bed, I stared down at the all-white covers. I thought of all the good times we shared on and under the silk sheets and faux-fur spread. I caught a vision of him standing behind me, my fat ass tooted up in the air while that nigga tapped the thick tip of his dick against my ass cheeks before easing every hard inch inside me. Pussy or ass. It didn't matter. The choice was always his, and sometimes he swapped between both. There wasn't shit off-limits.

I can't lie and say that old nigga couldn't fuck. True, his

was the only dick I ever had . . . but that nigga's dicking down completely fucked the game up for any other man. And *plenty* motherfuckas had tried.

Click.

I turned around. I knew what that sound meant.

Seconds later, Dyme walked into the bedroom. He looked like shit. His eyes were bloodshot. His fade and beard was fucked. His clothes wrinkled. And not a bit of jewelry on.

"Humph. Now you come here?" I asked with plenty attitude. "Too little, too fucking late. Get the fuck out."

Dyme took off his leather coat and flung it across the room onto a clothes-covered leather club chair in the corner before he walked up beside me. "I pay the rent on this motherfuck—"

WHAP!

My hand still stung from slapping the shit out of him. "Don't throw your money up in my face!"

WHAP!

He slapped me back just as quick before he grabbed my upper arms and picked me up to fling me onto the middle of the bed like I wasn't five-foot-seven and a solid hundred and fifty pounds. Before I rolled my ass out the way he landed on top of me, his weight locking me down beneath him. I closed my eyes to keep from looking up at him.

"Why you acting up, Goldie?" he asked, lowering his head to press a sizzling kiss to my neck.

I shivered like a dumb bitch. *No, do not let this old nigga fuck your head up, Goldie. Do not let this fool—*

I swallowed hard at the feel of his mouth lightly biting the top of my breast. That nigga knew I loved that. He knew that shit!

I squirmed away from him. Well, I tried to anyway. "I need more than D & D, Dyme," I snapped, locking my honey-colored eyes on him.

He looked down at me, all confused-looking and shit. "Huh?"

"Dick and Dough. That's all you got for me and that shit ain't enough no more."

Dyme smiled at me like he thought I was feeding him bullshit. "Damn, you looking good as hell in them little-ass shorts with your fat-ass pussy balled up like that," he moaned in my ear, completely ignoring my protests as he ground his hard dick against my flat stomach.

The dick. The titty kisses. The chemistry.

My pussy flooded.

I hated myself.

This nigga was my lifeline. Not just for money . . . but for everything I was. I'd been riding with this nigga, and fighting with this nigga, and fucking this nigga for six years. Six motherfuckin' years. My heart ain't on the same page with my head.

As much I hated him, I loved this nigga.

As much as he hurt me, I craved him.

As much as he lied, I wanted to trust and believe in his ass.

As much as he was married to another bitch, *I* wanted to be his wife. Fuck being wifey. Fuck the sideline shit. Second place is for motherfuckin' losers.

People talk about the danger of the dope game but the most dangerous game of all was love. I believed that on everything I was and everything I would ever be.

"I love you, Goldie," Dyme moaned against the row of tiny star tattoos as he shifted off the soft curves of my body and used his hands to tear the beater and the low-cut shorts I wore.

Dyme eyed my body from my head on down. "You think I'm gone let all this go? You a bad bitch, Goldie. The baddest bitch out there."

I looked up into his eyes as I shook my head and arched one threaded eyebrow.

"You can have whatever you like," Dyme sang off-key. T.I.'s song "Whatever You Like" was like our fucking anthem or something. He kept on giving me the hook while he rubbed his hands down my naked body and spread my thick thighs to finger my pussy.

My nipples and clit got hard. Throbbing. Aching. *Shit.*

"I want your body. I need your body. Long as you got me you won't need nobody," he said, touching me everywhere until I couldn't think straight.

"Stop tricking, Dyme," I said trying to sound hard while I fought like hell to ignore the way his fingers was stroking my clit.

He laughed all low in his throat. This tall bastard was cocky as he slipped two fingers deep inside of me to circle against my pussy walls. I gasped a little in the back of my throat, goose bumps racing up and down my body. He lowered his head and sucked deeply at one of my pointed nipples.

This nigga knew how to get all in my head. He knew me. He made me.

"I want you to go house shopping today."

My eyes shifted up to him. I bit my bottom lip. Was this nigga for real?

He eased his thick fingers from inside my pussy to dig in his pocket. I could smell the fresh scent of my juices on his fingers as he placed something cold and metal around one of my nipples.

My eyes shifted down.

A diamond engagement ring.

My eyes shifted back up to his.

"Marry me, Goldie," Dyme whispered against my lips as he lowered his head to press his mouth to mine.

And I caved. Just like that. Fuck it. I won. This motherfucka was mine. Finally.

My hands came up to grab the back of his smooth head as he sucked my tongue into his mouth. I felt his smile and I laughed softly. I felt like singing like Mary J. "We got that good love, that hood love. . . ."

"Is that a yes?" he asked.

I took the ring and slid it onto my left ring finger. "That's a hell yes."

I pushed him over onto his back and freed his dick from his pants. Once that hard motherfucka was in my hand, I straddled his hips and slid my pussy right down onto him.

We both gasped and bit our bottom lips.

I pulled the rest of my torn beater from my arms, leaning down to jiggle my big breasts in his face. My nipples rubbed against his lips before he moaned and sucked one into his mouth as his hands came up slap my ass as I twirled and worked my hips while making my wide ass clap.

Knowing what he liked, I kept riding that dick as I reached down and grabbed the rest of the blunt I smoked on last night before I fell asleep.

"Do that shit, Goldie. Goddamn I love this pussy. This *my* motherfuckin' pussy!"

I lit the blunt real quick and took a good hit, holding the smoke in my mouth, before I held it behind my back as I bent down and put my open mouth onto his. As I shot the weed smoke from my mouth into his, I rode that dick even harder, causing both of us to break into a sweat. The smoke drizzled from between our mouths as we kissed each other all deep and shit.

I blazed the blunt again, enjoying the weed and the feel of his dick stroking my walls as I rode him. Bending down again, I blew a stream of thick silver smoke into his nostrils.

Dyme loved this shit. He always complained his wife wouldn't smoke with him. Well, fuck that dumb bitch because this wife would.

My eyelids felt heavy as hell from the weed as I turned around with his dick still in me to ride that nigga backwards. Felt like his dick was in my damn stomach. I was just working my lower half into a split on his dick when the sound of a loud car horn blared off below my window.

Dyme stiffened.

I dropped the blunt back in the ashtray and popped my ass like I was try to give his dick CPR. It didn't take long for his hips to arch while his dick shot round after round of cum into me.

The horn sounded again.

Whoever the fuck it was was seriously killing my buzz and my fuck.

The horn sounded again. Longer. And it seemed louder.

"DAMION!"

We both froze.

"DAMION! Bring your no-good ass out here . . . NOW!"

He jumped up out the bed, knocking me off him, almost sending my ass over the side to the floor. "Shit," he cursed, creeping over to the window to peep out the suede-like curtains.

The weed and 'bout three nuts I bust on his dick had

me light-headed as hell, but I wobbled my ass over to the window. I pulled the curtain back wide as hell. He grabbed at me to pull me back but I brushed him the fuck off and stood right in *my* window of *my* bedroom in *my* apartment butt-naked looking down at his wife and her Benz blocking Dyme's Denali in the parking spot. She was decked out in a full-length sable with mink earmuffs, black leather gloves, and high-heeled boots. The bitch looked like the wife of a dude with money. *Old bitch.*

I watched as she reached through the open window of her Benz to lay on the horn again.

"DAMION!" she yelled again.

"Crazy bitch," I whispered against the window, looking down at the tall thick woman whose body was squared up like a fucking brick—not a *brick house*, just a fucking brick.

Mrs. Gunners, aka Frieda, was in my hood acting a straight fool. Everybody around here knew Dyme was my man, so they knew this was my fucking drama unfolding in King Court like some motherfuckin' ghetto-ass soap opera.

Her eyes settled on me and she frowned in distaste before she laid on the horn again.

I turned from the window. "Dyme, you better check that bitch before I—"

My room was empty. His clothes was gone and so was he. I didn't even know he had hauled ass.

"Oh *hell* to the no!" I snatched a pair of jeans and a T-shirt from the pile of dirty clothes on the chair. I was snatching them on even as I walked out my bedroom, across my living room, and out the door in my bare feet—which was mad dumb in the projects. Fuck it. All I knew was it was time for me and Frieda to meet and get to the real on this bullshit with Dyme.

I took them stairs two at a time and busted out the door. I hardly felt the icy-cold wind or my feet sinking into snow as I watched Dyme trying to block them blows she was giving him.

"I knew it. I knew it, you liar! I knew you were up to your freaking shenanigans, Damion."

Okay. I was racing over to them but I paused like a motherfucka at the sound of a white girl from the Jersey Shore escaping from this bitch's mouth. *What the fuck? Ugh!*

"You wrong, Frieda. I came here to check on one of my nieces," Dyme yelled back at her.

I came to a stop behind them and crossed my arms over my chest. No, this motherfucka did not think I was 'bout to cover for his lying ass. Picture that shit. Big nothing. I played his bullshit games in the past but no more. "Your niece, Dyme? I'm your niece?" I asked, attitude all up and through my voice while my heart beat crazy as hell.

He dropped his head at the sound of my voice and she leaned to look past him at me.

This moment was six years in the making. I seen her plenty around Newark—at the store, when I drove by her salon or their house. But she ain't know me. This shit was really 'bout go down. Fuck it. I'm ready. I *been* ready. She was cute enough with a smooth caramel complexion and long hair I could tell was hers. But she was no me. Never could be, not even on my worst fuckin' day.

"And who are you?" she asked.

I reached out my left arm into the cold air and wiggled my freezing fingers showing off my ring. "His fiancée."

Time went still for a few seconds.

Dyme turned and eyed me in disbelief . . . and anger?

Her eyes dropped to lock on my engagement ring.

Everyone looking on from their windows—and those bold enough to circle the drama—went "Ooooh," "Aaah," or "Oh shit." Some dude was singing the chorus to "It's Going Down."

Frieda eyed me from head to toe. I knew she took it all in. She saw the same thing a lot of women saw. A mixed chick with a smooth complexion, good hair, honey-colored eyes, and a body that could make most women—including her—look like a man.

Her eyes changed. Gone was the confusion and hurt, to be replaced by hate.

"So you're engaged, Damion?" she asked him, her voice calm. Too calm.

I grabbed his arm and jerked him around to look at me as he stood in the middle of his motherfuckin' lies. "Yes, *Dyme*, are you engaged?"

Real talk? I was nervous. My stomach felt like I might shit up myself and I knew he wanted me to just stay my ass in the crib and let him play his position but I *couldn't* do that. Not anymore. It was cold and lonely in some other bitch's shade.

Dyme looked at me a long-ass time and I eyed this man—my man—back with all the love and devotion I had for this nigga. All of it. I was standing in the cold and the fuckin' snow fighting for him.

"No," he said, turning to face his wife and turn his back on me.

My heart and my whole world felt crushed. This nigga? Humph. This nigga just fucked me all up.

"That's messed up, Dyme," some girl yelled from the crowd.

The sight of his back to me, iggin' me, pretending like I didn't exist, like we ain't shared six years, two abortions, and more bullshit than I can count, flipped my motherfuckin' switch from hurt to straight pissed the fuck off. With one jump I was on that nigga's back, clawing and fighting him like my life depended on it. Even as my tears flowed I tried to box the back of that nigga's head until the bells was ringing in his shit. Even while I knew this embarrassing shit was gone follow me in the hood, I fought until my arms hurt. Until my chest hurt. Until I was tired . . . and then tired of being tired.

"So you don't pay my rent either right? Huh, motherfucka? You don't take care of me? Huh?" Blow after blow after blow. I swung on that nigga like we were in warring gangs.

"Stop it, Goldie," Dyme roared as I scratched a layer of flesh from his cheek. Fuck it. I couldn't never hurt him as much as he hurt me.

He knocked me off his back and turned to swing on me. He missed because I fell back into the snow. The air was knocked out of me and I lay there with my eyes closed, trying to get my shit back together while the snow froze the shit out of my back and ass.

"If you want me and your family, then you tell her it's over. You tell her right here. Right now. Tell that slut she doesn't mean shit to you. Tell her it's over."

I opened my eyes at the sound of his feet eating up the snow. The fight in me was gone. I ain't feel like doing shit but crawling into a ball and bawling my eyes out.

He stood over me and I looked up at this man that I loved.

"Stay the fuck away from me, my wife, and our house. Don't fuckin' call me. Leave me the fuck alone." He turned his back on me again.

I slipped on the snow and the black ice as I climbed to my bare numb feet and grabbed the sleeve of his leather coat. "Dyme, you really standing there like you didn't just propose to me? Like we didn't just fuck? You really tryna handle me like that?"

"Just stay the fuck away from us," Dyme said, his voice colder then any winter storm on the East Coast.

Tears filled my eyes and I couldn't stop them from falling. "Dyme, all the shit I been through with your ass, and for your ass, and you really gone handle me like this?" I asked again, barely able to see him clearly through my tears.

Frieda walked up to us. "That's enough of this shit. I'll be damned if I'm going to watch my husband arguing with another woman, Damion."

I felt like I had an out-of-body experience or some shit. Everything about this reminded me of those days growing up when people would fuck with me . . . when the girls would pick with me.

Embarrassed. Ashamed. Hurt.

"And I'm not having my husband take money from our household to pay for a young and dumb piece of ass."

I heard her but my eyes were on Dyme. This the motherfucka who supposed to be my savior. This man standing there getting chumped by his wife was the same one who ain't do shit but lay the law and his hands on me?

"I don't want you no more. I don't need you. My wife is the most important thing to me."

I couldn't believe this shit. I couldn't understand how he could stand there, look down on me like shit on his Guccis, and tell me that shit.

Fuck him.

No backsliding and calling me tomorrow with expensive gifts and shit. This was it.

"I want that ring, Damion," his wife told him, her mouth twisted as she eyed me.

He closed his eyes and wiped his mouth with his hand. "Frieda—"

"Don't even," she snapped.

He reached out to grab my wrist, but I jerked away and swung on his punk ass, landing a solid right to his mouth, splitting it and causing blood to run down his lips and chin.

"You stupid bitch," he spat, raising his arm to swing.

But I stepped up and stared him dead in his eye. "You think after this bullshit that you can hurt me with your hands?"

Dyme dropped his arm and shifted his eyes away from mine.

"Six fucking years. I killed my babies for you, you lying son of a bitch, and you think fucking swinging out on me gone hurt more than this?" I was bitter and it showed in my voice. I was hurt and it came through in my eyes. I was betrayed and it shattered my heart into a million fucking pieces.

"Six years?! Babies?!" Frieda screeched. Two seconds later she was dead on his ass, swinging, kicking, fighting, and biting.

Real talk? I just didn't give a fuck about none of this shit no more. I turned away from them and for the first time noticed all the people standing in the courtyard watching my bizness. A few bitches look like they was happy my ass got played. Some of the fellas was straight clowning and cracking jokes. A few people's faces shown they was feeling sorry for me. More than a few had their cell phones in the air and I knew my shit was going right on YouTube or WorldStarr as a hood fight or some shit.

I made my way across the snow and icy asphalt toward the building.

"Stay the hell away from my husband, little girl," she hollered from behind me.

I turned. Dyme was busy trying to push her into her car.

"Bitch, please. Tell your husband to stay the fuck away from me."

Her eyes dropped down to the engagement ring on my finger and she laughed as she held up her own left hand. Her ring and wedding band glistened. Her rock was three times the size of mine. "You will never be me. Understand? Ne-*ver*. You little bitches don't get it. You ain't the first and you might not be the last, but trust me, I'm forever."

The shit that just went down, the way Dyme handled me like some side trick and kissed her ass . . . I knew she was right. What the fuck was left to say? I turned and walked into my building, finally noticing my feet aching from standing in the snow.

"Better go find you a job or a new sugar daddy to keep you up. It shouldn't be too hard to find somebody to pay the rent in this raggedy motherfucka!"

I ignored her words. I heard their vehicles crank up but I didn't dare turn to watch him and his wife drive out of the complex with all my self-esteem, self-respect, and love crushed under their tires.

The rest of my day was filled with plenty tears, plenty sad songs, plenty Nuvo, and plenty weed—all from the comfort of my sofa. I ain't been out my apartment since that shit went down that morning. That shit was mad embarrassing and I was laying low like a motherfucka.

In a perfect world I woulda strutted my ass out the door dressed to kill with my head held high, but I just didn't have that shit in me. I really loved Dyme. This man was my world for so many years and it was gone take more than some Gucci heels and a mink to get my mind right. My heart right.

That would take time.

What I didn't have time for was my bills or instead of being from the streets, my black ass was gonna be living on them. I didn't have a high school diploma and nathan on work experience. I was serious as hell about leaving Dyme's ass alone, so today I was deep in mourning, but tomorrow, getting my ass up to start a new life was going to give me life.

My apartment was dark except for the flickering lights from the forty-inch flat screen on my living room wall. I used the remote to flip through the channels, finally settling on one of them crazy-ass VH1 reality shows.

Bzzzzz.

I rolled my eyes and let go of a heavy breath at the incoming call. Yummy had been to my door to check on me but I didn't answer. I knew my bestest was trying to help, but I just wanted to be by my damn self.

My plan was to keep on chilling in my apartment, trying my best to get wasted as I minded my own. Reflected on some shit. Tried to find the moment where I fucked up so I didn't hit rewind on that dumb shit. I eyed my cell phone vibrating on the oversized chocolate leather ottoman I used as a coffee table. Sighing, I reached over and picked it up.

"Yeah."

The line stayed quiet.

I frowned like crazy, definitely not in the mood for no bullshit. "Hel-lo?"

"Goldie, don't hang up. It's me. It's Dam—Dyme. It's me, Dyme."

I held the phone from my face and checked the number on the caller ID. I didn't recognize it. I shook my head, biting my bottom lip, as I pressed the phone back to my ear. "What you want, Dyme? You made your choice in my parking lot today, remember?"

"You know I couldn't just let you go. You know I didn't mean that shit."

I sat up on the couch and reached for my sweating glass of Nuvo on crushed ice. I needed a little liquid courage to stay *that* bitch who wasn't takin' no shit from this nigga . . . or any other, for that matter. After a deep sip, I said, "The only thing I know for sure is I'm not wasting another minute of my life on you."

"Listen, baby girl, I need you to—"

"To what? Huh? To let you set me up to get played again? Sorry, dude, my days of being some dumb vic is over."

"Goldie—"

I hated the little bit of excitement I felt that he called. That he didn't want to be through. The shit just pissed me off even more. "Look, Dyme, I know you not calling me from a new number—probably some fuckin' prepaid joint—so your crazy ass bitch of a wife can't trace your calls. And no, you ain't moving me to another apartment or in a house 'cause your ass all scared to lay up in this motherfucka since she know where I live. And no, I don't need no fucking help with my bills. I don't need a vacation to nowhere. I don't need no more fucking jewelry or no more shopping sprees."

I didn't even realize I had jumped up to my feet, waving my finger like his tired ass was standing in front of me. "I don't need to be lied to, fucking played with, and played over. I don't need shit but for you to leave me the fuck alone, ya heard me?"

"You'll be back. Once you see just how comfy you had it out there and how different it's gone be without me. Humph, you'll be back."

I closed my cell phone and powered it off before I flung it across the room. My hand shook as I reached for my Nuvo and took it to the head like a forty.

The truth of my fears stung like a bitch.

4

Everyday I'm hustlin'
Everyday I'm hustlin'
Everyday I'm hustlin'
Everyday I'm hustlin'

—Rick Ross, "Hustlin'"

"I wrote the check and now it's time to cash it," I said, more to myself than my friends surrounding me at our table in Club 973. The sound of the music pressed against the walls and the bodies on the dance floor, drowning out any of my self-reflection bullshit.

Yummy leaned over toward me with the stirrer from her drink still between the lips of her peach-glossed mouth. The scent of weed, Newports, her body lotion, and the Henny & Coke she was drinking mingled together. "What you say?" she hollered, her short deep weave a bright ash blonde.

I just shook my head and took a sip from the Nuvo in my cup. No need fucking up her high wit my problems. Plus, I promised her that Dyme was a forbidden subject.

I frowned as the crowd suddenly circled around someone or something in the middle of the dance floor. Yummy and her cousin Kareema jumped to their feet and took they asses right over to see what was happening. Fight or what? Me? I dug deeper into my seat and crossed my legs. I already knew nine times out of ten that somebody was acting up and drawing attention to themselves.

I had nothing but money on my motherfuckin' mind.

I changed my house and cell number, e-mail and IM, blocked Dyme's motherfuckin' ass on Facebook, and booted him from my list of followers on Twitter. My ass was not playing about steering clear of Dyme. Two weeks down and a lifetime to go. But no Dyme meant a serious hurting on my cash flow. What little money I had would go quick with my bills. My ass needed a job. Did I want one? Hell to the no. But did I need one? Yes. Point-blank.

I wrote the check telling Dyme to take his D & D and now I had to cash it and rely on nobody but my motherfuckin' self.

The crowd went wild beneath the flickering lights. When I thought I heard "Go Yummy," I frowned and rose to my feet in the thigh-high leather boots I wore over black leggings with a sequin tank. I didn't miss the way the fellas were eyeing me. I'd be a liar if I said I didn't know I had hips, ass, and thick thighs for days. The short leather jacket I wore didn't do a damn thing to hide it.

Niggas stayed appreciating. Nothing new. I looked good. My blondish hair was moussed down and curly as shit. The goldish tones of my makeup and my extra-lush mink lashes only emphasized my eyes and high cheekbones.

I wasn't looking for dick or dough. But I liked the attention, especially since I never really was into the club. All of my free time used to be for Dyme, and Dyme's days in the club had been over a long time ago.

I eased between the crowd of bodies to stand beside Kareema's short pudgy ass in the inner circle just as the song switched to "How Low Can You Go" by Ludacris. I shook my head and laughed because Yummy was doing way too much on that dirty-ass floor.

She ran her hands over her quick weave as she slid into a split and then slammed the floor with her ass à la Chardonnay from *For the Love of Ray J*.

Kareema nudged me when two thirsty-for-attention chicks in see-through catsuits and thongs bust through the crowd. When one dropped to the floor and twisted her legs behind her head, I knew these bitches could have the floor. It wasn't even that serious. Flashes from camera phones were going on like crazy . . . especially when somebody pointed out her tampon string was showing and her inner thighs was mad ashy. Her ass was going straight to be clowned on Youknow youdeadazzwrong.com.

"Man, wheretheydothatat?" I said with attitude, turning to head back to our table. Yummy and Kareema followed.

Ignoring the hands pulling at my waist and wrist from dudes checking on a fine bitch, I checked my diamond watch. *Humph.* I tried to focus on the time and not on pawing that mug. It was after two in the morning. "I'm ready to be out. You two ready?" I asked, reaching in the pocket of my leather coat for my keys.

I was more than glad when they followed me out the club. At first the fresh winter air felt good after the heat and the smell of liquor, bodies, and weed, but after a few steps my thighs were freezing in these leggings.

"Let's go to Dino's," Kareema offered, her arms crossed over her chest with her microbraids twisted up in a knot atop her round chocolate face.

My stomach grumbled at the mention of the twenty-four-hour diner that was the spot to be after leaving the clubs. My ass was so busy singing the blues over Dyme that I wasn't even eating like I used to. My size-twelve pants were getting loose and I wasn't trying to lose none of my bottom.

Yummy said, "Let me roll one so I can be good and fucked up when we get to that bitch. Shit, y'all know how hungry I be after I blaze one."

"Yeah, bitch, you eat like a damn dude." Kareema joked. "Fuck that. I don't want your ass nowhere near my kitchen when you smoking."

We all laughed as we turned the corner. The streets were empty, and when a blacked-out van rolled up the street slow as hell we all paused. It was the perfect setup for some stickup kids. Empty street. Three females.

"Shit," we all swore together as the van eased over close to the curb.

I didn't know whether to break and run or what.

"And I just bought this damn leather coat," Yummy said, already unzipping it.

"This some bullshit for real," Kareema added, sounding mad and aggravated as hell.

The blacked-out passenger window rolled down.

My heart was beating like a motherfucka but Yummy and Kareema acted like this was some normal ish for them. I eyed these bitches steady undoing jewelry and shit while muttering under they breath. What the fuck?

"Whaddup, honeys. What's poppin'?"

We all looked up at Gunz smiling at us with his grillz gleaming against high yellow complexion and his left eye roaming in the socket like it was looking for something behind the damn lid. No one ever did have the balls to ask that nigga what happened to his fuckin' eye. But I heard everything from he was born that way to he was in a bad fight. Either way, I wished the motherfucka would wear a patch. Fuck it.

No doubt that he was a stickup kid, and if he didn't know us he woulda hopped out that van and ran our pockets for real. We wouldn't been left with shit but hurt fuckin' feelings. Gunz lived in King Court with his girlfriend, LoLo—this wannabe bougie bitch going to Essex County College for nursing. Nobody hated on her for going to college, but that bitch acted like she was better than somebody. LoLo didn't know that whenever Yummy called on that nigga he ran to get the pussy.

Yummy threw her hands up in the air, all "hell no" and shit. "Man, shit, you scared the shit out us rolling up like that."

I shook my head, glad the feeling of bubble guts eased off. "Damn, Gunz, what it do, baby?" I asked.

He eyed me from head to toe, pausing on my hips and thighs. "Good to see you out, ma. You a'ight?"

I nodded as I licked some of the gloss from my lips. I knew he was talking 'bout that shit that went down with Dyme and his wife. "I'm *real* good."

"You look it," the driver said in this deep-ass voice that made me think he could blow like Jaheim or something.

I stepped to the side a little bit and leaned over to try and look through the tinted mirror at some dude I didn't know. The tint was too dark and just asking for the police to pull they ass over. These niggas was riding suspect as hell. "Thank you," I said anyway, smiling because a situation like this could turn ugly in a hot second.

Gunz scratched in his crazy-ass uneven 'fro. "Where y'all

headed?" he asked, his eyes on Yummy in the leather bustier and short ruffled skirt she wore with ankle boots.

"We 'bout to go tear Dino's up. Y'all down?" she asked, getting her serious flirt on.

Gunz was cool and all, but what the fuck Yummy saw in that nigga was way beyond me. The eye. The robberies. The crazy rep. Man, fuck that. She always talking 'bout he had a dick big as a two-liter soda bottle. Humph, God had to bless that fool with something.

I didn't want to do shit but climb in my car and get the heat pumping. "I'm going to the car, Yummy, it's cold as shit out here," I said, already walking past her. "See you later, Gunz, and you too, Gunz's friend."

"'Bye, Gunz. 'Bye, Has," Kareema said, following right behind me while Yummy stepped closer to the van.

Beep-beep.

I deactivated the alarm.

"Has? You know him?" I asked Kareema as I climbed in the driver's seat and she slid in the back.

"Yeah, that his van. That nigga sell everything out that bitch. Pocketbooks, clothes, socks, fuckin' underwear, DVDs, CDs, MP3s, cell phones—"

I held up my hand, waving off the rest of Kareema's roll call. "I got you. Everything."

"Usually he be over in front of White Castle on Irvine Turner Boulevard." Kareema pulled her purse from beneath the passenger seat. Soon she was popping away on a stick of Juicy Fruit gum. "That nigga hella fine, too."

I cranked the Lexus, with my eyes on the shadow of his reflection in his rearview mirror. Sometimes life in the hood was all about the hustle. The grind. I had to get on mine and try to make money to take care of my damn self for the first time in all my twenty-two years.

"Hustlin'" had to be my new anthem.

I drove up and pulled to a stop behind the van. Leaving Kareema in the car, I climbed out and walked up to the driver's-side window feeling like that nigga eye was on me. The window lowered and thick weed smoke escaped into the cold night air.

"Has, right?" I asked, tilting my head to the side as I locked my honey-gold eyes on him. He *was* cute too, with his high cheekbones, slanted eyes, and long dreads but I was not looking for love—or nothing else.

"That's right," he said, his voice rough and deep. He stuck his blunt out the window at me.

Nada. I shook my head because I never smoked nothing I ain't seen rolled. Plenty motherfuckas be lacing they shit with dope or coke and I ain't even trying to get to that kind of high. "I don't smoke," I lied.

Gunz and Yummy started laughing. "Since when you stopped?" He asked with a "yeah right, you know your ass lying" face.

"Okay," Yummy agreed, now leaning inside the van.

"Idon'tsmokenomoreokay!" I snapped, my words running together as I eyed them two like I could straight slap they ass like I was they pimp and they had short me some money.

I smiled when I shifted my face back to look at Has. "Listen, I hear you got the best shit for sale, which means you got the best supplier, which means a lady like me tryna get down and get my own little hustle going. You know what I'm saying?" I was talking all soft and shit. It was my best hook-'em voice.

Has took a deep drag from his blunt, his already tigerlike eyes squinting as he released the smoke through the side of his mouth. "And why should I cut you in on my bizness?" he asked.

One thing I learned hanging up under Dyme all the time was any deal was all about the negotiation. You had to give something to get something. It's always about supply and motherfuckin' demand.

I was busy thinking even as I was shivering like a bitch from the biting cold wrapping around my body. I kept my eyes locked with his. It was all about trust too, and nothing said you was on the up-and-up like eye contact.

"Listen, Has, you don't need me. I know that—"

Has shifted in his seat to lean out the window. The scent of his cologne or body oils wafted to me. "Nah, I don't need you but I want you."

Boom. He laid it out there just like that.

I ain't gone lie. This nigga's vibe was mad sexy. I was even feeling the way his white teeth bit the end of the blunt.

It was the first time in six years that I ever felt that vibe with a dude other than Dyme. But being around Dyme taught me another lesson about business. Never mix it with pleasure.

"But I need you more than you want me," I began, picking my words carefully as I tried to slide our convo away from pleasure and back to the business at hand. A lot of the time, Dyme took me with him when he went to buy his merchandise for the store. Most dumb bitches woulda been listening to music in the car or playing with they acrylic tips. This bitch? I got right out with him, listened, and fucking learned how to handle business. Mama Bit always told me to keep my mouth shut and my ears open and I would learn something. She was right. I saw that nigga negotiate to get the best profit margin. Sometimes he even listened to my advice on what to buy and what to leave the fuck alone. Dyme was many things but dumb wasn't one of them. And neither was I. "So what I'm offering is like a hood franchise, you know. I pay you for your merchandise ten or fifteen percent above what it cost you. I agree not to sell shit in your vicinities. *And then* I give you ten percent of my profits . . . at first."

He was smoking, but I could tell Has wasn't all the way fucked up, because I saw the interest in his eyes.

"I know a lot of people and I used to shop a lot of stores. Let's make this money," I urged him, reaching out to touch his arm lightly.

He just watched me with those tiger eyes making me feel some kind of way that I ignored. Dyme's bullshit had fucked the game up for anyone even trying to come behind him. I was all about getting on up on my Giuseppe heels.

"I guess they call you Goldie because of your hair and your eyes?" Has asked.

I shrugged. "My ex gave me that name."

"Well, he shoulda called you Honey instead, because everything about you looks sweet as hell." His eyes dropped to my mouth. "Everythang."

Game always recognizes game and I felt all nervous, biting the sheer gloss from my bottom lip and shit.

"Give me your number and I'll think about it. A'ight?"

I nodded as he reached in the front pocket of his jeans for a BlackBerry. Even as I gave him my number and he programmed it in his phone, I tried to ignore the scent of his cologne floating in the night air around me.

"A'ight?" he said again.

I felt like I was being dismissed, so I gave him another soft smile before I walked back to my Lexus. And yes, I gave him the full sexy, extra up-and-down, side-to-side motion of my hips because I knew that nigga's sexy eyes was on me in his rearview mirror.

Yummy finally got in the car. "They ain't coming to Dino's," she said, reaching out to turn on the radio. The sound of Funkmaster Flex on Hot 97 filled the car.

The van pulled off and I checked the mirrors before I did a U-turn to take us downtown.

"What you see in that fool?" Kareema asked in between a rapid fire of gum pops, ripping the question from my own goddamn thoughts.

Yummy reached in her pocket and pulled out a sack of weed, holding it up to swing in the air like a bell. "And a dick big as your arm," she added with a neck roll and a little bounce of her shoulders before she reached in my glove compartment for a cigar. She busted it down the middle with her acrylic thumbnail. "I'm a blaze this sticky-icky-icky right now and I'll blaze that dick tomorrow. Whoot Whoot!"

We laughed at that bitch as I pressed the pedal of the Lex and sped toward Dino's.

It took almost three weeks for Has to call me. My rent and car insurance came due during that time. I tried some of every damn thang to make me some money.

First it was babysitting. That shit was a kibosh after a week. The shit Dyme bought for my apartment was too nice for spilt milk and sticky jelly prints and shit.

Next I hired these two chicks I know who could shoplift a penny outta nigga pocket without them feeling a thing. But them bitches wised up and backed out when they found out I was gonna sell the clothes and not buy them.

So then, fucking 'round with Yummy's scandalous ass, *we* hopped in the Lex and rode to Short Hills mall to shoplift some designer shit to sell back in the hood. One afternoon getting chased out the store and into the surrounding woods and I knew I wasn't fucking with *that* shit no more. I used to go in that mall and buy it up like money wasn't nothing. Now I'm boosting out that bitch?

Humph. I knew I officially fell the fuck off.

But I refused to run back to Dyme. Trust me, I knew he was waiting for me. The good life was waiting on me but I couldn't chance my heart with that nigga no more.

Plenty big-time dopeboys tried to holler, wanting to make me *that* bitch again. Even though my bills was chomping at my ass, I turned them down. Sent back the bottles of champagne in the club. Turned down offers to go on shopping sprees. Refused weekend trips to sunny locales. I wasn't putting my destiny and my livelihood in the hands of a man again. Fuck the dumb shit.

Mama Bit always said: "Fool me once, shame on you. Fool me twice, shame on me."

My lesson about being a kept woman was well learned. I was all about my own hustle. My own business. My own money. I would finally get what the fuck I been missing fucking around with Dyme these last six years. Money. Then the power. And then my respect.

"How low can you go . . . how low can you go . . ."

At the sound of my ringtone, I tightened my plush Egyptian cotton towel around my still-damp body before I scooped up my cell from the bed, hitting Send with my metallic gold Minx thumbnail.

"Whaddup, Has?"

"You as always."

My semi-crush on this nigga was helping me get over Dyme. I wasn't gonna act on it but it was nice knowing that I could have this big, fine, *young* motherfucka . . . if and when I wanted to.

Right now, though, I was on a dick break and his call was all about business. After almost a month of waiting, Has had finally came through. With the five hundred dollars I got from pawning a couple of my bracelets at Rich's on Broad Street, I was in the bootleg business.

When Has brought my first shipment by my apartment I had to admit I was impressed. The purses and handbags were decent enough knock-offs, the DVDs played clear as hell—none of that heads in front of the camera or people in the movie laughing and talking or half the screen cut off. His CDs were albums that hadn't even dropped yet and even had covers.

Word was already heavy on this side of the Bricks that I was the chick to get with for the best shit. I even had business cards and flyers drawn up with the number for a throwaway prepaid cell phone. Most times I sold my shit at events all over the tristate area, or people would call me and I'd meet them somewhere safe if they was looking to buy a good amount. My plan from the jump was to avoid standing on a street corner tryna sell like a crackhead. Me? Nada. Fuck that shit.

Even though I couldn't shop it up like when Dyme was financing my flyness, I still made it my business to stay dope. I made sure my ass was extra bossy when I went to the club or out to concerts or events. Outfit coordinated like a motherfucka, hair laid, makeup on point, perfume smelling up the air.

Bitches saw me, wanted to be me, and was willing to purchase what I had to sell to get like me.

Niggas saw me, wanted to be with me, and was willing to purchase what I had to get at me.

Humph. On some real shit, none of them was gonna get they way, but I got mine because I always sold out. *Always.* I stayed hustlin'.

"Goldie, you there?" Has asked, his voice just sounding like pure man.

I shook off the butterflies at the thought of his sexy self. "Yeah, I was getting the last of this merchandise ready to take with me to the comedy show at Symphony Hall tonight," I told him, moving out the bedroom to the kitchen in nothing but the plush towel I wrapped around my body after my bath.

I had finished taking inventory of the fake designer bags, logo scarves, and wallets on my laptop. All of my DVDs and CDs were sold out. Most of the people living in King Court copped those as soon as they heard I got some in.

"I didn't think you had it in you to hustle hard and get that shit sold," Has admitted, the sound of bass thumping in his background. "Thought yo ass was too bougie or some shit."

I smiled as I looked out the window in my kitchen to the sun setting and the streetlights flickering on. In another couple of weeks winter would finally be over and, like the seasons, I was all about fucking change.

"I came from nothing and I'm trying hella hard not to go back there, you know? So I'm doing what I gotta do to maintain," I admitted to him, my voice filled with it all. Mama Bit's death. No parents. No family. Plenty bullies. Dyme's heartbreak. My struggles. "There was a time you wouldn't caught me nowhere near these fake-ass bags, far less selling them. But I'm good, you know. Doin' what I gotta to take care of myself."

A bitch like me refused to go down that easy.

"I can respect that."

"So I'll be ready to pay you and buy some more shit tomorrow. You down?" I asked, moving past the leather Parson chair to grab a bottled water from my stainless-steel fridge.

"Actually, I was calling to see if you was down on some new shit, Mz. Boss."

"What's up?" I asked.

"If your money right, my supplier got a shipment of electronics coming in tonight."

Cha-ching. "You mean televisions, iPods—"

"Laptops, cell phones. The works. He doesn't get them in too often, so you gotta jump on it when he does."

I felt a little tingle shimmy up my pussy walls, but in that moment I didn't know if it was from Has or the idea of the money I could make. "Oh, I'm in. I. AM. IN."

Has laughed and I could hear his cocky-ass swagger. "A'ight, but these joints gone take more money."

I nodded, my mind already on selling. "So you'll bring me my shit and I'll pay you when you get here like always. You know I'm good for it."

"This time I'm gone need the money first."

Now *that* ish made me pause. There ain't too many motherfuckas I trusted—especially when it came to money. *My* money. Hell, this nigga hung out with Gunz, a known stickup kid. How I know I wasn't gonna be their latest vic or some shit? Damn. What if this was some crazy con game? Shit.

"The buy-in is too high for me to cop enough shit for me and you," he told, his deep voice sounding muffled before I heard the flick of a lighter.

Think, Goldie. Think.

"Hold on a sec."

I could tell he covered the cell phone while he talked to somebody else.

Think, Goldie. Think. What would Dyme do?

"A'ight, I'm back."

"So you don't trust me, Has?" I asked, moving through my kitchen and back into my bedroom. I dropped my towel to the floor. My outfit for the night was laid out across my faux-fur cover.

"Out here on these streets? I don't trust nobody . . . but this ain't even about that, Goldie. Either you in or you out."

His voice was hard, but I pressed on.

"I don't trust nobody either, Has. That money would wipe me the fuck out. And if something happened and I had to start over . . ." I said, pretending to sound confused and lost as I picked up a bottle of Bath & Body Works lotion from my dresser.

"I put you on . . . and *you* don't trust *me*?"

"I really need this hustle, Has," I said, tossing the lotion bottle over my shoulder before I reached for one of the dozen perfume bottles sitting on a tray on my dresser. "I want to go with you to meet the supplier."

"Nah. No haps, Goldie."

He was sounding all hesitant and shit but there was some shit that I figured out about Has. This nigga was all about his own grind, and money's always an issue with a hustler.

"I'll up what I pay you to twenty percent."

He laughed. "Nah."

Damn.

"Yo, you in or out?"

Biting my bottom lip, I cut my eyes to my reflection in the mirror. I knew I was taking a chance. Releasing a heavy-ass breath filled up with my nerves, I said, "I'm in."

"You need time to get your money straight?"

I had plans to open up a bank account, but I been so busy making money and then flipping the money that I usually kept my money stashed in my pillowcases. Something felt good as hell to me about sleeping with my head snuggled right above my cash. Plus, this bootleg business shit didn't exactly work on a nine-to-five schedule like the banks, and the ATMs had daily limits.

But that wasn't his motherfuckin' bizness all my loot was in my apartment. "I gotta go get it, so give me twenty minutes before you head this way," I lied.

"A'ight."

Click.

Snapping my phone closed, I tossed it on the bed and finished getting dressed for the show. My nerves was really fucking with me and I tried to get my mind right, but the risk of losing everything I had was scaring the shit out of me. For real.

The days of running through money because I knew Dyme would lace me with more was over. These days my ass was flying without a net. If I wanted to return to the days of shopping on a whim, I had to take this hood hustle to a whole 'nother level. One thing Dyme taught me over the last six years was how to . . .

"Make money money, make money money money," I sang as I turned in the mirror to double-check my appearance. Had to make sure I was looking right and tight.

My hair was pulled back in a low-slung ponytail that was so glossy my hair shimmered like real gold. I smoothed my hands over my hips and thighs in the fitted winter-white sweater-dress I wore. A matching cropped leather jacket with gold metal details and winter-white suede boots finished the outfit.

True, it was all from last winter because I sure didn't have the funds to buy a thousand-dollar outfit these days, but I wanted to look good. The diamond hoops Dyme gave me for Valentine's one year would finish the outfit off right.

I picked them up out of my jewelry box. I didn't want to think about him. I didn't want the good times fucking with my head. I hadn't really believed the day would ever come when me and Dyme stopped fucking with each other . . . but now I knew I was wrong.

Shaking it off, I put on the earrings and got the money from the pillow on my bed, shoving it deep into my Gucci crocodile purse just as there was a knock at my door.

It was either Has or Yummy.

My heels clicked against the tiled floors as I made my way to the front door. I checked the peephole and my heart did all kinds of flip-flops and shit to see that fine nigga leaning against the door frame. All cool. All confident. All cocky.

Just giving me plenty to ignore about his ass.

Come on, Goldie, I told myself, shoving my purse under my arm and using my index fingers to press down my nipples that just got hard as jail time at the sight of him. *This about dough. Fuck the dick. Right? Right.*

With one last shiver like a fiend 'bout to get that hit he worked all day to get by picking up cans or stealing pipes from basements, I took a deep breath and opened the door.

"Hey, Has. Whassup?"

As he strolled in past me, towering over me by at least six inches, I wondered if I was crazy to let this nigga into my apartment. Jonesing for his ass or not, I mighta just made my second dumb move of the day.

"Dayuuum, Goldie. Your shit hooked the fuck up."

Everyone said that shit whenever they came to my apartment for the first time. The chocolate and taupe décor was all stylish and sleek against the neutral-painted walls and tiled floors. Dyme always said I had good taste for my age.

I grabbed the envelope of money from my purse and turned to hand it to him. "When it came to spending money, my ex was real good to me."

Has took the envelope and slid it into the inside pocket of the charcoal-gray down jacket he wore over a thick sweater of the same color. "Yeah, Dyme's good people," he said, all casual and shit like he didn't just drop a bomb on me.

"You know Dyme?" I asked, trying like a motherfucka to sound all nonchalant and shit. And failing big time.

Has smiled down at me and suddenly he went from a tall dark figure that would scare a motherfucka in a dark alley to someone who could easily step onto the runway in anyway Sean John fashion show. "I know him. I used to own this record store on Hawthorne Avenue next to the beauty salon he bought for . . ."

My eyes dropped from his as my gut clenched with embarrassment. I been knew about the salon he bought Frieda but it was just another example of his fucking lies coming back to shame me. I'd thought I was a lady boss when I wasn't bossing a motherfuckin' thing but the dreams in my head. Dreams that was so far from reality.

"An-y-way," I said with this stiff-ass smile as I walked to the door.

Suddenly I felt Has's hand on my waist before he turned me to face him. "My bad, Goldie, I wasn't thinking a'ight. Man, fuck old dude. It's his loss."

See, what people failed to understand was that it wasn't just Dyme's loss that we were through. It was mine too. Fuck the jewels and the clothes and the promises of a house and the title of wife. I lost six years of my life to this nigga. Six fucking years that I couldn't get back.

It finally hit me that Has and I were kinda close. His hand was still on my lower back and my clit was pumping to life. I stepped away from that goddamn vibe, scared as hell that I was gonna push this nigga to the floor and strip him from the waist down and do work. "I'm straight," I said, keeping on toward the front door. "So what time you'll be through with the stuff?"

Back to business. All business.

He licked his lips and did that kinda cocky-ass smile like he knew I wanted to fuck. "About ten or eleven," he said, moving to the door.

"I'll still be at the comedy show at Symphony Hall. Just come straight there. Hit me on my cell and I'll come out. Cool?" I pulled the door open for him, and the noise of kids running somewhere in the building echoed.

He stepped past me into the hall but then turned in his all-black Timbs. "Goldie, yo, listen. How long you gone fight this?" Has asked me, his voice rough and sexy as he looked down on me with those eyes.

I knew what he meant. I knew exactly what he was talking about. That vibe was a motherfucka. "Fight what?" I lied.

He laughed before he nodded his head. "I can hold out long as you can." With that said, he turned and strolled down the brightly lit hall.

I stepped out into the hall and watched that fine nucka walk away.

Has pushed the door open at the end of the hall. "Long as you can, Goldie," he said again before he disappeared into the stairwell.

The winter chill had eased off and it was packed with people outside Symphony Hall. There were other people outside selling some of everything—especially pocketbooks, hanging from their arms in case they ass had to bail out real quick if the cops pulled up.

Yummy and I had already decided how to play our position and actually up the price of the bags to compete. There was no better way to catch the eye of them bougie bitches like me than to make them feel like a higher-priced bag was better—and trust, chicks like me feel like they want the best of what's available. All of 'em were faker than a quick weave on a bald-headed bitch, but ours were better quality. None of the clear glue showing from beneath edges where there shoulda been stitching. No bullshit zippers ready to split. None of that almost-look-like-the-right-kind-of-logo bullshit. Our product was on point.

Like always, the real Gucci or Louie or Prada I was wearing would set the convo off:

"I like your bag."

"Oooh, I love your bag, girl."

"Your bag is fly as hell."

"Damn, your bag is hot."

"Cute bag."

Yadda, yadda, fucking yadda.

Me? I eyed them, knowing that this body and my whole look was straight killing 'em, and I'd say: "This right here is real . . . but I got some bags for sale that I would carry if the real one wasn't in my budget. You know what I'm saying?"

Humph. Hook, line, sinker.

And fuck that carrying-around-bags-on-my-arms bullshit like some head or some shit. Nah. That's a done da-da for sure.

We parked the Lex down the street and was steady escorting people back and forth to that trunk to see what we had to offer. I gave out cards and let them know about all the electronics I would have real soon.

Straight hustling.

Yummy and me sold the rest of those purses before the comedy show even began. I even had orders for when I got in a new shipment. I gave her a cut on the dough for helping me and we was able to lamp and enjoy the comedy showcase.

"Why you keep checking your phone?" Yummy leaned over to ask me, talking all loud above the crowd laughing.

"Has was supposed to call me by now." There was no denying I was nervous as hell. If that Negro kept my money what I was gonna do, go to the police? Puh-leeze. Wind up with *my* ass in jail.

Where that nigga at?

I called his cell phone but it went straight to voice mail.

Something wasn't right.

And then Yummy's cell lit up in her purse. She was busy chuckling it up at Sommore on the stage while it was steady vibrating and flashing a bunch of colors like a disco ball.

"Right, right," she said agreeing with whatever the comedienne was saying before her ass pointed up at the stage, clapping like she saw President Obama, Michelle, the two kids, the grandmother, and the damn dog.

I didn't know what the fuck Sommore was saying, and really didn't give a flying fuck either. I wanted my money or my merchandise. Plain and simple.

Yummy's cell phone lit up again, vibrating like a dildo with extra-strength batteries.

"Yummy, see who calling you?" I snapped.

"It's just Gunz. I'll call that nigga later. I'm enjoying the goddamn show."

I snatched the phone from her purse and flipped it open. "Gunz?"

People starting shushing me and shit. Man, fuck them. I wanted my money.

"Yummy, yo, it's fucked up. Has got caught up in a fed raid for bootlegging. Shit, that nigga locked the fuck up."

My whole body went numb.

Has and my damn money was gone.

I couldn't do shit but drop the motherfuckin' phone.

5

Don't wanna cry over nobody else

No no no no I can do bad all by myself.

—Mary J. Blige, "I Can Do Bad All By Myself"

Three Months Later

I seen more than a lot at twenty-two years old. Okay, not as much as the ones who had to sell ass to eat, or fight memories of perverted motherfuckas making them feel grown before their time, or the ones lost to drugs and shit. I get that. My life coulda been worse. But I know damn well, plenty of suburb-living, college-attending, sorority chicks—black or white—wouldn't fuck with my life for shit.

Humph. I don't blame them.

My days laying up in bed with Dyme and not carrying my ass to school was coming back to bite me in the ass.

"Order up for table twelve."

I pushed some of my flyaway bangs behind my ear as I made my way between the tables in the diner. Two plates stacked high as hell with food waited for me.

Six months ago nobody coulda told a top-notch, boss-ass bitch like me that my ass would be up in Dino's twenty-four-hour diner working. For the last two months, our after-hours grub spot was where I made money to take care of myself.

Ain't life a bitch?

A sweaty, feet-aching, backbreaking, grease-funk-all-up-in-my-hair, lousy-tip-making bitch. Period. Dino's stayed crunk, and even with ten waitresses on duty to handle the fifty tables, I felt like I spent my whole shift humping.

I was sweating everywhere. Head. Under my titties. Between my thighs. I couldn't wait for my shift to be over at 6 A.M. so I could take it to the house.

Trust and believe this job was a last resort for me . . . and a wake-up call. It was hella hard looking for a job and all I had to offer was a pretty face. There was college grads out there willing to do clerical work because the job market was so fucked up. Why did I think a high school dropout like me without any typing skills and no work experience could compete? I didn't know a damn thing about writing a résumé and definitely ain't had shit to put on one anyway. Office work? Nope. Retail? Nada. Management? Definite hell to the no. And it took filling out a hundred applications to realize I had to shit or get off the pot. I needed funds. Ends. A damn job.

Any damn job.

In truth, it was hard for a bitch like me to admit that I was less than. Not enough. That pill was bitter as hell to swallow.

I stored all my eggs in Dyme's basket and he shattered them.

Either I could find me a new sugar daddy or get off my ass and take care of myself the best way I could.

Beggars couldn't be choosy.

I grabbed my plates, making sure to balance them joints

as I made my way back to the table. Last thing I needed was to dump a plate of pancakes and sausages on somebody's damn head . . . like I did the first damn night I worked.

Shit, it took time to get my shit straight. This was my very first job and I ain't know shit 'bout being no waitress.

It was summer in the city and the nights definitely were longer, still echoing outside. Even though it was almost three in the morning, the later it got, the more the diner filled up as the clubs closed down. People were hungry and not ready for their night of partying it up to end. Outside, the steady thump-thump of bass from of passing cars and the ones pulling into the parking lot sounded off. Out the glass windows, it looked like cars of all shapes, sizes, makes, and models were out there with chicks in flashy heels and dudes posted up. The parking lot was packed.

"Okay, here's your corn beef hash with eggs scrambled with cheese and home fries," I said, setting the plate in front of a big light-skinned dude breathing loud as hell like that shit was in fucking surround sound. I put the other plate in front of this other dude looking way too much like Biggie. "And a T-bone steak and cheese eggs," I said, about to ask his notorious-looking ass if he wanted a Welch's grape juice.

Them niggas tore into they food paying me no mind. "Can I get y'all anything else?" I asked, wiping the sweat from my hands on the back pockets of my jeans.

They both shook they head and waved me away. *Deuces then, nuckas.*

I was getting tickets for my customers while standing at the end of the long-ass counter running down the middle of the large restaurant, when the bell over the door rang. I looked up and into the diner walked Armina and two other chicks. Each one was dressed to the nines. You couldn't see the designer labels, but the cut and quality was there. Their heads was held high and their oversized designer bags swinging from their arms. These bitches reminded me of how fly I used to be. Glossy hair. Perfect makeup. Dope outfit. Banging bodies. Fuck-me heels. The whole set. My life.

Or the life I used to have.

My hand went to my raggedy ponytail. I barely had time to slap on some lip gloss when my shift started and I bit that shit off a long time ago. The black T-shirt and black jeans I wore was already crusted in spots. The heels were gone and a pair of comfy black Nikes was in their place. These days it felt like I ain't do shit but sleep away the mornings to get ready for work that night.

I was glad they strutted they asses on the other side of the diner . . . and out of my station. I ain't seen her or been anywhere near Dyme's downtown store. I didn't know if she heard about me and her moms bumping heads. Didn't really give a fuck. I just wasn't in the mood for no drama.

Pushing them aside, I saw Yummy and Gunz come walking into the diner all boo'ed up and pretty much fucked up from the glassy look of their eyes. Yummy was Yummy in all her colorful glory. Her ultra-short quick weave was jet-black with royal-blue highlights to match her outfit, shoes, nails and shades. I just shook my head. I ain't had the heart to tell that chick that she looked like Lady Smurf or some shit.

"Girl, you missed it. The club was packed!" Yummy did the Dougie in her royal-blue heels to her seat on the booth.

I just laughed at her. She always knew how to have fun.

Gunz was in his normal stickup-kid wear. All black. Humph. I wasn't sure this nigga *wouldn't* rob the joint. Gunz be wildin' like his brain was all over the place more than his eye. Yummy liked it, and if she liked it, I loved it. Fuck it.

I handed them one of the oversized plastic menus. "Next weekend I'm off I'm going," I told them, smelling the scent of weed around they ass. They had to just blew trees in the car 'cause I was about to get a contact just standing over them.

"Yo, Goldie, I talked to Has the other day, yo," Gunz said, pointing to the breakfast special on the menu before he handed it to me.

Has. My gut clenched as I tucked his menu under my arm and jotted down that he wanted ham and eggs. I didn't say shit and kept a blank-ass look on my face.

Gunz looked up at me and I made myself focus on his good eye. "He said he gone pay you back that money the feds took when he get out."

"And when that nigga 'posed to get out?" I asked, sounding like I really meant "whatthefuckeva."

Gunz shrugged. "I know he said he got a good lawyer."

"On a fed case?" I looked at this fool like he *was* a fool. When the feds swooped in they be ready, and Has had got caught up in some serious shit being in the wrong place at the wrong damn time.

"O-*kay*," Yummy agreed. "And let me have a sausage and cheese omelet. Bring us two lemonades, Goldie."

My mind was only half on jotting down her order when that bell sounded off again. I looked up.

In walked Rick, aka Slick Rick the Ruler, one of the baddest male strippers in the tristate area who "ruled" because that nigga had a twelve-inch dick. Over the years he made plenty money slinging, popping, and grinding that dick, and now he owned Club Naughty over on Clinton Ave.

Just like every other weekend night, Rick had just about all his female dancers with him. They came in after Club Naughty closed. There was tits, ass, glitter lotion, weave, long nails, and fake lashes for days.

Even though that nigga was dressed for business with his clean-cut fade and a black tailored suit with a black silk shirt that I recognized as Sean John, the way he moved his body was nothing but pure pleasure. Like he was still onstage and ready to pull away the suit and perform in nothing but a dick sock. Like he was built for fucking.

I looked away from his fine ass and walked away, heading into the kitchen. I didn't know my ass was in somebody's path until we walked right into each other.

"Damn, my bad." My steps paused when I looked up into Armina's face.

Her expression went from apologetic to pissed the hell off in two seconds flat.

She knew.

Fuck her, her mammy, and her no-good daddy.

I sidestepped her.

Armina stepped back in my path in her satin jumpsuit and heels. "Busting tables now that you ain't spending my daddy's money, bitch?"

"Bitch?" I snapped, my free hand already balling up into a fist to shoot this bitch one and lay her ass flat out.

Keep cool, Goldie. You need this job. You need this job.

Armina smirked as she circled me in the hall. "You sure look a *lot* different from when you was coming to the store."

Then she laughed in my face, filling my nostrils with the scent of liquor and Juicy Fruit.

I felt my anger building and I knew I would hurt this

bitch, lose my job, and probably catch a charge. My days of being played the chump *been* over. "I'm warning your ass, Armina, give me ten feet or—"

"Or what?" she asked, pushing her round face close to mine.

"Orders up!" Dominic, the cook and the owner of Dino's hollered out.

I brushed past her ass hard and walked into the kitchen to put my order in. Dominic barely eyed me as I gave him the orders and left. My mind was on Armina and straight cracking her jaw as I picked up my orders, took them to my customers, and then came back behind the counter to fix Yummy and Gunz's drinks.

Marcie, an extra-tall bleach blonde with long red nails came up to me. "Hey, Goldie. Table thirty-two requested you," she said, her Portuguese accent heavy.

Table thirty-two. I knew exactly who that was.

"We'll swap, baby, no biggie," Marcia said, taking the glasses from me to head to Yummy and Gunz's table. "Plus I'll help you out. Scoot."

Clearing my throat, I made sure my pen and pad was in the pocket of my black apron before I headed to the rear of the restaurant, feeling some kind of way about the request. Table thirty-two was really one of two private dining areas in the restaurant. The double doors to the room was closed.

I could already hear all the ruckus inside before I opened one of the doors and walked in. The TV in the corner was on and the girls were all chatting it up, but Rick's eyes was on me. The old Goldie, the one dressed to kill and confident as fuck woulda met his stare and gave back even more of my own. That Goldie was gone.

I cleared my throat, all nervous and shit, and took out my pen and pad. "How y'all doin'? My name's Goldie and I'll be your waitress. Can I start you off with drinks?"

They was seven people in the party at two tables pushed together. I started at one end and worked my way down until I was waiting on this short and thick brown-skinned chick sitting right next to Rick. Something about the way she leaned in toward him was like she was letting it be known they was fucking.

She looked up at me. "I want a lemonade with crushed ice. If you bring it and the ice ain't crushed, I don't want it."

I forced a smile and turned to Rick. He just stared at me. For the longest damn time, this fine nigga just sat there staring at me. "And what can I get you?" I asked, not missing the eyes going back and forth between my face and his.

"What's your name?" he asked.

"Goldie," I answered, avoiding the daggers Miz Crushed Ice was shooting me with her eyes.

Rick had this sweet brown complexion like caramel. His jet-black hair was freshly faded and framed up his round face. Even without his breaking a smile I could see this nigga had dimples for days.

He stood up and came around the table. Whatever cologne he was wearing surrounded me too. "You ever danced?" he asked.

"Huh?" I asked, my face frowned up.

He moved past me to sit back down in his seat. "You have the look to make some serious money dancing, Goldie. Whaddup?"

I looked at him like he was crazy. "No, no, *noooooo*. I'm good," I said, laughing as I tapped my pen on the pad. "Your drink?"

"Yes, Rick, give the *waitress* your drink."

"Chill out, Lick-Lick."

Lick-Lick? I looked at Miz Crushed Ice and this bitch released her tongue. It reached past her chin. She flicked the pointed tip. Ugh. What the fuck?

Rick reached in his pocket and this motherfucka pulled out a wad big enough to choke somebody. I remembered the days when Dyme gave me free rein to peel what I wanted off the money roll he kept. Then I think about all the emotional bullshit that money cost me. Moving on.

He peeled off four fifty-dollar bills and leaned forward to shove them in the pocket of my apron. "Dance for me."

What? No this motherfucka didn't!

"I serve up food, not ass," I told him, reaching in my pocket for the money to toss on the table in front of him.

Some of the strippers laughed, other ones talked shit. Like I really gave a fuck.

"Don't knock the hustle, boo."

"Better than smelling like fucking grease all damn day."

I felt my anger building but I held that shit in check. Fuck these hoes and the sweat-funky dollar bills they rode in on.

Rick picked up his money. "Get me a orange juice," he said.

I finished taking the drink orders and headed out the room for the fountains. *Me? A stripper? Nigga please.*

"I still can't believe you keep turning big-dick Slick Rick down."

I pulled the covers I had over my head down to glare at Yummy. "And I can't believe you woke me up to talk about this bullshit." My ass was so sleepy I sounded like a dude.

Yummy pulled out a pack of Newports and lit one before she dropped down on the edge of my bed. "How much he offer last night?" she asked, before she let out the smoke.

"Five hundred. Now get the fuck out, Yummy." Wanting her ass to get the hint, I pulled the covers back over my head.

"Five bills? Five motherfuckin' bills to dance. Sheee-it. Fuck the bullshit. Shake what ya mama gave you."

Seconds later that bitch slapped me on my ass. It jiggled and bounced.

I *still* ignored her.

Slick Rick was on a mission to see me strip for him, and night after night he reached in that wallet and upped his offer. Two hundred. Three hundred. Four hundred. Five. That nigga was straight wildin'. It wasn't even that serious. For real.

"You sure you can't get off next weekend? Shit, all women get in free with they Family First card or a child-support printout."

Damn, sometimes I forgot Yummy had a set of six-year-old twins, Mercedes and Lexus, 'cause she never had them. They lived with her mother and father over in Bradley Courts.

Now I've heard of some crazy shit in the hood, but getting a discount if you got a EBT or child-support papers? "Well, I ain't got neither one so I ain't missing shit." My voice was muffled by the covers.

"True, true." Yummy stood up. "I'm 'bout to be out, but if you still want to buy my food stamps hit me up."

"A'ight."

As soon as the front door to my apartment closed I flung back the covers and hopped up out of bed. I stood up in front of the mirror, checking myself out in the wife beater and thong I wore. Don't get me wrong. I knew I was fine and I been dealing with these curves since before Dyme, but all of the women working for Rick were fine with hella bodies. What made that nigga keep fucking with me?

I used to be some nigga's mistress but I ain't never been hot or fast or slutty. I never ended grinded up on some dude in the club. I could dance my ass off . . . but strip?

Turning in the mirror, I looked over my shoulder while I made my ass shake, clap, and wiggle. And it was a fine and firm twenty-two-year-old ass. None of them wrinkles, stretch marks, and fucking dimples. Just a smooth golden ass.

Me, strip?

I loosened my ponytail and let my brownish-gold hair fall around my shoulders. I could fuck. I knew that. Wife or not, my pussy moves had Dyme fucked up bad.

I turned around and imitated that nasty-ass tongue trick Lick-Lick did while I danced to the sound of a Pretty Rick–type song playing in my head.

Did I have the body to strip? Hell, yeah. The moves. Most def. The look? No question.

But get my half-naked ass up on a stage surrounded by hard-dick dudes waving dollars?

I frowned at my reflection and stopped my nasty wind.

Hell to the no. I would stay my ass right at Dino's 'til a better hustle came along.

After a good-ass nap, I got up and took me a long hot shower. It was time to get my ass to work. I hated that I thought about whether Rick was coming in to Dino's tonight. I hated it even more that I decided to mousse up my hair and wear it curly. I actually put on some mascara, blush, and gold-tinted lip gloss. And instead of the usual black tee I wore, I found one of my fitted Baby Phat tees and a snug pair of jeans.

I smoked me a blunt to mellow the fuck out and ate a sandwich before I grabbed my keys and my purse and bounced. It was summertime, so everything was live and popping 'round this bitch. People was outside in the courtyard. Dudes was balling on the court or just posted up hollering at chicks walking by—who was walking by to get hollered at. Kids playing. Fiends searching. Tricks tricking.

"Whaddup, Goldie."

I waved to whoever the fuck that was before I climbed into my car, cranked up, and reversed out the spot, making sure not to run over somebody's damn child as I did. In the summer there was no rules, and kids 'round here stayed out late as hell playing.

I let my windows down halfway and turned up the radio as I pulled to a red light. I loved my city but a chick like me wasn't crazy. One second I could be sitting at a red light minding my own and the next a Glock was being pushed through the window in my face. This wasn't no fucking war zone or some shit, but it was best to be on your guard . . . and not just from stickup kids. The cops done kill many a motherfucka chasing behind stolen cars and running over whoever got in they fucking way.

But see, even for twenty-two I knew that most of that shit people felt about Newark was a motherfuckin' stereotype. Fucking 'round with the news you would think everybody in the poorer parts of the city was selling drugs or ass, collecting welfare or stamps, just doing dirty shit to get by. But there was plenty motherfuckas like me working as they hustle. Plenty motherfuckas who owned they home. Plenty motherfuckas who got good grades in school and went to college.

I didn't know of them motherfuckas personally, but they ass was out there.

But I also understood them niggas hustlin' to survive. Them warriors that thought there was nothing better out there than dealin'. They saw dope as a commodity. Supply and motherfuckin' demand. They felt like there would always be fiends and junkies and somebody had to make money off they ass. In they mind it was like "Why not me?"

Robbers, killers, gangbangers. That shit I wasn't even trying to comprehend.

I eased off into traffic, enjoying the music and taking in the city I loved. I was passing by a small church sitting next to a liquor store on Springfield Avenue. The lit sign out front the church said, Pop, Lock, and Drop It . . . Into Church!

I just shook my damn head and laughed. In the hood you was likely to see all types of crazy shit.

I was making a right on Irvine Turner Boulevard when I spotted Dyme's Jag parked at the curb. All shiny and pretty with no sign that I took a bat to that bitch earlier this year. I ain't seen that nigga in so long. I missed the dick. Lawd knows I missed the money. The bullshit? Not so much.

I slowed down. "What he doing?" I wondered out loud to myself.

In my rearview mirror I saw a woman strutting up to the driver's door. I slammed on brakes.

A horn blared behind me and there was a squeal of tires to asphalt as whoever was driving behind me slammed on they brakes. But my eyes was on the bitch putting bags in the trunk, dressed in a pair of linen shorts with a tank and heels. It wasn't his wife.

I turned and looked over my shoulder through the rear glass of my Lexus.

It was that bitch Armina. Ever since that night she found out I worked there, her and her little friends come in Dino's and be straight handling my ass 'cause they know I don't want to lose my job. They always make sure to sit in my station and have me running and jumping through hoops for bullshit, all the while talking shit and doing dumb shit.

BAM! BAM! BAM!

My fucking heart damn near jumped out of my chest at the sound of someone banging on my window. I turned and saw a big nigga looking 'bout six-five and four hundred pounds or better.

"You almost caused an accident. You don't know how to drive?" he roared like a big old black-ass bear.

That nigga wasn't no thug. He still had on his uniform from working at Newark airport. Nah, just a little road rage.

I know my eyes was big as shit but I leaned right over to my glove compartment and reached for my cute pearl-handled .22 gun. "You know what, I *can't* drive but I *bet* you I can shoot this motherfucka right here though. Now what?"

Now his eyes got big.

"Poof. Pow. Begone. I got shit to do." I eased the window up in his face and pulled off with a squeal of my tires just far enough to whip a quick U-turn, speed back down the street, and park across from Dyme's Jag.

Armina was closing the trunk of the car and waving good-bye to somebody on the porch.

I put the gun back in my glove compartment, hopped out

of my Lex, locked it, and shoved the keys deep down into my pocket fast as hell as I made my way across the street.

"Hey, bitch. Now pop off. Huh? Talk all that shit now, bitch. I ain't at work."

Armina took a step back and damn near tripped on her heels as I stepped to her. "Girl, please, you better go somewhere with that bullshit."

She glanced back at the porch.

So did I.

Whoever had been on that porch was long gone and the front door shut tight as hell.

"All week long you been coming to my fucking job picking like the little punk bitch you is. Well I ain't work now, bitch. SO POP OFF NOW, BITCH!"

A crowd was gathering. People *loved* a hood fight.

Armina looked left and right at the people. I could tell she ain't want to get shamed. "Bitch, you just mad your little slutty ass working at Dino's 'cause you can't find another man to take care of your worthless ass."

I saw a hundred shades of red and I wanted to fuck this bitch up so bad that I could taste it. But see, if I whupped her ass the way I wanted to, I might catch a charge. I had to make this bitch swing first. I would even take a hit, but after that . . . oh, after that it was motherfuckin' on.

So I let my mouth straight run and this bitch ain't had shit on me when I was on a motherfuckin' roll. I delivered verbal blow. After blow. After blow. And the crowd hyped it up.

"And you just mad that your mama ain't had enough pussy to keep your daddy from fucking the shit out of me."

"DAMN!" went the crowd.

"I seen that Tasmanian devil–looking bitch. Fuck your mama wit her big back. Ole big back ho."

"OOOH!"

"And since you gettin' in your daddy bizness, bi-otch, your daddy missed your college graduation to lay up *all* day and get this pussy, bitch. That's right, his ass was sprung and didn't give a fuck about you or your diploma."

"DAMN, THAT'S FUCKED UP, DADDY!"

"Matter fact, ya mama ought to thank me because I can fuck your daddy whenever I get ready. That motherfucka was still calling me the same night his ass got caught at my house. Matter of fact, just because of you I'm gone fuck your daddy in your mama house on her purple sheets . . . AGAIN!"

"WHY, DADDY? WHY?" somebody's crazy ass hollered out, straight clowning.

And that bitch swung. I leaned into her shit. She barely grazed my chin but I staggered back making sure it was known she hit me first. Now it's on.

I stepped up and swung hard, landing two blows to her face.

"Spill water for me to pick up now, bitch."

Uppercut.

"Call me a bitch and a slut and a home wrecker now."

Elbow to the gut when she wrapped her arms around my neck.

"Leave me a penny tip now, bitch."

We fell to the ground landing on the curb. I made sure to get on top of that bitch and straight swing out.

She got all the anger I had for her, her daddy, and her fucking mama. For my money getting confiscated by the police when Has got caught in that fed sting. For me falling the fuck off. For me having to even work at Dino's.

For Mama Bit's death. For my mama leaving me and

Daddy never being the fuck there. For being hated cause I was mixed. For getting picked on.

All of that shit and more came out in the blows on her face and body.

Somebody pulled me off her and I still kicked at her ass as I watched some old dude help her to her feet. That bitch was lumped up and dazed. My hands stung.

I wasn't even no fighter type of bitch, but sometimes when you had enough, you just fucking had enough.

6

Gettin' money gettin' dough like a stripper
Countin' money makin' dough like a stripper.

—Keri Hilson, "Like a Stripper"

I ain't gone lie that I wasn't worried as hell that Armina would press charges. I wasn't even sure Dyme wasn't gonna come to Dino's and yoke my ass up for straight whupping his daughter's ass. Every time that aggravating bell rang over the door, I looked up expecting to see the cops or Dyme.

I didn't mean to fuck her up that bad, but I got a lot of shit on my plate and the last thing I needed was a spoiled daddy's girl tryna defend her daddy's wandering dick.

Since it was a Monday night, Dino's was kinda slow. I reached in my apron and counted my tip money. I used to blow money like this on dumb shit when Dyme was financing me, now I had to count every penny and make sure it wasn't wasted.

Sometimes I wondered what Mama Bit thought of me as she looked down from heaven. I missed her so much. There was so much time I could have spent with her if I didn't get so wrapped up in Dyme. Now Dyme was out of here and I ain't have nobody in this fucking world. Just me, myself, and I.

It's fucked up that I don't even know if my mama dead or alive.

I would never know if she gave a fuck about me or not.

And my daddy? Fuck him. Probably didn't even know he had a child out there.

It's cool. Fuck it. Every so often I get in that bullshit-ass reflective mood, but I knew I ain't had no kind of time to dwell on that shit. I had to take care of myself or be out there on the streets by myself.

Standing behind the counter I dropped my head in my hands and rubbed my fingertips over my eyes, ran my fingers through my hair. *Maybe Dom will let me go home and work Sunday night instead. . . .*

I stopped because I could almost smell the scent of cologne. It was familiar as hell.

"So this life is better than the one I gave you."

Dyme.

I took a deep breath, trying to settle myself and get my shit together, but nothing was gonna prepare me for the sight of him. Being near him. Having him standing before me. Nothing.

I finally looked up.

Same old Dyme. Tall. Looking good as hell and smelling even better.

"Hi, Dyme. Sure you have permission to be here or is your wife out in the bushes playing private eye?"

He turned his mouth downward and shoved his hands into the pockets of his linen slacks as he looked at me. Long and hard. Fucking with me—or tryin' to.

"Don't." I moved from behind the counter to walk to the back of the diner.

"Don't what?"

Feeling frustrated as hell, I turned and pointed my finger at him, ready to check his ass. "*Don't* look at me. *Don't* have your ass here. *Don't* fuck my life up any more than you already did."

"Let's sit down and talk."

I shook my head. "I thought you came here because of my fight wit your daughter."

"She told me about it. That's how I knew you worked here."

I looked at Dyme. I mean really looked at this nigga. Even after the abortions. Even with all the lies, disappointment, and bullshit he shot me over the years. Even after denying me in front of his wife and everybody living in King Court. I really saw this nigga for the first time and I didn't see shit.

"You know what, Dyme, you are the most selfish mu'fucka I ever seen."

"Selfish?!"

"I don't give a shit about your daughter or your wife, but I know damn well when they told you about your ex-mistress whuppin' her ass they damn sure ain't expect you to use the info to run your ass straight to me. Now did they?"

"Let me worry about my family, Goldie."

"And you let me worry about me. You know how you used to treat me like I was young and dumb and didn't know shit? Well, I know this much, that as you long as you can, you will say and do whatever whenever to get what the fuck you want . . . from your wife, your kids, and from a sixteen-year-old just tryna be grown."

"Goldie—"

"Man, roll up out my face, and if you come back I will go to your wife and tell her . . . and I mean it, Dyme. I *mean* it!"

"Your ass stay right here in some greasy-ass diner making minimum fucking wage." I must've struck a nerve in this nigga 'cause he was looking at me like he wanted to slap me.

"As long as I'm making my own money and taking care of myself so that I don't have to put up with your shit, then I'll clean dog shit if I have to."

Now *that* was a motherfuckin' lie . . . but his ass didn't know that.

"You'll be back," he said.

Cocky ass.

He used a finger to gently pull down the neck of my shirt and then grabbed my wrists and looked at my hands. "Where's all your jewelry I bought you?"

"I pawned it."

Dyme shook his head and looked at me like I crazy. "How much longer you gone hold out? When you gone realize again that you need me? Huh?"

I crossed my arms over my chest and looked at him. I saw some old dude in front of me that probably liked young girls so that he could control them. Manipulate them. Use them up. Use me up. This nigga was pathetic, and all the love I thought I had for him was gone. I was free of him and all my bullshit ideas about what love is.

Matter of fact, fuck love and fuck him. Both had me good and fucked up for the last six years of my life. No more.

Dyme reached into his front pocket and pulled out a gold and diamond money clip. He removed it and started to count the cash in front of me. "I remember how much you loved those designer purses and shoes. Going to the spa. Getting your hair and nails done every week. Living a good life."

I can't lie. I was countin' right along with that Negro and it was up to two grand.

"You like to be spoiled, Goldie. You like to be taken care of. And it's what you deserve."

Three grand.

"This penny-ante bullshit job keeping you laced the way you like, Goldie?" he asked, taking the money and dragging a trail between my titties.

I stepped back from that damn money. I had to before I took it.

"When the last time you been on a shopping spree? When the last time you ate at a nice restaurant? When the last time you pointed at something and it was yours?"

That was the life I knew for the last six years of my life. True, I was dumb as hell not to press to move my ass out of King Court, but I still had a good fucking life. No cash flow drama. No keeping track of every penny I made. No worrying about what was due and when.

My life was a bunch of bullshit now and Dyme knew that shit.

I wanted my life back. I wanted to stop stressing shit. I wanted to shop when the fuck I got ready. I wanted to spoil myself.

I wanted more control of what the fuck was going on in my life.

And everybody knew what it cost to be a boss.

This diner bullshit wasn't cutting it.

My feet hurt. My back hurt. And my motherfuckin' pockets stayed hurt.

"You know what, Dyme. You right. This shit ain't for me. This ain't my life."

This nigga took his time folding his wad and putting it

back in the clip as he smiled down at me, showing all them expensive-ass veneers he got.

"I want my shit back on point."

Dyme reached out to touch my face.

I reached out just as quick and snatched up his wrist, keeping his hands off me. "But I don't need you to have it. I will get it on my own. Watch me."

That shocked the shit out of him and it felt damn good.

Giving him one last look. "Selfish ass," I muttered before I walked past him and out the front doors of the restaurant. I just felt like I needed some air, a blunt, and some Rémy. The air was gone have to do for now.

I walked around to the side of the stone-front restaurant and leaned against the building waiting for Dyme to finally walk his no-good ass out the restaurant and back out of my life. A horn blew behind me.

I jumped, completely surprised and freaked the fuck out, before I turned.

A black-on-black Range Rover with some boss-ass twenty-two-inch rims was sitting there with its lights on me. I covered my eyes with my hands. "Damn, you blindin' me."

The black-tinted driver's-side window came down and Rick leaned out to smile at me. "A fine chick like you should be used to the spotlight."

He cut the lights and pulled up until he was beside me.

My eyes looked past him to the passenger seat, but there wasn't shit but a shiny black gun sitting there. "Where's your entourage?"

He laughed and them dimples took center stage. "They coming. I left early."

I turned and peeked around the corner. Dyme's Jag was gone. Good.

"Goldie!"

Turning around, I looked at Rick. I already knew what was coming. "Don't," I said, feeling aggravated as hell.

"Listen, you got the body and the look without even trying. Even smelling like old French fries you hot as hell. I could imagine if you tried hard."

"Listen, I ain't no stripper."

"So you wouldn't want to make the same money and more in one fucking night instead of two weeks."

"Nah, I'm good," I told him, stepping back from the Rover and everything he was tryin' to talk my ass into.

I turned and walked fast as hell back into the diner. I ain't had time for Rick and his shit. That shit wasn't even on my mind because I was already thinking of a master plan to take my cash flow higher.

One thing Dyme said was right: I wanted my life back, because this below-minimum-wage, shucking-for-tips bullshit wasn't cutting it.

It's clear as an unflawed diamond that I fucked up big-time by dropping my ass out of school. There was jobs out there for people without a drop of experience and no high school, but shit, them motherfuckas worked twice as hard and made less than half the money. And what would be the purpose of leaving Dino's to find another job flipping burgers or taking orders?

I wanted to be in charge. Run my own shit. Tell other people what to do. Okay. I'm twenty-two, broke, a high school dropout who ain't got shit going for me but my body, my looks, and my desire to hustle and grind.

And that's why I was actually standing my fine ass up in

this private room, filled with women who made they money grindin' on poles, actually thinking about using what I got to get what the fuck I want. Money makes the world go 'round and does way more than make me cum.

"So whaddup, Goldie? Is a thousand dollars enough for you to shake dat ass for me or not?"

I focused my eyes back on Rick's fine ass sitting in the center of his dancers like a motherfuckin' pimp.

My eyes shifted to the hundred-dollar bills sitting on the table next to his half-eaten plate of pancakes and bacon. My eyes shifted again to Lick-Lick, still in her spot damn near glued to his side, looking at me like she wished she could fuck me up.

"Look here, boo, go on and carry your little dusty, grease-smelling ass and get me a refill on my juice." Lick-Lick leaned forward and pushed her glass to the end of the table toward me. "Leave the dancing to the pros."

Some of the girls giggled.

I hated that bitch and I knew she hated me.

Arching my used-to-be-threaded brow at her, I turned, and walked over to the corner to step up on a chair and change the channel on the TV hanging. I stopped on BET.

The video for Ester Dean's "Drop It Low" was on.

Hopping back down to the floor, I worked my sneakers off my feet, kicking them away before I pulled my shirt over my head and took off my jeans.

"Oh, shit. Here we go."

I was soooo nervous. I was shaking. I felt like I was going to pass out.

I couldn't believe I was doing this shit.

In nothing but a black lace bra and thong I strutted over

to the table and snatched up my grand. I kept my eyes off of everybody and turned my back to them, closing my eyes, tryna pretend I was alone as I started to grind and wind like them chicks I saw in videos. My heart was beating like a motherfucka. I knew he probably wanted me to turn around but I couldn't.

Esther sang, "Drop, drop, drop, drop . . ."

And I dropped down into a split on Dino's wet-smelling carpet before I worked my back muscles and popped my ass against the floor.

I wonder how long I gotta do this shit?

In my head I could hear Keyshia Cole singing, "I just want it to be over."

I jumped up to my bare feet and turned long enough to grab a chair and turn back around and slide down onto it backwards. I pretended there was some big-dick dude sitting beneath it and rode that chair like I would a dick. I didn't know if that shit looked dumb or not. I just knew I had to do something because of the thousand dollars I had balled up in my hand.

I bent backwards and arched up on my toes, still grinding and popping my hips against the chair. This was a move I fucked Dyme's head up with a few times. Believable and fucking achievable.

Deciding I had enough, I kicked my legs over my head and landed in a split on the floor in front of the chair.

Clap. Clap. Clap.

"It wasn't all that."

I stood up and looked at Lick-Lick even as Rick continued to clap. This bitch was a fucking motivator.

I looked better than her.

I had a better body than her.

"You still couldn't top me on my worst fucking day."

I settled my low-cut bikini on my curved hips, not even giving a fuck that Rick was eyeing my fat bald pussy and big nipples through the sheer lace.

"Are we done?" I asked him, folding the money and sliding it into my bra.

Rick eye's took in all of me. From my bare feet to the top of my head. "You and me just getting started."

Our eyes locked.

Real talk? I forgot anybody else was even up in that piece for a sec. So I shook myself a little and turned away from him to grab my clothes and get dressed. I grabbed my apron and pulled out my pad to put his bill facedown on the table.

This world was mad crazy, because Rick and the dancers all went back to eating they food like some woman hadn't just put on a strip show in a restaurant. Like *I* hadn't just strip for they ass. That shit kinda freaked me out even more than what I did. These motherfuckas was way too blasé about this shit.

It felt like I auditioned or some shit and now they was waiting on me to leave the room to discuss my performance. I really don't know what I expected, but for sure it wasn't for this motherfucker to be eating on his pancakes. *What the hell? Fuck 'em, I got my money.*

I turned and walked out, patting the money in my bra.

I didn't carry my ass back in that room, either. They had they food with entertainment. They got they bill. My job was done.

"So you wouldn't want to make the same money and more in one fucking night instead of two weeks."

A thousand dollars. I reached in my bra and pulled out

the short stack. Back in the day I would of straight blew all that gwap on a bag or an outfit with shoes in a second. Now I was gone take my ass to the bank and deposit it. Keep it for a rainy fucking day. Like a fucking senior citizen or some shit. I was twenty-two and single. I should be having fun.

No, fuck that. I should be making even *more* money, to have fun *and* save bank.

How? A bitch like me had to get back, and to get back I had to get on my motherfuckin' grind. No more settling. Fuck the dumb shit.

When I heard a little ruckus coming from the rear room, I politely turned and headed for the employee break room off the hall. I didn't need to see any of them.

And for sure they ass see way more of me than they needed to.

I took my money out and counted it. I couldn't lie, it felt good as shit to have some money again. The last six months been hard as hell for a chick used to balling out. I couldn't remember the last time I went shopping. Or had a day of nothing but my favorite beauty treatments. Shit, life was a real bitch right now. A real bald-headed, getting sprayed all day bitch.

I still can't believe my ass damn near got butt-naked and danced in front of room of strippers and they boss. Did I look dumb? Did them bitches give me side-eyes and shit? Did they think I was a joke?

"So you wouldn't want to make the same money and more in one fucking night instead of two weeks."

Knowing I needed to get back to work, I pushed my money back in my bra and pushed Rick's nagging-ass voice out of my head. The diner was still half-empty. As I was headed back to that rear room I was thinking about asking Dom or his wife, Maria, the manager, if I could leave early. I had a grand in my hand. Working only half a shift wasn't gone hurt me.

I walked in the room, feeling sure as hell Rick and his bag of tricks was gone. I was wrong. Rick was scrolling through his iPhone while he sat at the cleared table. He looked up at me for a second and then looked back down at his phone.

I let the door swing closed behind me. I just wanted to get my tip and bounce. Thousand dollars or not, money was money.

Rick set the phone down on the table. "You ready to make this money, Goldie?"

I patted my titty. "I already did."

"You could make close to that or more every week if you work those tips right."

"Really?"

He nodded before he smiled, and those dimples just made this nigga sexier. "I never thought you would do it," he finally said to me, wiping his eyes like he was tired.

"Shit, neither did I."

"You did good as hell." He stood and stepped over in front of me. The smell of cologne was sexy as hell and it surrounded me, fucking my head all up. "Everything about you is dope . . . especially that body. Goddamn!"

I didn't say shit. I just stood there. I didn't step back, though. I stood my ground. This nigga made nervous all up on me. But I didn't back down.

"You deserve to be spoiled. I want to spoil you, do you know that?"

Everything he said breathed against my mouth. I had to fight not to lick my lips just to take some of him into me. "No, I didn't know that. I'm smelling like French-fry grease, remember?" I asked him, my voice soft as his eyes dropped to my mouth.

I licked my lips just to fuck with him.

"Are you gonna let me take of care of you?" Rick reached out and grabbed my hips, pressing his lower half against mine.

Damn! I could feel his dick, all hard and thick running down his thigh. "Listen, I'm a keep it funky with you. I'm just twenty-two years old and I been down the road before with letting a nigga take care of me . . . until his wife made him choose. And since my ass workin' at Dino's you should know how that went."

"Man, fuck him. I ain't that nigga, I'm *that* dude that will take care of my lady." He pressed his mouth to mine.

My clit swelled. My panties got soaked. And my thick nipples got hard as the diamonds Dyme used to lace me with. This nigga was tryna fuck and my body was right there with his big-dick self. Shit.

I leaned back to look up at this Negro like he was straight lying or just crazy. "Oh, you want me to be your lady but you been hypin' me up to strip for other dudes. Man, miss me with that bullshit."

"I don't give a fuck, Goldie, I know this bullshit-ass job don't suit you. It don't fit you. This motherfucka looking real small on you." His hands shifted down to my ass and I could feel the heat as he gripped them cheeks like he was scared he was gone drop 'em or some shit.

The door to the room squeaked open. I didn't bother to move, and neither did Rick. I was feeling more bold and cocky than I had in a long-ass time.

"Goldie?! What are you two doing in here?"

“I’m quitting, Maria,” I told her, glancing over my shoulder at her before I turned back to Slick Rick the Ruler.

“Quitting?”

I smiled a little—just a little—before I leaned my head and kissed that nigga. My mouth on his mouth. My tongue slipping inside his mouth to stroke his tongue. My hands easing down to grab his ass just as hard as he was grabbing mine. He moaned. I moaned. He bit my lip a little. I bit his right back.

Rick was the first man besides Dyme that I kissed. Shit. It was awesome.

“If you quit, then get the hell out, Goldie!” Maria yelled from behind me.

I ended the kiss. “Thanks for the offer, Rick, but I choose to spoil myself,” I whispered to him.

My pussy was throbbing harder than my fucking heart when I stepped away from Rick and strutted across the room as fly as I could with wobbly legs. Maria eyed me like I was shit on her shoe. I just smiled. Fuck her. Fuck Dom. Fuck the whole damn Dino’s crew.

It was time to get my life back.

“I’ll be by your club tonight, Rick.”

I breezed past Maria and walked out that greasy motherfucker for the last damn time.

It felt good as a motherfucka.

Usually after a night working, I would put in some earplugs to block out the constant noises of King Court, and my ass would sleep hard ’til about two. But not this time. I took a hot but quick shower, pulled my hair up into a topknot, and got dressed before I left my apartment. It was summertime and the hallways was hot as hell, even hotter than out the door.

I slipped my shades on. A few kids was playing outside, and struggling dopeboys was supplying their customers, but it was quiet for a summer day. Give it two more hours and shit would be mad hectic and crowded outside until late into the night.

As soon as I unlocked my car door I felt the heat rush out to press against me. The leather seats burned the back of my thighs and my back in the peach silk strapless romper I wore. "Damn, it's hot as hell."

I let the windows down and turned the AC on full blast, feeling sweat already making the silk cling to my damn body. But I didn't give a shit if it got up to a hundred and fifty degrees. A bitch like me had shit to do and money burning my pocket to get spent. Especially since I was gonna make more . . . stripping?!

If I was gonna do it, I planned on doing it right. It was time for a beauty day to get my shit back together.

First I hit up a tanning salon on Ferry Street down neck. Just five little minutes had my skin even more golden. A full Brazilian bikini wax on Pulaski. Mani-pedi on Broad. My eyebrows threaded. A stone massage. And finally my hair glossy and laid as I strutted out the doobie spot on Halsey. Nobody could do my hair better than Dominicans, and Martha's was the shit. Period. Point-blank.

Everybody was glad to see me after so long and I was glad to see them. I paused in opening the door to my Lexus to peep my reflection in the driver's-side window of my car. Playing around and shit, feeling damn good, I blew myself a kiss before I climbed inside the car.

Oh, this boss bitch was back on point. I looked and felt damn good.

Power

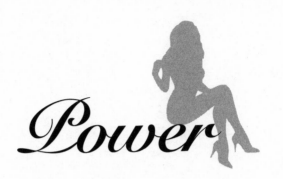

7

Every day a star is born
(Clap for 'em, clap for 'em, clap for 'em
clap for 'em, HEY!)

—Jay-Z, "A Star Is Born"

Club Naughty looked like any other bar in the hood. Brick building. Glass windows with a lit neon sign. The bass of the music beating against the walls and echoing into the concrete streets. Men smoking a cigarette or a blunt outside, laughing with each other or trying to holla at some chick passing by them. Cars lining both sides of the street.

I sat in my Lex, blazing a blunt and watching Club Naughty throw the thick-ass smoke. My ass been sitting there for damn near an hour, trying to get the clit to go inside. I was all bold and shit when I quit my job that morning. I was even bolder when I told Rick I would dance at his club.

Titling my head back I blew smoke rings, definitely feelin' good from that kush.

Knock-knock.

I jumped and dropped my damn blunt at somebody knocking on my window, I swore it was the cops.

"Goldie, calm your scary ass down."

I looked up at Rick bending down to look inside my car. That feeling like I was gonna shit up myself passed as I opened the car door. "Damn, don't scare me like that." I snapped, pissed the hell off while I reached down to grab the blunt. That shit burnt a hole in my rug just that damn quick.

"Yo, how long you gone sit out here?" He took the blunt from me and dropped it into the gutter water. It went out after a long sisss. *"You don't need that bullshit. You too fine to be smokin' fuckin' weed like a dude. And your lips taste too good to have 'em black as hell."*

That kiss. Just the thought of it made my nipples hard.

I didn't really say shit. Plus, I had enough to knock off the edge and the blunt was 'bout done anyway. Yummy's crazy ass smoked it 'til she damn near burnt her fingers, but it wasn't even that fucking serious.

"Damn, I thought you was fine as hell smelling like grease. Shit, you looking like a champ right about now, Goldie." Rick reached in and grabbed my hand to pull me up out the car onto the street. Right there he twirled me, getting the full 360 degrees on me. I even did a little pose like his ass was taking pictures.

At the sounds of sirens and squealing tires we both turned and looked. A red Honda Accord sped up the street and then turned the corner wild as hell, almost flipping the stolen car on its side. The police was hot as hell on they tracks.

Everybody's head went from left to right watching the chase go down. The crazy shit is how everybody outside just went back to talking once the chase was out of they sight. It wasn't nothing to see cops dead on the ass of a stolen car.

"You ready to do this?" Rick asked me, eyeing me up and down like I was just as half-naked as I was during my strip-tease at the diner earlier on.

"Tonight?" Oh no, hell no! "I didn't bring nothing to dance in. I was just coming to see when you wanted me to start."

"I got plenty new outfits and shit in my office."

This nigga gots to be crazy. Fine as hell, but even crazier.

I looked past his shoulders at the club.

Was I ready to shake that ass, pop that coochie, drop it low, and all that shit to make that money? Could I do it?

If I didn't think of the shit I knew Dyme would talk when he heard.

If I didn't worry about what the streets might say.

If I didn't worry about what my Mama Bit would say.

Rick stepped off the curb and turned to look back at me.

I didn't want to go back to Dino's. I didn't want to bust my ass for weeks to bring home just enough to pay my bills. I didn't want to get wrapped up in another dude. Not Dyme. Not Has before he got locked up. And not Slick Rick with the dick big as a ruler.

Could I do it? And how much Henny and weed would it take for me not give a fuck?

It was time to find out.

I tossed my hair over my shoulder and followed Rick across the street to Club Naughty. My strut didn't show how nervous I was about this shit.

And it didn't show that I knew once I walked my ass through that door into the skin game that my life would never ever be the same. . . .

I focused on my reflection in the mirror, the lip gloss wand still in my hand. I remembered that night—my first night—like it was yesterday and not three months ago. All of that bullshit I went through—all them nerves and shit—was gone.

Long gone.

Gone like a motherfucka.

The steady thump of the bass from the club was hittin' against the walls of my little-ass dressing room. I looked around. This tiny motherfucker was even smaller than my bedroom at Mama Bit's and it had boxes of liquor lined up against the wall, but this motherfucka was all mine. No sharing. Sometimes the big dressing room smelled like fried fish and cheese mixed with all the body oils and cheap perfume them chicks be wearing. I ain't had shit in this piece but a little table with a mirror and a cracked pleather sofa, but fuck, it was mine. Them other bitches hated it, but real always recognizes real, and whether they liked it or not, they knew who the star was in this bitch.

Nothing was like what I thought it would be and I made it my bizness to make it everything I wanted it to be. Fuck it. I got into this game to make money. Point-blank. So I made it my bizness to make as much money as I could by being the best the club had to offer.

The best the East Coast had to offer. More than just shaking my tits and ass, but giving a performance. A fucking show.

Better music. Better costumes. Better routines.

I made myself the boss up in this bitch. They could follow suit and step they game up or get run the fuck over. I left most of them bitches with tracks on they back. Fuck 'em.

My sets was so good, me and Rick figured out the less I performed the bigger the shows. Word of mouth was the best advertising and them niggas spread the word that there was a five-star chick taking the strip game to another level. I hustled my show the way dudes hustled dope.

Just three nights a week and I made way more money than some of these chicks made booty-tooting for five days. On my days off I worked on my business, remembering how Dyme would think out of the box to be successful. I would go to the gym and plan out my shows, making sure I kept my body and my skin game tight. I did a professional photo shoot and used the sexy pictures to set up my own website, postcards, and business cards promoting the private shows and bachelor parties I did up and down the East Coast. That brought in more money and got my name out there. I was straight grinding.

Plenty niggas tried to fuck, but giving up ass wasn't part of my hustle.

I finished putting on my makeup, going all out with the smoky eye and glossy lips that looked good against my rod-set hair. I rubbed this bad-ass body down with glitter lotion with a real heavy, sexy scent that made my golden body glow when I was under that spotlight.

I stood up to adjust my hot-pink fringed bikini and then stepped into the matching suede fringed ankle boots to finish it off.

Knock-knock.

The door opened and Rick walked in. "No, Rick," I said, holding out my hand to his chest when I saw that "I wanna fuck" look in his eyes, his dick already hard in his slacks, and a Magnum packet in his hand.

"Shit, I want me some of that good-ass pussy." He grabbed my hips and pushed my body against the wall while he kissed me, bringing up all that heat we made anytime we was next to each other. Heat that I stopped fighting two weeks after I started stripping at Club Naughty. After a while I told myself fuck it.

I had to admit Rick taught me a lot about giving a good show. That nigga really put me on. And we had a good-ass time fucking each other. I mean damn good. That nigga made me forget Dyme and whatever vibe I thought I had with Has.

He sucked on my neck, not giving a fuck all the glitter lotion I had on. My pussy stood and clapped for this nigga just like that, but I wasn't even trying to go onstage smelling like sex. That was a bird-ass move that Goldie wasn't even going for.

I grabbed his face and gave him a deep-ass kiss, sucking his tongue and all, but when his hands pushed my thong bikini to the side and stroked my clit, I pushed him back just enough to move from him.

"Rick, you know I go on in a minute so chill out," I told him, strutting in my four-inch heels back to my table to replace the lotion now on the front of his silk shirt. "How's the crowd?"

I watched in the mirror while he unzipped his pants and pulled that twelve-inch monster free, jacking it while he walked the few steps to drop down on my chair. I ain't gone lie, watching that nigga was turning me the fuck on. Damn.

His eyes was closed, his head tilted back, he was biting his bottom lip and grinding his hips while he stroked and choked that snake. It long, thick, and curved.

Uhm. Uhm. Uhm.

I knew firsthand how good that hook felt against pussy walls.

Focus, Goldie. Focus. I had to keep telling myself that as I turned around and enjoyed the show. His hand was vibrating up and down on just the tip and I knew that nigga was 'bout to nut.

Fuck *that* shit. If I had to wait 'til after my set to bust mine, he was gone wait too.

I grabbed the pillow from my seat and tossed it at his ass. It slammed right into his dick. Rick sat straight up looking at me like I was crazy. "What?" he asked, before he got right back at it.

I reached in my purse for my Taser and flipped that switch to turn it on with a loud-ass *buzz*. "Damn, nigga, I'll be done dancing in like ten minutes, you can't wait?" I asked.

Rick laughed. "Man, put that shit up."

I turned it off and dropped it back in my oversized black patent leather LV tote. I bought the Taser a few weeks ago to take with me during private gigs. Sometimes a motherfucker just needed a few wake-up volts and not a bullet.

"As soon as you step offstage, you gone come to my office and ride this dick down?" he asked, working his still-half-hard dick back into his pants.

I turned around and worked my ass muscles the way he liked while I looked at him over my shoulder. Shit, he wasn't the only one love it. I was known for my ass tricks.

Knock-knock.

We was laughing and barely heard the knock at the door. The sounds of T-Pain's "I'm N Luv wit a Stripper" got loud as hell as Lick-Lick opened the door in a lace bodysuit with nothing but a thong underneath. She rolled her eyes at me but I just gave her a sad face 'cause I know she salty as hell that I'm the headliner . . . in the club and in Rick's bed.

"Rick, you got a phone call." She turned to step her short ass back out.

"Hey, Lick-Lick, next time wait for me to tell you to

come into *my* dressing room. Shit, you don't know what you almost saw." I eyed that bitch, never forgetting how shiesty she used to act up in Dino's *and* when I first started working with her.

"Bitch, you ain't *all* that." Lick-Lick said, her face pissed off.

"I can't tell."

Rick stood up and finished zipping his pants. "Man, don't start y'all shit."

I just laughed at that bitch and turned to pick up the tightly rolled magazine I needed for my set. Rick followed her out the room. I wouldn't doubt Rick was side-fucking Lick-Lick or one of these thirsty chicks. I didn't really give a fuck. Dyme made my heart hard as hell and the only thing I wanted from Rick was between his thighs. He wanted more. I didn't. Point-blank.

Fuck love and relationship and all that goody-good bullshit that blows up in your face and leaves you hurting behind a motherfucka and his lies.

I'm about this money.

I'm about my grind.

I left my little-ass dressing room, strutting down that hall like I owned Club Naughty. Like I ran this joint. Like I had a camera on me and I was starring in a video. Like music played and I catwalked to the bass.

Like I was the shit . . . because I am.

My eyes wasn't on shit but the curtain leading onto the stage. My stage. I owned that motherfucker. And anybody that came before me was my opening act. The appetizer to the main show. The bullshit before the real shit.

G-Man, the DJ and announcer, saw me coming from his

glass booth on the other side of the stage. He pointed at me and I pointed back with a smile and a flick of my golden hair over my shoulder. The sounds of my song for the night started. It wasn't none of that bass-heavy, fast shit. Not tonight.

I'm gone fuck they head up with some old-school shit. "Darling Nikki" by Prince. I tapped the magazine against my thigh as I strutted up the steps. Humph, I'm a show these niggas darling Nikki wasn't the only one who could masturbate behind a magazine.

"Here's the one y'all been waiting for, fellas . . . and ladies. Ha-*ha*! Coming to the stage . . . our own million-dollar baby . . . *Goldie*!!!"

Damn right. I stepped through the curtain and struck a pose with the magazine between my thighs, pressed against my pussy, just before the spotlight shone on me.

The crowd went wild. Just like any other night I performed, the club was packed.

They came to see the star.

The days of Rick taking the girls to eat after the club closed was over. I had something else for him to feast on. Ya dig?

We were in the Land Rover, headed to our favorite spot, the Hilton down by Penn Station. He always wanted to go to his apartment, but I felt like that shit would really fuck with his head on that relationship shit.

It was three in the morning and downtown Newark was damn near empty. We were both quiet. I guess both of us had a lot on our minds. I know I did. I was trying to figure out the right time to let Rick know I wanted a flat percentage of the door receipts on the nights I performed. If his crowd damn near doubled only on the nights I was shaking my ass on the stage, then only a dumb motherfucka couldn't see I was pulling them niggas in. That meant more door money and more liquor sales . . . for Rick.

But before we get to business, I'm ready to get to pleasure.

I didn't forget that Dyme said don't mix business with pleasure. I didn't forget at all . . . I just didn't give a fuck.

I didn't know if Rick knew it but I was always extra horny on the nights I performed. I didn't want any of them niggas wanting me, but I did feel some kind of way to have all the dudes wanting me.

On the elevator, I leaned against the wall across from him and watched Rick's face while he played on his iPhone. My pussy throbbed and I wanted the feel and taste of his dick against my tongue. In my mouth. Teasing my throat.

In an instant, I had an image of him fucking me doggy style right there in the elevator, not giving a fuck who might walk in or who watched. I felt horny as hell. Hornier than I had felt in a long, long time. I wanted to fuck, or rather, I wanted to be fucked. Hard. Fast. Furious.

My eyes darted down to his mouth. This nigga had the kinda lips made to suck my pussy whole until I filled his mouth with cum.

"Rick," I called over to him, tired as hell that the iPhone was feeling his touch and all his attention. Not me. I dropped my LV tote to the floor and opened the ivory sweater-dress I wore.

He looked up at me and then his eyes dropped down to my open mouth and then down to where sweat made the silk of my black bra cling to my titties. I licked my lips as I watched his eyes get hot.

"Fuck me," I told him, not giving a fuck.

Humph. That nigga crossed that elevator in two big-ass steps.

I took his hands and brought them up to my breasts as I stepped up and lifted my lips to his.

"Shit, Goldie," he swore against my mouth as his fingers squeezed and rolled my nipples just the way I liked.

I tried to swallow his tasty tongue as I grabbed the back of his head and pressed his face closer to mine. His hands shifted down to grab my bare ass cheeks as he roughly lifted my body upward. My legs surrounded him. He pressed his hard dick against my open pussy in my moist panties.

I cried out as he bent his head to suck my thick, hard nipples through the silk with a low growl as his fingers slipped down below to play in the slick, wet folds of my aching pussy. I tightened my fingers around his shirt collar as he stroked my swollen and sensitive clit with his thumb. I needed this.

I brought my hands down to unbutton his shirt with trembling fingers. "Suck my nipples," I whispered to him as he undid the latch on the front of my bra to free my titties.

His wet tongue slickly circled the nipple and I felt the juices pour from my pussy until my ass felt wet. He moved from one soft breast to the other as he slid one finger into my tight pussy and then his thumb into my ass.

A jolt pierced my body and I cried out hoarsely as he slid another finger in and out of me. It shocked me that the finger buried deep in my ass felt good. So good that I begged, "Deeper," as my head thrashed from side to side on the elevator wall.

"Feels good?" he asked throatily, watching the emotions run across my face as he pushed his fingers deeper into me.

"Yes," I whispered. "Yes."

He bent down to his knees and placed one of my legs on each of his strong shoulders. When he stood my back slid up the wall as my body rose with him. At his full height, he looked up at me as he used his chin to split my pussy lips open.

"Smells good," he whispered, his words feathering against my pussy, ass, and thighs.

"Eat me," I commanded, feeling bold. Fuck it.

The first touch of the firm tip of his tongue to my clit brought tears to my eyes but I blinked them away. He fucked deep inside me with his tongue and I enjoyed the way my pussy walls closed around it. Fast and furious flickers of his tongue against my clit had my whole ass and legs hot as I filled his mouth once and then twice with my cum as the tears I tried to hold back streamed down my cheek. I circled my hips against his face.

"Suck it. Suck my clit."

He obliged with a deep motion that was noisy and erotic as I wilted forward to press my breasts against the top his head. "Your pussy taste so good," he said, licking me from my ass to my bald pussy.

He released me and I slid down the wall until our eyes were level. We stared at each other as he kissed me deeply.

I moaned at the taste of my pussy juices on his tongue.

Rick wrapped his arm around my waist and laughed. "You know we missed our floor?"

I ain't give a fuck that we went up to the top floor and then all the way down to sit in the lobby. I felt good as a motherfucka right about now.

Rick pushed the button for the fifth floor and I closed my sweaterdress, ready to get to the room and get finished.

"What you want?" he asked me, all sexy and shit, before he stepped back to unbutton his slacks and let them fall around his narrow hips along with his boxers.

My eyes dropped to take in his dick. *The* dick. It was thick and long, with a wicked hook. It was as dark as milk chocolate . . . just like the rest of his body.

"You want it?" Rick asked, wrapping his hand around the base of his dick before he wiggled that one-eyed snake at me.

I dropped to my knees and moved forward to grasp his buttocks. Like he was blessing me with rain I lifted my face as he lightly tapped the heavy tip of his dick against my lips and cheeks. Ready for more, I used my hands on his ass to guide his dick into my mouth. The smooth tip stroked my tongue as my lips surrounded him firmly. I inhaled deeply of the scent of him as I sucked in as much of him as I could.

He shifted his hips back to ease his dick from my mouth. "Easy, baby. Easy."

Slowly I began to lick and then suck his dick, enjoying the feel of the hardness beneath the smoothness of his skin. The vein running along the side of it throbbed with authority against my tongue. I enjoyed the way his thighs trembled with each suck I gave the smooth tip. He leaned forward slightly and his hands pushed against the wall behind me with his head hanging down between his arms as I sucked his dick like I was giving him life.

"This is our floor. Come on, let's get to the room," he said, pushing my forehead and pulling back his hips to free his big dick from my mouth.

I got up off my knees, grabbed my tote, and followed him off the elevator to our suite. As soon as we walked in that bitch, I turned from him and leaned forward against the wall, the coolness tickling my throbbing nipples as I used my hand to spread my ass and expose my pussy to him. "Fuck me," I said, looking at him over my shoulder.

Rick stepped forward, rolling a Magnum on his dick with his eyes locked on me. "Turn around. I want to look right in your face when I put this dick in you."

And I turned, raising my hands to squeeze his shoulders as I lifted my leg over his bent arm. He bent his knees to guide that big hard motherfucka into me. The size of his dick always made me nervous as hell, but my desire to fuck and be fucked overruled all that bullshit.

In husky tones he kept talkin' to me as he slid inch by inch of his dick in me until my walls felt the pressure. I gasped and arched my back, tightening my grip on his shoulder. With a moan I flexed my pussy walls, tightening and then releasing that dick.

His teeth clenched and sweat coated his brow. "Your pussy's so tight," he whispered against my cheek before he kissed it softly.

Rick began to work his hips to flex his hard buttocks and press his rigid dick against my slippery wet clit.

He locked his eyes on my face. "Is this what you want?" he asked in a voice that made me want him—want *this*—even more.

"Yes . . . yes." I gasped as he circled his narrow hips, making his penis shift against the sides of my walls. "You don't hear me sayin' stop."

We laughed a little together at that. I'm not sure when the distance between us disappeared but the feel of his mouth on mine made my heart pound just as loudly as his. We shared tiny kisses and deep suckles, small bites of the lip, and little licks of the tongue as we used our hips to create a wicked slow grind.

Our eyes locked and stayed locked as he fucked me against that wall like I was the last woman alive. At that moment I felt like I had the best pussy God ever created. I felt like Juicy had him going crazy as I got wetter and wetter until I felt my juices drizzling down my inner thighs.

His hands rose to squeeze my breasts and twist my nipples between his fingers. I began to grind my hips right along with his again, working for the nut I *had* to have.

I purred. He growled. We fucked.

I cried. He comforted. We fucked some more.

Right against the wall, we both started cummin' like we were starved for it. I cried out hoarsely, tilting my chin up as his dick throbbed with each squirt of his cum filling the condom.

We held on to each other tight as hell, breathing like we was having an asthma attack and our hearts beating so hard I thought I was gone pass out. He eased his dick out of me, making sure to hold the rolled end of the condom.

Shit, I felt good. The "ride" was just what I needed. "I ain't gone lie, Rick, if I had a blunt right now I'd have blazed that bitch by myself," I told him, swallowing hard to ease the dryness I felt in my throat.

He looked at me a long time before he stepped out his pants and drawers and walked to the bathroom to flush the condom.

I stretched and let out a big yawn before I stripped out my clothes and lingerie, heading straight for the bedroom. I didn't forget the business but right that sec pleasure had me sleepy as a motherfucka. I promised myself me and Rick was gone have a come-to-Jesus meeting before we left the suite in the morning. It was time for me to get on my business grind even more.

I just hoped me and that nigga was on the same page, or a bitch like me was making moves.

Good dick or not.

By the time Rick got out of bed that morning, I was showered and back in my sweater-dress with my dirty lingerie in my bag. I was sitting in the living room of the suite flipping through the channels of the flat screen on the wall, not really watching it because my mind was occupied with more important shit.

I reached in my bag and pulled out my cell phone. "Oh, shit."

A missed call from Yummy. "Damn."

I called her back but her phone went straight to voice mail. "Yum-Yum! Whaddup, *bitch*? I ain't heard from you in a minute since you moved but I'm glad you called me. So, yo, hit me up when you get this message and let's go get something to eat or go shopping. You know how we do. I miss your crazy ass. A'ight then. Deuces."

I ended the call and dropped the phone back into my purse, thinking of my friend I ain't seen in almost a month.

"Goldie?" Rick called from the bedroom.

"I'm out here," I called back, crossing my legs.

Naked, big dick swinging like a broken fucking tree limb, Rick strolled into the living room. "Damn, why you up so early?" he asked, stretching.

I didn't let myself focus on the body or the dick. It was time to punch in, so to speak. Straight nine-to-five it. Business.

"Listen, I want to thank you for putting me on, but I think we need to peep the fact that I got the club bust wide open with dudes any night I perform. I mean, straight up, I've hopped in my car and rode through the set, you know what I'm sayin', when I'm not working the numbers are not the same."

He didn't show shit on his face while I laid out nothing but straight facts. "So what's your point? What are you after?"

I locked my eyes on his, stiffening my back because this nigga sounded annoyed. "I'm after what I deserve to receive. On the nights I perform I want a percentage of the door. We can negotiate the—"

"Can we talk about this later?"

I started to trip. I started to flip. I started to press the issue. But fuck it. I laid it out for him. The ball was in his court and if he took too long, then I had to do what the fuck I had to do. See, I wasn't crazy, because whether he wanted to admit it or not, I knew I was bringing major money into the club and in this negotiation that gave me the power.

Period. Point-blank.

8

Always stays fly, keeps it so real.

But behind closed doors she a nasty girl (yup).

—Ludacris, "Nasty Girl"

One Month Later

When I realized that Rick wasn't feeling making the right moves and running me money from the door, I made a few moves of my own. Fuck all them stalling tactics. If he couldn't deliver, then neither would I . . . in Club Naughty, anyway.

I glanced at the clock on my bedroom wall. It was 10 P.M. Time to make that money. I walked out, careful not to trip in the metallic gold thigh-high boots I had on with an itty-bitty gold bikini.

Fuck Club Naughty. I had Club Goldie in full effect right in my apartment. Thursday through Saturday with two shows a night, my apartment was the place to be for all these hood niggaz. To keep shit from getting too crazy since my living room wasn't that big, I kept it at no more than twenty dudes at a show. Every last one of these niggas paid twenty-five bones just to get in for the thirty-minute show, and lap dances was fifty. No cameras, camera phones, or videotaping allowed. Between the door money, the liquor, and food sales I was pulling in a minimum of two grand a weekend for three hours' worth of work.

That didn't include the money I brought in from doing private shows and parties.

I stood behind the black silk sheets hanging from the ceiling like a curtain, blocking off the entrance to the hall, the bathroom, and two bedrooms of my apartment. I playfully winked at Mr. Wilson in the small kitchen, busy frying chicken wings and pork chops for sale, and serving up liquor for a dollar a shot. Plus he took the money at the door.

I hit the play button on the radio sitting on the edge of the kitchen counter. "Nasty Girl" by Vanity came on. Another classic. I had way, way less stage than at the club, so I didn't have the room to do my usual tricks, but that was cool 'cause these niggas was just looking for ass tricks and a few grinds on the pole.

The dudes started shushing, getting ready for me to make my appearance. As soon as I came through the sheets, the smell of men, weed, alcohol, and food hit me harder. I ignored all that shit, focused on my body and the music, and walked up the short aisle made with the chairs surrounding the stripper pole in the center of the living room. Focused on entertaining these niggas. In fulfilling their fantasy. To make them either want to fuck me or to get 'em horny enough to go home and fuck they wife or girlfriend.

Them niggas' eyes didn't know where to go, 'cause I could move my hips, ass, thighs, and arms all in a thousand different directions that just screamed sexy. I dropped to my knees and backed my ass up to the pole, working that cool steel like it was dick. And I hopped up on the pole and flipped my body upside down and worked my ass muscles and my hips before I flipped back down and slid into a split. I flipped back up and locked my ankles around the pole while I stood on my head, doing a Beyoncé-type hip movement that made them niggas make money rain down on me and around me on the stage.

I already recorded the CD with the chorus on repeat because anytime the song got to the chorus, I would pick a nigga to look dead in the eye, point to him, and then dance in front of him singing along, *"Do you think I'm a nasty girl?"*

Dude after dude. After dude. After dude.

"Do you think I'm a nasty girl?"

This old dude I recognized as one of the maintenance men for the Housing Authority was still in his uniform and holding up a fifty-dollar bill. I danced my way over to him and straddled his hips. His dropped his hands like deadweight. Smart move.

Mr. Wilson explained at the door that touching was not allowed. Anybody that violated would be banned.

Didn't matter, because I tried to make him feel like his funky-breath ass was the only nigga in the room.

That's my job.

And I knew I was one of the baddest bitches at it.

It was around 1 A.M. when I finally closed and locked my door for the night. After a very hot and very long bath, I threw on a silk robe, poured me a glass of wine, and stood at my living room window looking down at the city. Off in the distance was the Hudson River separating Newark from New York. The bright lights of the Big Apple looked like stars against the dark sky.

I always thought it was good that Newark and New York sat across from each other, because in many ways they were mirror images of each other. Same vibe. Same drama. Same bullshit. Same hopes and dreams.

Knock-knock.

I took a deep sip of the wine, still trying to get into the taste of it, and turned to look at the door. I can't front and say I didn't get nervous as hell. I sat my glass on the counter and then reached behind it for my .22 sitting on the top shelf.

Suddenly the sound of my cell phone ringing from somewhere in my bedroom made me jump. I made my way to the door, hitting the switch to turn on the lights. Up on my toes, I looked out the peephole.

What the fuck Rick want?

I let my head drop to the door before I stepped back and opened it. My heart was beating fast as hell. I ain't seen this nigga since I quit dancing at Club Naughty.

Two weeks apart ain't did nothing to make my body stop wanting him, but my head wasn't in the mood since he tried to fuck me over with the money.

"Whassup, Rick?"

He gave me a head nod before he strolled in, his cell phone in his hand. I figured that was him calling me. I closed the door and turned around to see him staring at the stripper pole and all the fold-up chairs in my living room.

"I heard you doing shows in your apartment, but I thought that was some bullshit 'cause you smarter than that." Rick shoved his hands in his pockets as he looked down at me.

"Here we go." I strolled my ass over to the counter to pick up my wine and set the gun back in its spot.

"Yo, you damn right here we go, Goldie. What the fuck are you thinking?"

I set the goblet back down and walked back over to his ass. My robe opened and I didn't bother closing it. How the fuck was I gone be a prude now when I just picked up and then pushed out a Heineken bottle with my pussy walls in a room full of niggas?

"I'm thinking that this dude I was working for and fucking shoulda respected all the extra money I was making his ass . . . and *cut me in*!"

Rick shook his faded head, his eyes dropping down to take in all the goodies on display. "Is that a new tattoo?" he asked, using his finger to pull the robe back more to take in the tiny row of stars on my hip.

"Yup. And I'm getting Dyme's name covered over next week." I turned, bent over, flipped my robe over my head and wiggled my ass at him. "I know how much you hated to look at it when you giving me all that dick."

Rick slapped my ass and then rubbed it before he pulled my robe back down. "I ain't come here for pussy, Goldie."

"That's good, 'cause you wasn't getting none," I told him over my shoulder, strutting over to the counter to pull out the plate of weed and blunts. "You can tell Lick-Lick to thank me later."

That motherfucka's eyes shifted to the left.

My eyes locked on him. Hard. "So you *is* fucking that big-tongue bitch."

"You left."

That's all that nigga said, like it was enough. It wasn't. What it was to me was just more proof that niggas wasn't shit. I didn't love him. I would never be a sucker-ass duck for love again. I didn't put no claims on his ass. But this the shit. He always claimed to want a relationship. He always claimed to want more. He always claimed that he could see us together, more than just fuck buddies . . . if I would just say the word. He said he could see himself falling in love with me. Now he was back fucking his ex-ho that quick? That shit pissed me the hell off. Real talk. To me he was a lying motherfucka just like Dyme.

And . . . and I almost fell for his shit. Almost, I admitted to myself, hating the truth.

"Goldie, look, it's risky as a motherfucka running a strip club out your apartment."

"Look, motherfucka, I ain't crazy. I know the risks, a'ight?" I lit the blunt I just rolled. I just smoked it 'cause I know his ass didn't like it. Fuck him and his big-tongue, freaky-looking, short-ass, wanna-be-on-the-come-up bitch.

"You don't know shit." Rick strode over strong as hell and snatched the blunt from my mouth. "What if you get put out? What if one or more of these niggas act up and try some shady shit with you in here?"

I got that. I got all of that. I just didn't give a fuck what this nigga had to say, especially since he was back fucking Lick-Lick . . . or never stopped fucking that weirdo bitch.

"Anytime dudes and liquor is both in play, anything could pop off 'round this bitch."

I looked at him as I dropped the silk robe from my golden body. I stood before him and kicked my leg up to rest on his shoulder while I wound my hips.

His hands came up to rest on my ass, and even though his touch was sexy hot . . . even though my pussy jumped to life . . . even though my nipples got hard as hell . . . my heart pounded . . . my breath caught in my throat. Even though . . .

"I hope Lick-Lick can freak-fuck you like I did since you ain't getting no more of this here pussy," I whispered against his mouth before I dropped my leg and moved away from him with one last stroke to his rock-hard dick. That nigga wanted me and there wasn't shit Lick-Lick could do about that.

"Get the fuck outta here. You don't give a fuck about me. You just want that money. Well I'm pocketing that gwap right now. Me. I'm running this shit. Me. I'm sorry Lick-Lick and the rest of them birds ain't drawing in the crowds."

He watched me while I grabbed the wine and downed it all in one gulp—the same way I used to swallow every drop from his dick. "You really think that's the only reason I'm here?" he asked, his voice low and deep.

"Yup."

"You think I don't care about you and want to take care of you?"

"Hell to the no or you would run me my money."

Rick shook his head. The apartment got quiet. We could hear the faint sounds of the sirens of police cars or ambulances. I had a vision of Lick-Lick's big nasty tongue swirling around his dick.

"Look, Rick, just get the fuck outta here. Go get your bitch to give you a sponge bath with that big-ass tongue."

"Stop being childish, Goldie," he snapped, finally dropping the blunt to the floor and then squashing it beneath his Gucci shoe.

I twisted my shoulder-length hair up into a loose knot and bent down to snatch up my robe. "Childish? No, I'm being a grown-ass woman taking care of herself. I'm the boss instead of waiting on one to take care of my fine ass. Well, I can take care of myself, Rick. If I had got off my ass and did that from the jump then Dyme, Has, or you couldn't fuck me over. My days of sitting around waiting on a motherfucka is a done da-da and I can promise you that shit."

Rick turned and walked to the door. I pulled on my robe, tying it as I watched him. He turned. "Okay, fine. Stop doing this crazy shit. Come back to the club, and I'll give you a percentage of the door."

I had plans. Big plans. And they didn't include Club Naughty or Rick, not anymore. Not now. "Nah, I'm good," I told him, rolling another blunt. "If I'm out there doing all the work, then *all* the money might as well be mine."

He opened the front door and the bright lights from the hall took away some of the darkness of the apartment. "Life ain't just about money, Goldie. Damn."

And he was gone.

The next morning I woke up with a mad crazy Henny-and-blunt hangover that had me feeling pretty much fucked up. It took a hot-ass shower and a handful of Advil to get my mind and body halfway right. I wouldn't have got up at all but me and Yummy was supposed to have a spa day and just chill like we used to. I felt like shit but I was ready to see my friend.

I turned the flat screen on and flipped to the news. It was October on the East Coast and the weather could be warm one minute and then cold as fuck the next. I wasn't tryna get caught out there sweating like a dope fiend or freezing like an Eskimo.

In my closet, my hand fell on the ivory sweater-dress I wore that last night me and Rick spent at the Hilton. If that bitch didn't run me three hundred dollars I woulda threw it in the trash and hopefully all the memories along with it.

I sucked air between my teeth. "Man, fuck him."

Pushing thoughts of him away, I grabbed a crisp striped

cotton shirt with a cute rose detail near the collar, a pair of dark skinny jeans, and my navy leather ankle boots. My lightweight ruffled leather jacket would work if it got chilly.

I was combing the last of my curls in my hair into a side ponytail while I listened to a news story about the kid of some idiot asshole who took drugs to school thinking it was candy. I was glad when the top of the hour was over because they never got to the positive shit going on in the city until they blazed through the crime and bullshit first.

Knock-knock.

My heels clicked against the tile while I strutted to the door and snapped on my new oversized gold hoops. Thinking it was Yummy, I snatched the door open. *Oh shit.*

I stepped out into the hall damn near knocking the exterminator the fuck back. I knew most of the Housing Authority workers and they all was cool and didn't give a fuck what I did in here. But this tall white dude with the thick-ass glasses might be a snitch-bitch.

"Yes?"

"I'm here to exterminate."

Nothing. I shook my head and pulled the door closed behind me. "I'm allergic to that, so I'll pass. Plus it don't do shit but feed the roaches anyway."

He shrugged and walked to Mr. Wilson's apartment. He was probably just another one of them white dudes living in the 'burbs but making that fifty grand a year or better in the hood. He didn't give a fuck if we had roaches, rats, or anything else.

"Gol-*die!*"

Yummy's roll call echoed down the hall loud as hell, even blocking out the sound of her heels on the tile.

"Yum-*my*!" I answered, just as loud.

"Shut *up*!" somebody hollered from around the corner.

We just laughed and hugged like Celie and Nettie in this bitch. It was hard finding a real friend sometimes, and I knew Yummy was the type of bitch that would take my secrets to the grave. I'd do the same for her.

We walked into the apartment. "I'm almost ready."

Yummy pulled out a pack of Newports and lit one. "Girl, only a bold bitch like you would open a strip club in your apartment. This is some wild shit, Goldie."

I laughed while I went in my bedroom to grab a vintage navy logo Gucci bag that I found on the Internet. It *was* bold and wild. And this weekend shit was making me money. Niggas had to respect the hustle and envy my grind.

Back in the living room, my eyes fell on Yummy. She looked way different than how she looked since I saw her a few weeks back. Her hair was cut ultra short and was just gelled down hard to her head. She was just wearing a black sweater and jeans. All the color and fun that made her Yummy was gone. Beneath her eyes were dark spots and she looked tired as hell. "You okay, girl? You look sick."

She smiled at me before she pulled a sack of weed and a scented Philly from her pocketbook and set them on the countertop. "Girl, I ain't gone lie. I been feeling drained like a motherfucka. Like I'm anemic or some shit."

"Maybe you should carry your ass to the doctor."

"That's what my moms said too." Just that quick that bitch had that motherfucka split, rolled, and lit. "You gone hit it?"

"Nah, I'm still getting over last night. Plus. I don't smoke like I used to."

Yummy laughed like that was the funniest shit she ever heard. "Fuck it. I'll smoke enough for both of us."

She walked across the room to step up onto the mini stage

holding the pole that was screwed into the ceiling. "Maybe I should dance and make me some money," Yummy said, sounding like the old crazy-ass Yummy before she twirled on the pole and then bent over backward to blow smoke rings to the ceiling.

I transferred all the shit from the camel Coach I carried yesterday into the blue Gucci. "Girl, Gunz ain't going for that shit."

"Right." Yummy dropped down from the stage and then sat on the end of it to smoke.

I grabbed my keys. "You ready to ride? I have got to get my hair done for this bachelor party I got in Livingston tonight."

"Livingston?"

I snapped my fingers and rolled my hips. "Hell, yeah. And with the money them white dudes is paying they getting nothing but top-notch treatment."

Yummy stood up. "I can't hang out too long 'cause I drove Gunz's van over here and he need it later, plus I told my moms I'd get my kids for a little while today."

"I bet they so big. I ain't seen they little bad asses in a minute." We walked out the door and I locked it.

She took a deep drag on the blunt. "They bad and growing and steady needing shit."

"Yo, Yum-Yum, if you do need to make some extra money, I need somebody else I can trust to work the door."

Yummy threw her arm around my shoulder. "Uhm, thanks but I'll pass on watching you booty-toot all damn night. That's way more of you than I need to see."

I couldn't do shit but laugh.

* * *

Brrrnnnggg.

I was somewhere in that zone between sleep and not being asleep, not sure if that ringing was just in my dreams or not.

Brrrnnnggg.

Until it kept ringing.

"Damn it." I rolled over and reached my hand down to the floor to pick up my cordless phone from the base to press to my face. "Hello."

"Goldie? Goldie, hey, this is Shavonne. Yummy's mother."

I shot straight up in bed in the darkness. My heart slammed against my chest. A phone call late in the night? This shit couldn't be good. "What happened? Where's Yummy?"

"She's at UMDNJ and she asked for you."

I heard tears in her mama's voice. "What happened?"

"That fool Gunz got my baby hooked on that shit, Goldie. She had a stroke and he just left her in the house. He just left her."

I started shaking. Straight trembling. I barely heard her mother give me the room number. "I'm on the way."

Yummy on drugs? Yeah, we blazed trees together and I couldn't lie that she loved a blunt, but drugs? Her mama wasn't lying—it had to be Gunz's crazy-eye ass put her on that shit. I sat up on the edge of the bed and tried get my mind straight while I rubbed my hands together to keep them from shaking so bad. Right 'bout now I looked like a fucking junkie needing a fix.

"Damn." I jumped up on my feet and crossed the room to hit the light switch. Quick as hell, I pulled on jeans and the off-the-shoulder black sweater I wore earlier. I barely zipped on my over-the-knee boots before I grabbed my keys and bust out the door. The halls were quiet as hell for a change. My heels beat against the tiled floor while I hurried my ass out the building and down the stairwell.

The October chill was in the air, especially with the sun gone, but I forgot to grab my damn jacket so I just dealt with it. I pulled out of King Court and floored it, speeding across town on a definite mission.

It reminded of that night Yummy rode with me when I went and fucked Dyme's car up for lying to me. I almost crashed and she went off.

"I know Dyme is a . . . a lying, old-ass, uncircumcised-dick no-good motherfucka but how 'bout we keep from being two dead motherfuckas? You feel me?"

I could hear clear as hell like she was in the car with me right then.

I looked over at the passenger seat. It was empty. I didn't know if my ram would ever ride shotgun again.

Because of Gunz.

As soon as I came to a red light, I grabbed a hair band from my ashtray and pulled my hair up into a ponytail. Fuck my new do.

Turning down Irvine Turner Boulevard, I sped through the empty streets until I came to the big apartment building on the corner across from Weequahic Park. I slammed on my brakes in front of the apartment building, grabbed my purse, and jumped out to strut into the building, and I had to pause. People talk shit about the projects, but this tall motherfucka looked—and smelled—way worse. Dirty-ass scuffed floors. Graffiti on the walls. The smell of piss in the air. Glass broken out one of the front doors. What the fuck? I got on the elevator and had to cover my nose with my sweater just to fucking breathe.

I been to Yummy and Gunz's apartment once since they moved in together and I couldn't wait to get to that motherfucka now. The closer I got to the door the more I heard music. And that shit was coming from their fucking apartment.

I banged on the door with my fist.

This crazy motherfucka was partying while Yummy was laid up in the hospital?

I banged even harder.

The door opened and some glassy-eyed bitch was standing there in nothing but a fucking sheet. I reached in my bag for my gun and tapped the barrel against her forehead. "You got 'til the count of three to haul ass."

Her eyes got big as shit. "Gunz said you was in the hospital."

"Getthefuckouttahere," I snapped, reaching out to yoke her ass by the throat and pull her into the hall.

I stepped in the dark apartment, the sounds of some Gucci Mane song loud as hell, and walked back to the bedroom. That nigga was sitting in the middle of the bed snortin' powder from a picture. I stepped into the room, lifted the gun, removed the safety, and cocked it. "Don't move, Gunz," I told him, my voice as cold as ice.

He lifted his head, looking at me with the one good eye while the other one was steady shifting left, right, up, and down. That motherfucka was high as hell. He was so zooted that when he did say something that shit sounded like fucking gibberish.

I walked closer to the bed. "Stay the fuck away from Yummy. This is my first and my final warning."

He laughed, his nose covered with fine white dust.

I reached back in my bag for my Taser, flicked it on, and stuck it to his neck, that motherfucka crackling and popping.

Buzzzz.

That nigga dropped like deadweight on his side, his crispy ass to me with his black-ass nuts jammed between his thighs. The picture frame and his coke flew to the floor. Fuck him. I thought about Yummy and stuck the motherfucka again . . . dead in his nuts.

Buzzz.

His body shook like a motherfucka.

I leaned over him.

"Pack your shit and be out of this motherfucka by morning or me and the cops gone have fun getting you the fuck outta here," I whispered in his ear.

I was headed back out the room when I caught sight of the picture in the frame. I turned and picked it up, using the sleeve of my sweater to wipe the coke residue from it. It was Yummy and her kids.

Shooting his ass one last nasty look, I turned and tucked it under my arm before I strutted from the apartment, slamming the door behind me hard enough to shake the whole raggedy motherfuckin' building.

I couldn't believe that was Yummy laying in the bed. She looked thin as hell. Her caramel skin was gray looking. Her short hair was running crazy all over her head. And her mouth was twisted at a weird ass angle to the left.

I took the cleaned picture and set it on the bedside table for her to see whenever she woke up in the morning. Taking her hand in my mine, I sat down in the chair by her bed. I wasn't going nowhere until she was better.

And Gunz better hope she pulled through or I swore I would stick my gun in his ass and blow his fucking brains out next time.

9

We got grands in this bitch, girl come and get you some
(Money make me cum, money, money make me cum).
—Rick Ross, "Money Make Me Cum"

One week later

Between sitting with Yummy in the mornings and still trying to run my hustle in the evenings I was more tired than a junkie who been hooked and running behind drugs for fifty years. Pulling into King Court, I didn't want to do shit but wash and get in my bed.

Yummy's condition wasn't no better, and thankfully, Gunz hadn't brought his ass nowhere near the hospital. Word on the street was he got robbed. It's cool with me if that nigga either didn't want people to know it was me that fucked him up or he was too fucked up to remember. What the fuck ever.

I grabbed my purse and stepped out the Lexus, hitting the switch to lock the doors and set the alarm. I walked to my building, the golden tips of my hair shining in the fall sun.

"Oooh, Goldie, girl, how *you* doing?"

I stopped and turned around to find Big CiCi walking

toward me. I laughed at her Wendy Williams imitation. "I'm good. How *you* doin'?"

"I'm blessed to be so big and fine all the time." Big CiCi paused and then walked the rest of the way to me like her ass was on *America's Next Top Model.*

She was damn six feet and every bit of three hundred pounds or better but she did have a real cute face. I wasn't hating on a big girl with confidence.

"Listen, I heard about your little bizness and hey, I think its time to get a little help and have something on the menu for the chubby chasers."

Did Big CiCi just offer to strip for me? What the fuck? That shit made me do a double take like "Say what? Say motherfuckin' who?"

"Uhmmmm, CiCi, girl I just came from the hospital sitting with Yummy—"

"Oooh yeah, how she doin'?"

"The same. But . . . but listen. Uhm. Girl, I'm wore the fuck out. Let me just go get a little nap and . . . uhm I'll get back to you. Okay?" I smiled and reached out to squeeze her hand before I turned and run-walked like a pit bull was loose on my Marc Jacobs heels.

"Hey, Goldie."

"Shit." I had just made it to the door and my hand was on the handle. I looked over my shoulder and Big CiCi started doing the stanky leg . . . horribly.

Uhm. Lawd. I smiled and pointed at her. "You better work it girl. I'll catch up with you, okay?"

In the building, I shook my head while my stilettos ate them stairs up. Funny shit was, CiCi wasn't the first chick to hit me up about dancing. Thursday through Saturday my shows had the neighborhood on lock. Word was spreading like a STD but that was a good and bad thing.

The crowds was a sign that the money was flowing lovely, but the more people who knew, the more risk I took getting busted. I really wanted to rent my own club and move my business out my apartment. With more room I could really get loose setting up the T & A spot for the fellas to relax and spend that money. I was so busy with Yummy and helping her mom with the kids that I ain't had time to look for a place or nothing.

If me and Rick wasn't beefing I knew he could really help me get my shit together, but that nigga wasn't even feeling me right about now. What would I call it? I wondered, pausing on the stairs. Club Orgasm? The Golden Experience? The Gentleman's Club? Goldie's Girls? *Hmmm. I like it. I like it a lot.*

Walking into my place, I looked around at the makeshift strip club. For so many years I was happy in this place because I thought Dyme was going to move me to better. Five years later I finally got the message. If—no, *when*—I got my own gentlemen's club and turned a big enough profit, I was moving to a luxury apartment building or big dream house I always wanted Dyme to give me. This bitch was gonna do it for herself. My own hustle. My own grind. My own goddamn money.

But for now, I knew I had to get serious about scouting dancers. Some real chicks with potential to be top-dollar pros just like me.

With more girls dancing with me, I could charge more money. My eyes lit up. More money was always a good thing. *Cha-ching!*

I grabbed my cell phone from my purse and did something bold as hell. Fuck it.

"Club Naughty."

"Is Luscious or Missy working today?" I asked, changing my voice so that whoever answered didn't recognize it.

"They both here. Which one you want?"

My mouth turned the fuck up when I recognized Lick-Lick's voice. "Can I talk to Luscious real quick?"

The phone dropped to the table. That bitch probably thought she really owned Club Naughty now. "Fuck, I'll go fuck Rick right onstage during her set, little dumb-ass. Ugh. I hate her," I whispered to myself.

"Hello."

Luscious's voice was swoll up with plenty of attitude. "Damn, Luscious, what's up, boo?" I said, smiling.

"Who this?" she asked, attitude still heavy as hell.

"Girl, this Goldie but don't let nobody know it's me."

She started laughing. "Shit, I thought you was one of them sickening-ass bill collectors. Girl, I was about to go off."

I rolled my eyes at her goofy ass. "I know that's right. Listen, I need to holla at you and Missy 'bout something. When can y'all meet me?"

"You know Rick still got us on that busted-ass early shift, so we done for the motherfuckin' day."

I arched my brow and two-stepped. That's exactly why I picked them. They been complaining about not getting one of the late shifts. That's where all the money was to be made.

"Guess we'll take our whack-ass tips and blow 'em on a bottle of Goose or some dumb shit."

"That's why I'm calling you. Y'all know how I do, and if you want in on making some money, then y'all meet me in an hour at Pages restaurant downtown on Halsey. And don't tell nobody."

"I don't know 'bout Missy but I'll be there."

"Good."

I ended the call and rushed into my room to wash and get changed. To lure them bitches I had to be fresh to def, and like anything else I do there was no half-stepping. Plus, if I could pull two of Rick's bitches? That would serve his ass right for Lick-Lick and my money.

Both of them was cute with the necessary big titties and ass, but unless they upped the game since I left, I knew they just needed to work on the set and get rid of the "dead-ass eye" like them chicks in a bad porno video. And there was nothing worse than watching somebody get fucked who looked like they rather be anywhere else.

Once them two learned to look like they was just as horny as they were making they clients, then they ass would make more than motherfuckin' pocket change.

Since I needed them just as much as they needed me, I was willing to do what the fuck I wouldn't do when I was at Club Naughty—teach them better so they could do better.

In thirty minutes I was strolling back out the door, feeling tired as hell but looking damn good with my hair moussed and curly as hell around my face, wearing a black suede strapless dress with a short leather trench and boots. The diamond cross I wore was snuggled in my cleavage and my bracelets shimmered like ice around my wrist. The sun was still beaming at nearly four in the afternoon so I slid on my black oversized Ralph Lauren shades and headed out the door, down the hall, the stairwell, and into my car.

"Whaddup, Goldie?"

For a second I thought it was Gunz coming for revenge. I slid my hand inside my purse and closed it around my gun. I didn't release my burner even as I eyed a group of teenage boys sitting on the bench by the basketball court. I eyed them as they giggled like bitches and kept nudging each other.

"I got ten dollars, can I get a lap dance?" a little short and cocky one with a fucked 'fro said, eyeing me up and down and looking every bit of thirteen.

"No, but you need to get your little bad ass a haircut."

His boys started clowning him and I actually felt bad. It reminded me of getting picked on. I could tell he was embarrassed like a motherfucker. He was just a kid.

I walked over to them—my hand still in my purse and my eyes on their hands because kids be strapped these days. I pulled fifty dollars from my pocket. They eyes showed how nervous they was like they ain't trust me either but they braced up like they would slap the shit out of me just to prove something to each other. "I meant *all* y'all needed a fucking haircut." I gave the cocky one the money. "Jaman on the third floor in my building cut hair for like ten dollars. Y'all go handle that and stay outta grown folks business, okay?"

"Thank you," they all said, running past me and into the building back to being kids instead of tryna front like they grown.

I made my way back to my car and climbed in. As I drove toward downtown, I thought about the shit people was probably talking about me. I learned not to give a fuck. These niggas wasn't feeding me or fuckin' me, so fuck them.

It didn't take me long at all to get downtown. I just hated to park anywhere near Halsey Street because it meant paying to park and walking a block to get to anything worthwhile.

By the time I walked into the crowded restaurant in the Prudential Mall, I was surprised to see Luscious and Missy already there sitting in a booth.

"Whassup, ladies," I said, dropping my bag onto the booth seat before I sat down next to Luscious. "Y'all hungry?"

"More curious than hungry," Missy said, flipping her Pocahontas-style black weave over her shoulder.

Luscious Lee nodded. "Yeah, Goldie. What's the deal?"

I sat back against the booth and eyed both these chicks. "I want you two to come work for me."

They eyed each other before they both eyed me.

"I do strip shows in my apartment on the weekends and private shows. I could use help with both."

"In your apartment?" they said, both sounding skeptical as hell.

"Just until I open my own club." I leaned in close and locked my eyes with one and then the other. It was time to get to the bottom line. "Listen, it may sound like bullshit but it ain't no worse than working day shift in Rick's club. *That*'s some second-rate bullshit. Plus, I'm getting way more requests for private shows than I can handle via my website and all the promoting I get done. So I will set you up with my photographer, get some real pretty pictures down, get you up on my site, and book you for parties. Help you get your look and your shows together. Show y'all how to get this money . . . just like me."

Humph, I didn't miss the way either one of 'em eyed the shit out of my clothes, jewelry, and handbag. They knew they wanted to get like me. They knew it.

I had to keep myself from rolling my eyes. "Listen, you'll make much more fucking with me than you making with Rick."

"Yeah, but your apartment, Goldie? That's some wild shit," Luscious said, drumming her long bright pink acrylic nails on the table.

"I ain't got time for games and doubts. I'm a take this skin game to a whole 'nother level. I plan on hiring plenty of bitches to dance for me. Y'all just the first two I fucked with. I just thought I'd give you chicks a chance to make some real money. Hey, get on or get off. Choice is yours."

I stood up, grabbed my bag, and walked away like I owned the fucking world. Fuck begging these broke bitches. They needed me more than I needed them. Plus, I saw Dyme pull that "leave them in your dust" stunt with many a motherfucka he wanted to do things his way.

Most times it worked.

"Goldie!!"

I smiled as I stopped at the glass door, more than ready to walk out on they ass. Fuck the dumb shit for real.

"We down," Missy said, as I slowly turned around to face them.

I nodded. "Good, let's grab something to eat and then we talk makeovers," I said, eyeing them from head to toe. "Cool?"

They nodded.

"Good."

That Friday I was amped that Luscious Lee and Missy was joining my show. Word was already out that two more girls was performing and Mr. Wilson had to turn niggas away. It was so packed up in this bitch that we had to put up the chairs and let these hardheads stand up with their bodies pressed to the walls. Requests via my website for parties and events jumped up too.

Bringing these bitches on was the best thing I ever did.

Once I was dressed in my rhinestone bralette and thong with a matching choker and clear stilettos—and feeling like the headliner bitch that I was—I locked my bedroom door, hid the key above the door frame, and made my way to the bathroom. I knocked once and walked in. "Y'all ready to make this money?" I asked them.

They stepped out into the hall.

"Yeah," Luscious Lee said, looking real pretty with her new jet-black hair, blunt-cut bangs, and weave to her lower back. It looked perfect against her chocolate complexion, with her makeup emphasizing her high cheekbones and full lips. The sheer black mesh chemise she wore high as hell on her thighs with a thong beat the hell out of them regular-ass twelve-dollar bikini bathing suits she usually wore.

"I'm ready." Missy's short 'do was dyed a pretty auburn that matched her caramel complexion. Her strappy lace teddy was sexy as shit with the back made of nothing but looping strings. I did her makeup too, with a lot of emphasis on her big-ass eyes.

"Remember, it's all in the eyes. Connect wit these niggas, make 'em think you feeling 'em. Make them feel like they the only motherfucker in the room."

Luscious leaned over to peek through the silk sheets. Her mouth fell the fuck open. "Damn, Goldie, it's more niggas out there than be at Naughty during the day."

"It's just like doing a private party." I waved my hand at they nerves. "Stop acting like y'all ain't never been on the motherfuckin' pole and go make that money. Anything y'all don't get I will have stuffed in my bra and thong when I close the night out. I promise you that."

They nodded.

I hit the Play button on the CD player and the sounds of Shareefa's "Mr. Incredible" filled the speakers in the corners of the living room. "A'ight, Missy, that's you."

She stepped through the sheets and the crowd went wild. I moved over to peep through the curtain and watch her, making sure this bitch don't fuck up. Everything they do and don't do reflected on me.

"You know Rick is pissed that we quit," Luscious told me, adjusting her chemise higher up on her hips.

"So y'all was supposed to just stay making chump change?"

Luscious laughed before she looked like she remembered something and then grabbed my wrist. "Yo, when I leave here I'm headed straight to Club Infinity in New York. Hell, shit don't really start jumpin' off 'til one anyway. They said all the celebrities and shit be in there. You wanna ride?"

"It's been a minute since I hit the club but I'll pass. I got to get some sleep before I go check on my friend in the hospital." I peeked out at Missy. When she looked my way I pointed to my eyes.

"It'll just be a couple hours before the club closes and we need to celebrate, right? I know Missy will go. That bitch don't miss a chance to party, but I want you to go too." Luscious started dancing to Missy's music.

"I'll go, but I'm driving. When I'm ready to bounce, I'm out."

"Girl, we gone have fun. Watch."

I drowned out the rest of her conversation. I noticed that Luscious didn't be talking 'bout shit but she stayed talking. Man, fuck that. I had a friend in Yummy and I wasn't looking for no more. Period. Point-blank.

* * *

As soon we finished up for the night we each took turns taking a shower and getting dressed to jet to New York. Since we ain't had much time and they didn't bring a change of clothes I let them borrow outfits from me, but I made it clear they couldn't have them. I don't play the sharing-clothes bullshit, plus I ain't know them like that.

I had to admit that it was fun gossiping and getting dressed to go out. It reminded me of the days after Dyme and me ended that Yummy made me get over him by living life to the fullest. I felt my age in those days. I could only hope that she pulled through so we could have fun together again.

We made it into the city and to the club in thirty minutes. The line to get in was still halfway down the block.

"Man, we not getting in there tonight." Missy said, looking cute in my silver strapless dress as she turned in the rear seat to look out the window at the crowd.

Luscious shook her head and waved her hand before she reached in her bag for her flip cell phone. "Just park, Goldielocks, my cousin will get us in."

I sped up and turned the corner to circle the block. "I ain't tryna get embarrassed, Luscious."

Luscious put her phone to her ear and turned down the sounds of a new Shareefa song on the radio. "I got this. I *got* this."

I just eyed that bitch like "you better." We parked near the corner and made our way up the street. Car horns were blown and men hollered out passing cars definitely checking for us. We did look good. I looked good. The truth is just the truth.

Me with my golden skin and glossy hair in the leather strapless dress I wore with a short ostrich feather jacket that framed my face. I wore my hair up in a loose and messy top-knot with these flashy, oversized rhinestone hoops. Nobody had to tell me I was straight top rung. I made it my business to be nothing less.

All eyes were on us as we walked past the line and straight to the door where sure enough the bouncer in the black suit and black turtleneck waved us right on in. I can't lie. As soon as we stepped inside I had to stop and take it all in. The music was loud and filled with bass that seemed to beat inside our bodies. The darkness of the club was broken up by flashing neon lights and spots of colorful smoke. Up on platforms women dressed only in bikinis danced like they was trying to save their lives. The spot was huge and it was packed.

I was loving that ish. Loving it.

This wasn't shit like them bullshit clubs we used to go to. Nothing at all.

"You lost?" someone whispered close to my ear.

I turned and some tall dark-skinned cutie in a fitted shirt with a butter-soft leather coat was smiling down at me with a drink in his hands. He looked familiar. Something about him . . .

My smile spread like warm butter. "You're Reginald 'the Damager' Franks," I said, easing up on the tips of my platform sandals so this multimillion-dollar professional football player could hear me.

He held out his hand to me, flashing his Super Bowl ring, and smiled right back at me. "And you are beautiful."

I slid my hand in his. "And thirsty," I hinted playfully.

He laughed and even with the loud music it was deep as hell. He stepped back and waved toward the bar.

I turned to make sure Luscious and Missy were following me straight to these free drinks, but I didn't see them anywhere. Figuring they got lost in the crowd or hooked up with Luscious's cousin, I shrugged. Fuck it. I was a loner anyway.

He made room for us at the circular bar in the middle of the floor. "What you having?"

"Just an amaretto and orange juice."

He ordered the drink and paid for it. "What's your name?"

"Kaeyla . . . but everybody calls me Goldie." I took a sip of my drink, knowing it was more about quenching a thirst than catching a buzz. It would take a whole lot more than amaretto to get a bitch like me fucked up.

"So what do you do, Goldie? You a model, one of them video chicks—"

"Why can't I be a nurse or a lawyer?" I asked him, leaning my fine ass on the bar while I looked up at him with my golden eyes.

The Damager held up his beefy hands. "My bad. My bad. You're right. Just because you fine don't mean you're not smart."

"I own and operate my own strip club."

That changed his whole face game. "Word?" he said, tilting his head to the side to look down at me.

I laughed and reached inside my clutch for one my business cards. "Word."

He took the card and looked at that motherfucker hard. "So I wasn't *too* far off."

The way he said it made me laugh.

"Private shows, huh?"

Sipping my drink, I nodded and danced a little in my spot to the sound of a club remix of Mary J. Blige's "I'm Fine."

"Is 'private show' a code word for 'more'? You know, like 'massages'?"

"We sell the fantasy, not the reality." *No pussy for sale, nigga. Sorry.*

He eyed me up and down. "You sure?"

Truth. He was rich, famous, and cute in that big cuddly teddy bear kind of way, but the Damager wasn't my type. I wasn't gonna fuck this nigga for free or otherwise. I locked my eyes with his and tilted my head back to drain my cup. "Positive," I told him, setting the cup on the bar.

"Too bad."

A dude dressed in all black walked up to the Damager and whispered in his ear. He nodded. "I gotta run but your drinks on me all night," he told me, reaching in his wad to hand the bartender two hundred dollars. He held my business card up between two of his beefy fingers. "I got your number, Goldie."

He turned and soon the crowd surrounded him and he was gone.

"What you having next?" the bartender asked, holding up the two bills.

"Whatever bottle of champagne blows the whole two hundred," I told him, reaching in my clutch for my cell phone. I had six missed calls from Missy.

"One bottle of Cristal coming up."

"Yeah, uh-huh." I dialed back Missy's number.

"Goldie, where you at?"

"Downstairs by the bar. Where y'all at?"

"In VIP! Look up."

I turned and looked up. I saw the VIP section on the second level, but I couldn't spot Missy and Luscious. "I don't see y'all, but I'm headed that way."

"Luscious left with some rapper named Make Money or some shit."

I frowned up my face. That was some groupie type of move . . . and behind some motherfucka I ain't never heard of. There was plenty sucka-ass motherfuckas with fake diamonds and a mic who thought because they could rhyme "at" and "sat" that they was the next fucking Jay-Z.

Luscious had to do better.

I couldn't do shit but shake my damn head, grab my bottle of champagne, and head to the VIP.

It was damn near six in the morning when I finally dragged my ass in the house. Shee-it, I danced, drank, and partied my ass off. But no matter how tired I was, I slept for like two hours then got my ass up to shower and head straight to the hospital to give Yummy's mom a break.

I knocked twice before I opened the door and walked in. There was a lot of medical personnel around the bed and my fucking heart dropped to my boots. I dropped all my shit to the floor and rushed through them to get to her side.

When I looked down at her I gasped, because her eyes were open and she was looking up at me. "Yummy, girl."

I felt weak. My legs gave out and somebody strong led my ass to a chair in the corner. I don't think I ever felt so emotional in all my life. By the time I got myself back together the doctors and nurses had all left.

Yummy's mom was sitting by the bed with her head down

and her shoulders shaking. I stepped over by the bed on her right side and took her hand in mine. She tried her best to squeeze it back. "Girl, you scared us, Yummy. You really scared us girl," I said to her, trying hard not to stare at the whole left side of her face twisted down.

Her moms started crying harder. I bent down and closed my eyes and whispered, "Don't you worry, I put something on Gunz his ass will never forget."

Suddenly her grip on my hand tightened and I lifted up to look down at her just as Yummy looked at me and winked with her good eye.

Remembering how I put that Taser to that crazy motherfucka's nuts, I smiled and winked right back.

"She winked at me, Miss Calhoun," I said, happy as hell for the small sign that Yummy might be okay one day. I was already planning to fill her room with all the flowers and balloons money could buy.

Her moms stood up on her left side.

Yummy's eyes shifted to her.

"We getting the hell out this city. Me, you, and the kids."

That shit made my stomach drop and my eyes shifted over to her.

"Your Uncle Norris just bought a house down in South Carolina and he said we could live in his trailer 'til we get on our feet. It got a big old yard for the kids and he said he'll build a ramp onto it for us."

"Miss Calhoun, you sure about this?" I asked, not trying to be disrespectful but not even trying to lose my friend.

She looked up at me with red-rimmed eyes. "I appreciate you sticking by my baby, but these streets got her 'bout dead from drugs, not knowing if she ever gone recover from a stroke. If I gots to take her to the other end of this earth to give her a chance to get better, then I will do it."

Yummy squeezed my hand.

I looked down at her. My best friend got hooked on coke and I didn't know shit about it until she had a stroke and almost died. How the fuck could I protest whatever decision her family made for her and the kids?

One thing about the hood—any hood—it's made up of people who thrive or people who struggle every day just to survive. The life is fast and if you fuck around and get hooked on drugs, the pace goes even faster until the very things you crave runs you over and over and over like a Mack truck. The hood ain't for everybody. These streets can drag you and leave nothing but a shell of the person you used to be.

Yummy was almost a casualty.

A tear raced down her cheek and I knew she wanted to go. She knew she had to go.

"If there is anything I can do for you, name it and it's yours, Miss Calhoun. Just take good care of my friend."

Miss Calhoun reached across Yummy and took my hand in hers, forming a circle. She dropped her head. I did the same. Yummy closed her good eye.

We all said our silent prayers.

10

But bitch, I got money to blow
I'm gettin' in, letting these bills fall
All over your skin.

—Birdman and Lil' Wayne, "Money to Blow"

Five Months Later

Business was booming and life was sweet as hell.

I didn't bring on any more dancers for the weekend shows at my apartment, but I now had fifteen bad bitches on my roll call for private gigs from here to Philly. I trained them all to deliver top-notch, unique-as-they-could-get-it, asstainment. Chicks was clamoring to be a Goldie Girl.

Between the weekend shows at the apartment and our private gigs, my take was an easy four to five grand a week after my payroll and expenses. I was far from rich, but it wasn't bad for a twenty-three-year-old chick without a high school diploma. I can't front that after sending Yummy and her mommy money in South Carolina, that most of it didn't go to getting back into the lifestyle Dyme raised me on. I partied hard and shopped even harder. All of the members of my beauty squad were back on speed dial. I was the boss bitch again and the more I made, the more I spent. I treated myself often as a toast to my grind.

It felt good to walk into Short Hills mall and be able to shop 'til I dropped again. It felt even better to be meeting a real estate agent to look at business and residential properties. It was time to make my shit legit and to get the hell out the PJs.

My Louis Vuitton heels clicked against the hardwood floors, sounding like a clock in a quiet room or some shit as I walked around the empty living room of the four-bedroom, three-and-a-half bathroom home in the Vailsburg section of Newark just on the border of South Orange. I wasn't crazy. I knew I was being mad ambitious but it was what I wanted, and lately, by hook or by fucking crook, I was getting used to getting just what the fuck I wanted. Including the bar on West Kinney that was for rent and just the perfect spot for Goldie's . . . or whatever name I came up with for my strip club/lounge.

I figured the mortgage and rent would be under three grand a month, and I spent that on handbags and shoes easily.

I stopped in front of the windows and pulled the blinds to the side. It was just like the neighborhood where Dyme's lying ass was having his happily-ever-after with the Tasmanian devil. He lied and said he would get it for me, but it felt damn good to get this motherfucka for myself. My eyes focused on my reflection in the glass and I reached up to smooth my hair, shiny and straight and bust down the middle. A golden Pocahontas dressed in Gucci shades.

The sound of something coming through on the fax made me turn to the Realtor, some white chick named Amanda

Millstone, who was sitting at the little black card table in the corner.

"Miss Dennis, I had my assistant fax over your credit report." She looked like she belonged in one of the big-ass office buildings in Manhattan, with red square-frame glasses and a suit.

"And?"

She looked up at me over the rim of the glasses. "*And*," she said, sounding disappointed as hell, "you don't have any established credit, nor do you have a verifiable source of income."

"A verifiable source of income." So all the dollars pushed in my thong don't count?

"Where do you work?" she asked, picking up her pen.

"I dance."

Amanda pushed her glasses up with her finger. "Ooh, that is fabulous. Are you on Broadway or in a troupe?"

I frowned. *A troop? The fuck she talkin' 'bout?*

"No, I dance," I said, turning sideways and booty popped. "You know, strip?" *Duh, bitch.*

"Oh, oh, okay," she said, looking surprised.

"Don't knock it 'til you try it," I said at the look on her face.

I didn't say shit else. I was busy thinking, busy fighting off the disappointment I was feeling. It was true I ain't had shit in my name that I ever made payments on, and the Housing Authority damn sure wasn't reporting my bullshit rental payments to no damn body. Dyme paid cash for everything. I didn't even have credit cards.

Amanda pushed some papers inside her crocodile briefcase and stood up. "Let me give you some advice. Put something in you name and work on building a credit profile. Then file taxes on your . . . your, uh . . . *income* this year. Maybe get into a first-time home-buyer program."

We walked out my dream house together and I stopped on the brick steps to look at the quiet tree-lined neighborhood that didn't look shit like where I grew up and nothing at all like where I lived now.

I might run my business under the table, but I couldn't buy a house or lease a decent club that way. I was young and still had a lot to learn, but fuck it, I tried. I didn't want to rent some fucked-up hole-in-the-wall for my strip club, but it looked like I might have to until I got my credit and income straight. Still, next time this bitch saw me, I would be ready.

I slid in Mary J. Blige's classic CD *My Life* as I pulled off in my Lexus behind her red convertible Volvo. At the corner I made the right onto South Orange Avenue and headed straight for some retail therapy at Short Hills mall. It wasn't but a twenty-minute ride, and Mary J. sang me right on there while I just cruised and took my time.

My cell phone rang on the console just as I pulled into a space in the parking deck. Checking the caller ID, I was surprised to see the number to Club Naughty. I started to ignore the call and whateva drama it was about to bring into my life. I *started* to.

"Hello."

"So you stole Luscious and Missy to dance for you."

Rick. I rolled my eyes. "Nigga, you late. They been dancing with me for a while now," I told him, grabbing my Chanel patent leather satchel. "Who *just* told you? Or why you just coming at me wit it?"

"Don't worry about that shit. Just stay out of my club recruiting, Goldie, that's some fucked-up shit."

I stopped my strut across the deck. "You know what, I learned a long time ago, Rick, the whole world is fucked up and ain't shit to do but keep it movin'."

Click.

I hung the phone up right in his face. Get outta here with that bullshit. I ain't got time for a motherfucka whining in my ear. The only thing on my mind is my money and how to make more of it.

And for one, I had to seriously holla at Luscious. Ever since she hooked up with that washed-up rapper fool at the club she been fucking up big-time. She missed a couple private gigs and even missed a night or two during our weekend shows. Then last week the bitch had the nerve to invite me to her birthday party tonight. I couldn't believe her nerve when she had just skipped a bachelor party I booked. She wasn't shit but a warm-up for "the Goldie Experience," but she was still on some unprofessional bullshit talking 'bout she in love.

Humph. Dumb bitch. Love don't love no motherfuckin' body.

A man wasn't good for shit but dick. Fuck it, I got a black-ass dildo twice the size of Rick's dick and half the fuckin' heartache *and* headache.

I ain't had nobody in this world. Nobody. I could cry over it like I did about shit when I was just a punk-ass kid or I could keep it moving. I didn't even let myself get to the pain I felt about not keeping any of my babies. That shit cut like a razor blade.

"That looks good on you, baby."

I froze in the dressing room of Macy's.

"You think I should get it, Damion?"

I *thought* that was that motherfucka's voice, and from the sound of it, he had the Tazmanian devil with him. *Man, shit, first that real estate bullshit, then Rick calling me, now I run into these two geriatric mofos. What the fuck next?*

Shaking my head, I turned to face the mirror in the lace and leather bustier I was trying on. I flipped my gold-tipped hair over my shoulder while I checked out my reflection. I tried to imagine the bustier with a pair of leggings or skinny jeans.

But it was hard to focus.

"That dress will look good for our anniversary party, baby."

"After I caught you in that bitch's house, I thought we wasn't gone see another year, Damion."

I got tense. My face scrunched up while I ear hustled like a motherfucka.

"Man, listen, I don't want to talk about that bullshit. And that's what it was, some bullshit. I made a mistake. You are my wife, and when I said I do, I meant forever."

Some bullshit, huh? Dyme's shit didn't hurt me anymore. There was a time those words woulda fucked my world up and had me crying and shit. Now? I just stuck my finger in my mouth and pretended to gag. They dumb.

I took off the bustier and got dressed, grabbing all the clothes I tried on and was going to buy. I stepped out the dressing room and walked right into Dyme. His eyes got big as shit.

I just stepped past his ass and he stepped in front of me and tried to grab my arm to pull me out the dressing room outer area. I eyed this motherfucka and then I leaned over to knock on the dressing room door. "Please get your husband," I said, loud as hell and not giving a fuck.

With one last "how you like me now" look, I breezed to the register. I didn't even turn around when I heard them arguing, but I know she spotted me. Fuck it. Fuck him. Fuck them.

I was way over they shit.

"Your total is one thousand, one hundred and five dollars and eight cents," the salesgirl said to me, even though her eyes were on the commotion in front of the dressing room.

And it was a hot-ass, motherfuckin' mess.

"That bitch" this.

"That ho" that.

I pulled out my matching Chanel wallet and counted out twelve hundred dollars to hand her. I just wanted out of there and as soon as she handed me my change, I rammed that shit in my wallet, took my garment bags with a smile, and notched my head high as I strolled out that motherfucka like I owned it.

Before I could get to the door, I felt a hand on my arm. I looked down at the female hand and then up at the pissed-off face of Dyme's wife, Frieda. I jerked away from her touch. My first reaction was to swing on this fool.

"Did Damion tell you to meet him here?"

"Look here, lady, the days of *Damion* telling me to do anything is over, so leave me out y'all bullshit." I mean-mugged her ass and turned to walk out the store.

This bitch grabbed at me again. "Oh, so you just happen to be in here the same time as us?" she asked.

"Look, you old enough to be my mama and I'm trying not to knock you the fuck out, bitch, but if you lay hands on me 'gain . . . it's on."

Dyme's no-good ass was nowhere to be seen. Triflin' nigga.

"Why don't you leave me and my family alone?" she said, loud as hell and all hysterical and shit. White folks was straight staring at the Negroes.

I felt like stomping my foot and screaming in frustration like Pinky the record store owner in *Next Friday*. "Leave y'all alone? Leave *me* the fuck alone. Your daughter got fucked up for her mouth and now if you don't stop harassing me you 'bout to get yours just like she got hers. And your husband still calling begging for the pussy, wanting me to spend that money like I used to."

She looked at me like she wanted to spit in my face. "I hate you."

"Don't hate me because you got to learn just like I did that Dyme ain't shit, never was shit, and ain't gone ever be shit. He is what the fuck he is. Trust me, *Frieda*. I. DON'T. WANT. HIM."

"There's no way Damion been messing with you for six years. You lying."

I shook my head. I really wasn't all about hurting this bitch, but she was floating in that river called denial. "Whatever," I said, just waving my hand like *fuck it*.

I calmly dug in my purse, pulled out my keys, threw up a deuce, and turned to finally leave the mall.

I pulled into King Court and parked. I spotted some chicks lounging on the benches by the basketball court. Even though I didn't really fuck with too many females around King Court, I raised my hand to speak but none of them spoke back. Matter fact, all them bitches threw me glares like they was ready to do something. Me being me, I shot them all the same glare back. It reminded me of being in elementary school and putting fists to your eyes to let somebody know you was gone whup they ass the first chance you got.

What the fuck eva.

I made a big to-do out of gathering all my bags from the trunk and locking the doors to my Lex. Motherfuckas always threw shade 'cause they hated to see somebody else shine.

I walked into the building. Nina and her husband, Hector, was leading their triplets down the stairs. He looked at me, his eyes dipped down to my body—probably reminiscing on that lap dance I gave his ass last week. Hector's little short ass was a regular. He didn't miss a Friday night.

Nina looked at him and followed his line of vision.

WHAP!

My mouth fell open. She slapped the shit out of him and the Spanish words flying out her mouth had to be cuss words. I eased right past that motherfuckin' drama and jogged up the stairs leaving them to *they* mess.

Word was getting out to the women and I could tell they was getting restless. Plus Mr. Wilson told me some of the older tenants was fucking complaining about all the traffic in and out the building on the weekends. If the ladies didn't know what the fuck was goin' on, they ass was curious about it.

Yummy's old building was straight run by dopeboys and they mad at what's popping off in *my* apartment?

I paused as I neared my door. "What the fuck?"

Mr. Wilson's door opened and he stepped into the hall with rubber gloves on and a bucket in his hand. "I was gonna clean that up before you saw it."

Taped to the door was a screen shot of the WorldStarHip-

Hop site showing the video of me, Dyme, and his wife wilding out in the courtyard. Spit that somebody hawked from they guts ran down the door in a dozen different spots. Shit was smeared in ugly, funky brown streaks. Eggs and the cracked shells were everywhere.

I covered my mouth feeling like I was going to throw the fuck up.

All of it was nasty as hell . . . and only on my door.

I reached in my wallet and pulled out five crisp one-hundred-dollar bills to hand to Mr. Wilson. He took it and used the key in my hand to unlock the door and push it open wide for me to step my ass over the threshold without getting all that hate on me.

I had this bullshit coming at me 360 degrees today. What the fuck?

"You still gone open up tonight?" he asked.

"Damn right, Mr. Wilson," I told him, my eyes hard as I locked them on him. "One ignorant-ass shit-, egg- and spit-throwing monkey don't stop no show."

Shit that went down in the hood wasn't that different than shit that went on in the suburbs, in the south, or in the country. Drugs. Prostitution. Car thefts. Gang violence. Robbery. It's just shit in the hood seemed more hectic because there was a lot of people living in the hood.

One of my neighbors ain't had but a three-bedroom but I know damn well it's about fifteen strong living in that motherfucker. I sat down, took my time, and counted one day.

Still, even though you hear crazy hood shit. Even though you see crazy hood shit. Even though you live through crazy hood shit. It never ceases to amaze me that motherfuckas find a way to shock the shit of out people in the hood.

That's what the fuck I was thinking when three niggas dressed in all black threw they hoods back, revealing they had on ski masks while they stood up and showed their guns. "Don't nobody move. Y'all know what this is!" one of them shouted.

"Damn it." I was just in the middle of my show and straight froze on that pole. When a nigga—far less three niggas—with a gun said freeze there wasn't nothing to do but get like ice.

I cut my eyes across the room. Missy and Luscious was stiff as mannequins too. They had been helping Mr. Wilson out by serving the liquor and food to keep niggas from moving around too much.

Mr. Wilson's hands was already up and them niggas ain't even ask for all that. Probably one of them stickup kids pointing a gun dead at him made him say fuck it.

My gun and Taser was hidden behind the speaker to my left, but I wasn't crazy enough to think I could outshoot three motherfuckas with guns.

I knew there was a chance niggas would stick me up, but I banked on all these fools knowing me and letting me slide. I banked wrong as hell. It wasn't like I had metal detectors to find out they was strapped.

All I could think about was all the money I was 'bout to be hit for. *Damn it. Shit. Motherfuckas. Goddamn bullshit. Crazy sons of bitches. Shit. Fuck.*

They pulled Dollar Store plastic bags from they pockets. The one standing by the door spoke up. "A'ight, let's run them motherfuckin' pockets. All your money. All your jewelry. Your cell phones, BlackBerries, iPods. Even them little bullshit prepaid joints. Superman, grab the cash box from the old dude. Batman, you work the crowd and get all the tips she worked so hard for over there."

God damn it.

"Let's make sure we the only superheroes in this bitch!"

While I stood there watching these niggas rob me I wished like hell they would shoot the speaker and put an end to the replay of the damn song. That shit was irking my nerves bad.

The one called Batman, the short chubby one, walked through the thick-ass crowd toward me. He stood there eyeing me in my rhinestone bikini. I know it seems dumb as hell, but that shit made me feel naked and exposed. I watched him like a hawk, my face not showing the fear or the anger I felt at the bullshit going down.

He reached out to me with his gun and stroked the barrel up my thigh and then nuzzled it against my pussy before he looked up at me. Something in his eyes made me think he wasn't right in the head.

That scared the shit out of me. I didn't move. Either Missy or Luscious cried out.

"Shut the fuck up!" the leader shouted, pointing one of the guns to the ceiling. "Batman, get the money and stop fucking with that ho, man."

I shot him a nasty look at calling me out my name.

"Just to make sure y'all don't go running outta here trying to catch us, I want everybody to stand the fuck up and strip."

"Strip?" everybody said together. If the shit wasn't sad and aggravating it woulda been fucking comical.

Superman laughed.

Batman finally took his gun from between my damn thighs.

The leader laughed. "This a bullshit-ass strip club, ain't it?"

"Nigga watching too many old movies and fucking *Martin* episodes and shit," somebody muttered.

Whoever said it was damn right. Me and Dyme talked about the same robbery scene in some old seventies movie he made me watch called *Let's Do It Again*. When I told him I saw this shit on *Martin*, he set me straight and told me where the fuck the TV show got it from first.

Old copycat-ass nigga.

From my spot on the stage I watched grown-ass men stripping down to nothing. I ain't never seen so many dicks in my life. Most men tried to cover they shit with they hands but a few cocky big-dick niggas just stood there with they tree limbs swinging.

"Tricks too."

Batman stood there waiting on me to strip butt-naked. I refused to cry. I refused to let these niggas known that no man except Dyme and Rick had seen *all* of my goodies. I refused to let these niggas see I was scared they was gone rape me or the other girls.

I reached behind me and unclasped the rhinestone bra. It fell to the stage. I pulled my bikini down over my Beyoncé-like hips. It fell on top of the bikini top.

Batman massaged his hard-on with the gun while he watched me.

"Let's go, fellas."

I didn't relax until them niggas backed out the door and soon the sound of their sneakered feet running down the hallway echoed. Missy rushed over and handed me a towel. I wrapped it around my body.

The men was all pissed and riled up. I couldn't blame them. Some of them just got stuck for the money from they paycheck. Two weeks' worth of working down the drain.

The men starting filing out the door, still talking mad shit about me, my club, and the stickup kids.

What the fuck could I say?

"That one over by us? It was so crazy how one minute he had two eyes and the next I ain't see shit but like white and shit," Luscious said walking up to us in another one of my towels wrapped around her body.

Mr. Wilson had walked up too. Me and him looked at each other. "Gunz," we both said.

Damn. Payback *is* a bitch.

11

Put the needle on a record and I make her get lower than a Lamborghini
And if she really getting low then I'm a shoot a video and put it all on TV. . . .

—Ludacris, "How Low Can You Go?"

I can't front. That robbery fucked my game up for a minute. Anything coulda happened that night. Anything. Murda couldn't be counted out. Rape. Total mayhem. Really, we was all lucky to get out of that bitch alive. Everybody realized that and was scared. For the last two weekends I could count our clients on one hand. Mr. Wilson flat-out advised me to stop and definitely pulled hisself out of the equation, saying the only gun he wanted pointed at him had to have a set of balls and be loaded with cum . . . not bullets.

I would shut the shows down for a few weeks and spread the word that I was hiring security for the door when I reopened. It wasn't like we all wasn't still busy. We stayed making that money from our private shows. Hopefully a few weeks of realizing what they were missing and my clients would be swarming around my door again.

I wasn't out of my own race to the finish line, just had to

find a detour. Nothing or no one was stopping me from getting what I wanted. Point-blank.

And anybody that got in my way was going to get run the fuck over.

The dark Newark streets were lit in spots by tall streetlamps. The air was cold even for February and people were bundled in sweater hats, gloves, and coats. Cars constantly eased up and down the long stretch of Irvine Turner Boulevard. From where I sat in my Lexus, my golden eyes shifted between the building on the corner and the oncoming traffic on the street.

My golden hair was wrapped up beneath a black silk scarf and I was dressed head to toe in black leather. Perfect gear for a stake-out.

I sat up straighter when the door to the building opened. My breath held in my throat until I saw Gunz walk out to stand on the street. He was smoking a cigarette, holding it with just his index finger while he looked up and down the street like he was waiting for something or somebody. He turned to the wall and lowered his head. I knew he was snortin'. Hatred for that roaming-eye motherfucka burned in my guts as I picked up the throwaway cell phone and dialed a number.

"Yo."

"He's outside," I said, my eyes locked on him.

The phone hung up.

Two seconds later a blacked-out Ford Focus pulled out a parking spot in front of a corner store and passed by me to pull in front of the building.

Gunz looked up in surprise just before the three bulky dudes in black jumped out the car with the door wide open.

I sat in my car, smoking a 'port and watching them straight stomp a hole in his ass . . . just like I paid them to. This nigga had to learn not to fuck with me. I'm not taking shit no more, and I felt no regret watching them kick, punch, and stomp that fool. His head. His ribs. His face. Punch after punch. Kick after fucking kick. Fuck him.

He had to learn I ain't the one to fuck with. He was going to respect me and mines.

People started to holler and scream for them to stop. They hopped back in the stolen Focus and pulled off.

I tossed my cigarette out the window and pulled off, making the left turn to cruise by the front of the building. He was sitting on the concrete, brushing away the hands of people trying to help him.

I tooted the horn.

He looked up. His face was a red bloody mess.

I lowered the window and waved before I pushed the gas and sped away. I didn't slow down until I came to a red light.

I felt anxious and excited about what went down. I didn't know what was coming next, but I would be more than ready for that motherfucka. He was lucky, 'cause Red and his boys was willing to straight kill his ass. Lucky for Gunz I didn't think none of this shit was *that* serious.

Bzzzzz.

I picked up my cell phone. "Yeah?"

"Goldie, where you at?"

BAM!

I dropped my cell phone as my body flew forward against the steering wheel. I shook my head to clear it and looked up in the rearview mirror.

The sight of Gunz's van backing up to ram into me again

made me scream out and floor my gas, shooting out into oncoming traffic. A Ford Explorer swerved to miss me but I kept going because I had a lunatic behind me.

"What the fuck?"

I sped down Irvine Turner ducking and diving in between cars, my eyes going back and forth between the rearview mirror and the city streets in front of me. He ducked and dived behind me. Cars blowing they horn as we barely missed hitting people and cars.

I turned the corner, damn near on just two tires, hoping to shake this motherfucka. I didn't even know what street I was on, but I knew Frelinghuysen was coming up at the intersection. I knew I had to outrace this fool. I knew I was scared as shit. And I knew if he caught up to me I was dead.

I checked the mirror. He was behind me on the brick-paved streets. I beat the wheel. "What the *hell*?" I screamed at the top of my lungs.

BOOM!

I gasped and looked in my mirror. Gunz's van was wrapped around a light pole outside an abandoned factory. Glass and metal was everywhere. Smoke was coming up from under the hood. And the steady wail of his horn let me know his body was laying on the wheel.

I slammed on my brakes. My heart pounded as I gripped the wheel like a motherfucka. "Oh shit, oh shit, oh shit, oh shit."

I had to get out of there. "Go," I urged myself.

Just as I sped off and made the left onto Frelinghuysen I glanced out the driver's-side window just as the van exploded and burst into flames.

The war was over.

* * *

That scene with Gunz showed me I wasn't nearly as hard as I thought I was. I didn't want the nigga to die . . . especially like that.

A vision of the wreckage fucked with me constantly over the last hour since it all went down. I had to shake my damn self to turn it loose. Truth was, I didn't know if Gunz was dead or alive. I hauled ass with a quickness. For all I know that nigga climbed out that fucking burning van and was somewhere getting his shit together to come get me.

I was second-guessing my last-minute decision to come to Luscious's birthday party. I came straight from the accident here figuring I might need a damn alibi. I closed my eyes and tapped the top of the bar at the Key Club in downtown Newark. Soon the bartender sat my third shot of Henny in front of me. I swallowed it down and tried my best—my very fucking best—to calm down. *What the fuck I done got myself into?*

Nobody told that nigga to leave my friend to die.

Nobody told that nigga to rob me and my clients.

Nobody told that nigga to chase behind me and try to run me off the fucking street.

Hell, he crashed into the fucking pole chasing *me* to kill *me*.

Right?

A hand landed on my shoulder. I screamed out and turned at the same time pressing my back to the bar. I laughed all nervous and crazy and shit at Luscious standing behind me.

"Damn, Goldie, what's up with you?"

Calm the fuck down. "My mind was somewhere else."

"I thought you wasn't coming again," Luscious said, looking real cute in the deep purple strapless leather ruffle dress she wore. Her hair was pulled back into a severe ponytail that swung down past her ass.

Neither did I, I thought giving her a fake-ass smile as I pushed away the vision of Gunz's van exploding. I was up to a blunt packed with kush and four shots of Henny. My hands was still shaking like crazy. Nothing helped me from being afraid that someone spotted my bright red Lexus leaving the scene.

"Listen, my friend. Make$ is here and well, I kinda told him I stopped stripping," she said to me as she led me back to the table.

I side-eyed her. "So you lied?" I asked her, knowing I was being smart at the mouth and not really giving a flying fuck.

"Listen, we just really started talkin' and that nigga ain't paying all my bills yet. It cost to be the boss."

I shrugged. The only thing Luscious's ass could do for me was get to her shows on time so I could get the fee I charged for booking all of 'em. I didn't really give a fuck what she told her one-hit-wonder rapper. After he dropped his first single, "Get Like Me," last year I ain't heard shit else from his ass. Fuck going gold off a single and people don't give a fuck about nothing else on your whole CD. Nigga please. ONE. HIT. WONDER.

"Yeah, okay, Luscious. Whateva."

I wasn't even gone come to her party but I felt like my ass needed an alibi and so here the fuck I was. The sight of the bar and the liquor sidetracked me like a motherfucka.

Get your shit together, Goldie. I knew I looked a fucking mess. I barely took time out in the car to snatch off my scarf and the bobby pins to finger-comb my doobie-wrapped hair down around my face and shoulders. I grabbed a tube of my IMAN lip gloss from my pocketbook and slathered it on my lips before I unzipped my fitted leather racing jacket, exposing the diamond-encrusted heart pendant snuggled just above my cleavage.

This was the best I could do . . . and real talk, it was shit, but it was still a gazillion times better than most bitches look on the average day.

Luscious left my side as soon as we got to the tables. She went toward this crowd of niggas. I assumed it was her boo and his entourage. There was about twenty other people sitting at the tables. She didn't bother to introduce me and I just threw up a half-ass wave to these people I didn't know before I grabbed the empty seat next to Missy.

"Looks like you're having fun," I drawled.

Missy's already slanted eyes looked even smaller. "I'm fucked up."

"You look it," I told her, hanging my handbag on the back of the chair.

Missy just laughed and held her drink up in the air like "heeey."

Luscious moved onto the dance floor and my eyes shifted to the dude she pulled behind her. *So this Make "$" up close and personal, huh?* "Get Like Me" started playing and the crowd went crazy when he took the mic the DJ handed him and started performing.

Shit looked planned like a motherfucka to me.

This mofo was redder than me, with tattoos all over his neck and arms. He wasn't but five-foot-eight and thin as hell with his jeans sagging—even with a Gucci belt on. His big-ass shades hid most of his face and a toothpick was working overtime shifting from one side of his mouth to the other.

If Luscious liked it, I loved it. Fuck it.

I tried like hell to get into the music and enjoy the drinks and food that I ordered but I couldn't. Plus, some of the dudes in Luscious's family kept staring at me and Missy like we was on the pole booty-butt-naked. They was pissing me off and I started to take out a titty and charge these mother-fuckas for the peep show.

I leaned across the table toward Missy. "I'm outta here. Tell Luscious I left." I stood up and grabbed my bag. It wasn't but ten thirty, but I was way over Luscious's party.

Plus, I had other shit on my mind.

Tossing my hair over my shoulder, I walked out the Key Club grabbing my cell phone to call and check on Yummy. I wished like I hell I could talk to her and tell her about Gunz—she was the *only* person I'd trust with that info.

"So you're Goldie?"

I turned around and eyed Make Money—no, excuse the fuck outta me, Make$—leaning against the side of the building smoking a cigarette. "The one and only," I said, shooting him this "why are you talkin' to me" look before I headed toward my car.

"I heard about you."

I paused, shoving my hands into the pockets of my jacket as I faced him on the street. "Wish I could say the same about you." Nope, I WAS NOT in the mood.

He laughed, letting out a stream of smoke. "They say you was bad as hell and know it."

"They who? Who is they?" I snapped, my gold eyes flashing.

"I like your look," he said, ignoring my question, all eyeing me up and down.

"And what about Luscious?" I told his little ass, shaking off the hair the wind blew against my face.

Make$ dropped the Newport to the street and squashed it beneath the toe of his custom-made crocodile leather Nikes. "She straight . . . but I don't want my boys watching her strip."

If this motherfucka wanted to believe Luscious wasn't shaking her ass to make money, that's *they* drama. "Look, that's y'all's situation. I'm out."

"Word is you a female hustla all about your business."

I locked eyes with this nigga trying to figure out his angle. "That's one hundred."

"I'm throwing a big party and I need you and four more strippers for the VIP section."

This nigga wanted to hire me? First thing that strolled through my mind: *How much*? Fuck what you heard or if you ain't heard it, but money make the world—my world—go 'round. If the money was right, then fuck everything else—including Luscious. That bitch don't pay my bills.

"Any particular look you like . . . *other* than mine?" I asked, already figuring what I'd charge his ass and who I'd get to work the night for me. If this one-hit-wonder wanted to throw away money hiring dancers and throwing a big party like he fucking Jay-Z or some shit, that his business.

Make$ nodded his head. "I want another Latin chick, you know—"

"Another?" I asked, crossing my arms over my chest.

"Yeah, I figured you was Puerto Rican or Dominican or something."

I just shrugged. Hell, what the fuck else could I do? I didn't know what the fuck was all mixed up in me. Didn't know if I ever would. Didn't know if I would ever stop giving a fuck. Didn't know if my past would stop hurting. One day maybe I'd take the time and try to get it all figured the fuck out. But for now? The present? That was all in my control.

I reached in my purse and pulled out a business card. "Call me and we'll work out the details . . . like my money."

Make$ reached for the card.

I pulled it back. "Where does Luscious fall in all this?"

"She won't be there *and* this business right here is none of her business." He reached and snatched the card.

"Secrets cost extra," I shot right back at his ass. Drama came at a price.

"Goldie, you leaving already?"

I watched as Make$ slipped my card into the inside pocket of his leather coat before I looked over at Luscious easing up to him. They hugged up.

"Yeah, I got a lot to do tomorrow," I told her, trying to ignore that Make$'s hands was under Luscious's skirt, exposing her ass to the cold and whoever the fuck walked or drove by.

But this nigga don't want her to strip? Man, miss me with the bullshit.

Luscious rubbed on Make$ all possessive and shit, staking claim. "What was y'all chitchatting about?" she asked.

I eyed this bitch. Jealousy wasn't cute on her ass, and before I flipped and slapped the shit out of her, I threw up a deuce and turned to walk to my car, my heels beating the street. I really wasn't in the mood for they shit. Straight the fuck up. Me and Luscious was cool and we made plenty money together but I ain't missing that she is seriously not feeling me anywhere near her man. That shit let me know that bitch didn't trust one or both of us. Considering the deal that just went down I guess most people wouldn't blame her, but this was all about money for me. Her nigga and his dick was safer than a motherfucka. So fuck her. Fuck him. Double fuck them.

I left him to come up with a lie for her ass. I'm not being questioned by no bitch. Especially when I have money and mayhem on my mind.

I climbed into my car and soon I was headed toward King Court. I turned off the radio blasting some old-school slow jams and put my cell phone on silent. I needed quiet to think and focus. As I drove through the busy traffic of the streets, my eyes would look at the rearview mirror and expect to see the bright round lights of Gunz's van behind me. Ramming me. Trying to hurt me.

I flinched.

The false images of the lights transformed to the fiery explosion of his van.

Was Gunz dead?

And if he wasn't, what the fuck would he have in store for me?

I ran my hand through my hair and cruised through the streets of my city. If Gunz was begging forgiveness at the pearly gates or cruising straight into the pit of hell, I just needed to know where the fuck I stood in all this.

I glanced at my gold watch. It was still early. Just a little after eleven. *I just might make it . . .*

As soon as I walked into my apartment, I grabbed the remote and turned on the flat screen on the wall. I kicked off my heels and moved in front of the stripper pole blocking some of my view of the screen.

"*. . . the victim of the fatal van explosion in Newark that we reported earlier has been identified as Robert—*"

My heart damn near burst. I used the remote to up the volume as an image of the burnt van shown. "This gots to be it," I said, biting my bottom lip.

"No other vehicles were involved in the head-on collision. Preliminary reports are sketchy as authorities await the autopsy of the victim. More details will be reported as they become available to us in the newsroom."

Click.

I turned the television off and headed over to the bar to grab a bottle of Cîroc vodka. At the kitchen sink I poured out a shot for Gunz and did an even longer pour for Yummy. He was dead, and with her stroke, I know she felt like she might as well be dead.

Did I want Gunz to pay for leaving Yummy to die and for robbing my set?

Hell yeah.

Did I want that nigga to die?

No . . . not necessarily.

But was I glad the mini war I started with Gunz was over?

I took a drink straight from the bottle to toast to that. *He fucked with my friend and he fucked with my money. Two thumbs in a bucket . . . fuck it.*

It took over a week for the images of Gunz's van blowing up to stop chasing me. I tried to focus on getting the girls, costumes, and routine ready for Make$'s party, but that shit stayed heavy as hell in the back of my thoughts. I didn't start to feel any better until I caught the news that the streets was laying most of the blame for his death at his own reckless, wild-living door. They figured he hopped in his van after getting jumped and blacked out behind the wheel or he was so wasted on liquor and 'caine that he crashed.

When people mentioned Gunz's death, the fact that that nigga lived his life straight jacking people and doing crazy shit wasn't too far off from coming out their mouth. The whole "live by the sword, die by the sword" and "reaping what you sow" mentality.

Regardless, *this* bitch was in the clear and my life had to go on. No more mayhem. It's time for my money.

I looked around the small-ass dressing room they stuck us in at the club. The steady *thump-thump* of the music echoed through the walls. Five chicks getting ready in one room was mad hectic but we was making it work. Thankfully, the room smelled of nothing but our various perfumes and lotions. Any chick dancing for me knew of my shower-first policy. No fish-smelling bitches on my team. Unnecessary. Unprofessional. Motherfuckin' unsanitary.

My Mama Bit always taught me that if a woman didn't wash her ass on the regular, her cha-cha would tell it. Wasn't nothing worse than the smell of a rank pussy.

"Mama Bit," I whispered, ignoring the chill that raced over my body as I avoided my own eyes in the mirror.

I raised you better than this, Kaeyla.

Yes you did, Mama Bit. You sure did. My eyes shifted up to take in my reflection. The sleek hair, the makeup, the big titties pushed high in the black leather bikinis we all wore.

But I wasn't turning my back on my hustle. I went from being broke and ridiculed to spoiled and pampered and back to broke again. Now I was making my own gwap, buying what I wanted when I wanted. Not putting up with a motherfucka's bullshit.

Sorry, Mama Bit, but I'm gone shake this ass.

I turned and peeped my goods, 'cause all these bitches was to me was something to sell. "Y'all ready to do this?" I asked.

Make$ asked for more *boriquas* but I was planning to fuck his shit all the way up with my own version of a rainbow coalition. Everything from white to Asian.

Ming had those shots to make her ass big and round and knew how to work her hips to make a nigga "love her long time."

Ice was this thick white chick who wasn't shit but silicone and bleached blonde hair, but she loved black dudes and they loved her ass right on back.

Marisol, aka Spanish Fly, was built like a Coke bottle and flexible as hell.

Coko lived up to her name with skin that was damn near black but smooth as hell with a body that was killa and a china-doll face.

"I heard there's supposed to be some celebs in the house," Ice said, her Harlem accent sounding mad crazy out her mouth as she rubbed lotion on gravity-defying triple-D tits.

"Like who? I ain't never heard of no Make$ motherfucka," Coko shot at her, waving her hand with her four-inch nails slicing the air.

"More like Make No Money," Ming added, twisting and turning her ass in the mirror to see how her black leather thong fit.

"Girl, you remember that song "Get Like Me," Ice said, flipping her blonde extensions over her shoulder before she sang the hook.

Coko's face changed. "Oooh, that was my jam last summer."

Ice nodded her head, eyeing each one of us. "I read online somewhere that Make$ might be signing a big deal real soon with Platinum Records. Fuck what you heard, but that nigga still touring like crazy and making money off that shit."

I wasn't really payin' none of they ass no attention until I heard "Platinum Records." Shit, who the fuck ain't heard of *them* niggas? They was straight running the rap game right now. *That's* who Make$ might be getting down with?

Say what? Say fucking who?

Even as we left the dressing room and climbed the private stairwell to the VIP area, my mind was working like a motherfucka. Sometimes it ain't what you know but who you know.

The VIP section of the club had its own private entrance with one-way mirrors surrounding the circular second floor. Them niggas inside could see down but there wasn't shit anybody could see in. Make$ already told me it was a no-holds-barred lockdown. Once we were behind that velvet rope, nobody was getting in or leaving until the show was over.

The door opened and a big tall and buff dude with this mean-ass mug held it open for us. I sent Ice first, then Ming, Marisol, me, and then Coko stepped into the room last. Niggas, liquor bottles, and the thick smell of weed, cigars, and cigarettes was heavy in the air.

Five chairs sat in the middle of the room and the sounds of that classic stripper joint "Juicy Fruit" by Mtume played . . . just like I asked.

"A'ight fellas, the real show you been waiting on. Welcome the baddest entertainment on the East Coast . . . Goldie's Girls."

Everything we did was in unison, and I knew that seeing

five fine bitches in nothing but black leather bikinis was fucking these niggas' heads up. This wasn't that everyday shake-and-vibrate-your-ass kinda shit; we did all that and more. I always tried to give a nigga an experience, something he'd remember, something he would spread the word about.

That's why my shows was the best on the East Coast.

I eyed the crowd even as we worked our hips and squatted like we was on a dick. When we moved in the hollering crowd to pick a nigga to grind, I headed for the dark corner to my left and held my hand out.

Half a second later, Make$ slid his hand in mine and I led that little nigga to one of the chairs in the middle of the floor.

"Juicy fruit . . ."

I snapped my fingers and at the same time each of us straddled the dude we picked's hips.

Make$'s hands came up to grab my hips as I snaked my upper body to the floor, grabbed his ankles and then ticked my hips right along with my girls.

"Dayum!" Them niggas went wild and money rained down on us.

"Juicy fruit . . ."

Right on cue we flipped off they laps and into a split in front of them. I locked my eyes on Make$'s face. I knew that even behind them shades that nigga was looking right back at me. I had him hooked.

We jumped up on our stilettos, kicked high, and landed our thighs on their shoulders.

"I'll be your lollipop . . ."

Pussy was straight in they face.

"You can lick me everywhere."

Make$ slapped my ass, making it jiggle in a thousand different directions. Luscious wasn't on my mind, and I knew for damn sure she wasn't on his either.

I climbed back on his lap, grinding against his hard dick with my arms around his neck. His hands dug into my ass hard as hell but I just smiled. "I think you and I need to talk to some real business."

"Oh yeah?" he asked, the scent of liquor on his breath.

I raised my arm and snapped my fingers twice. Two seconds later, them four other niggas was left with hard dicks in their chairs as the girls came over to surround Make$.

"Dayum, y'all gone do a nigga like that, huh?" he asked with a big ass Kool-Aid grin as the room went crazy.

That nigga had all shades of titties, ass, and thighs surrounding him. His dick was hard as hell beneath me.

I leaned back. Ming and Coko bent down in front of him and kissed each other, moaning as they sucked each other's tongues. Them bitches was freaks. Dick or pussy—they didn't give a fuck.

Make$ tilted his head back and howled to the ceiling.

I had him.

With the robbery and the females 'round King Court wildin' out, maybe it was time for a new grind. Some new shit. I hadn't worked out all the details yet but I knew I needed this nigga to make it pop off.

A bitch like me just had to come up with a plan to make sure that I came out on top.

Respect

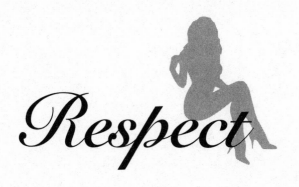

12

You done got a rapper, I see ya vision
And one of the best too that's ambition . . .

—Clipse, "Dirty Money"

Three Months Later

Make$ had to be sick of performing "Get Like Me," because after two months of performing with that nucka I was thoroughly sick of that shit.

Me, Coko, and Ming took our spots on the stage in some Connecticut club packed with mostly white folks. Just like every other show. In their minds, Make$ was still fuckin' relevant. Whatever.

My plan to step up my Goldie's Girls brand worked. I had to offer for me and two of my best girls to perform free during any shows close enough to drive to. Of course that nigga went for it.

I took a risk paying the girls out my own pocket, then hiring a choreographer and a stylist to get us ready for the stage. Thank God that shit paid off.

Word spread fast that Make$ added some stripper chicks to his show and he started selling even more tickets and booking more shows. Now we were paid by Make$'s people, and they even flew us out with him to some of the bigger venues. This summer was going to be on and poppin'.

My grind was ridiculous. Between my girls still dancing for me at private shows and some club events up and down the East Coast, plus the team doing Make$'s shows with me, I was making money and enjoying the power. My website got more and more traffic every day. My cell phone and e-mail stayed blowing up with people wanting to work with my crew. I definitely had the baddest bitches on the East Coast, and I made it my business to teach them how to be even badder.

Next up? I wanted to get some of the badder Goldie's Girls in videos for other artists. My chicks fit the bill for video vixens . . . just like me. Tall and thick as hell, pretty as a motherfucka, and able to move in a way that said "I'm so sexy you either want me or want to be me."

"Make$!" The crowd went wild when he strolled onto the stage shirtless with his jeans down around his ass showing off his black Gucci boxers.

We started our routine, keepin' in sync with the music and one another. Three fine bitches dressed in thong bikinis booty-clapping, grinding, and acting up in unison to one of their favorite rappers performing was tearing the crowd up. I enjoyed the roar of the crowd and the hot feel of the stage lights.

Make$ took center stage and motioned for us to come to him. On cue, I dropped down to a split in front of him and ass-pounded the floor. Ming and Coko both grinded one side of him before bending over backward. He took the champagne bottle in his hands and poured it over us.

"Get like me!" Make$ dropped the mic to the floor and walked off the stage.

The lights went out.

Show over. Money made.

We ran off the stage and my heart was beating so fast. Being on that stage was a fucking rush for me. I can't front and say I didn't love it.

"Listen, Goldie, talk to your boy about the fucking champagne," Coko said, as soon as we walked into our "dressing room" that wasn't shit but a storage area, just like in my days at Rick's club. "I ain't got that wash-and-wear hair like you and Kung Fu Pussy. He ain't paying enough for me to get this weave washed."

Ming just laughed. "Don't hate, bitch."

My mind was on telling Make$ that I needed my own fucking dressing room. I ain't give a fuck if it was a stall in a fucking bathroom long as I was on my own and not having to hear this bullshit-ass complaining. Truthfully, though, he could kill that champagne shower. "I feel sticky as hell from that shit. I'll talk to him."

Coko lit a cigarette while she undressed. "I'm ready to get to the room and wash my ass."

I eyed Ming reach in a small metal can and pop something into her mouth. She looked up and saw me watching her and just shrugged.

"I'm off the clock, Goldie."

The bitch sounded all defensive and shit. That let me know that shit wasn't no fucking Altoid mint.

"It's just Ecstasy, Goldie," Coko said, all blasé and shit, before she reached over with a laugh and tweaked one of Ming's brown nipples.

I couldn't keep the nasty frown off my face looking at these two bisexual, sometimes dykin', pill-popping freak bitches. I didn't need no fuckin' users 'round me. Next them bitches be stealing.

Or worse, spike my drink and double-team my pussy. Nothing. Strictly dickly—even though it been months since I had some. My hustle was my lover and I fucked my grind.

"Goldie!"

Somebody was hollering my name through the door. Two seconds later it opened. I barely covered my titties with my hands when Make$'s manager, Chill Will, walked in. He paused in the doorway and watched Ming and Coko touching on each other. Them freak bitches giggled as they both eyed him and then rubbed their titties lightly against the other's.

Fucked his head all up.

"What's up, Will?" I asked him, ignoring them because I knew them bitches acted way worse when somebody paid they asses some attention.

"Will," I called out again, when his ass just stood there like Ming and Coko was his own private porno show.

I looked down at him, and that short, pudgy nigga was rubbing his dick like he might nut up his pants.

Ming and Coko slapped hands and laughed like crazy.

"Make$ and me need to talk to you," he said at last, finally focusing his big round eyes on me.

"Let me finish getting dressed. I'll be right there."

With one last look at Ming and Coko, he left the room. I decided to handle what the fuck ever was in that can when we got back to Jersey in the morning. Right now business was on my mind. The last time I met with Make$ and Will, they started paying me and the girls to perform. No more freebie shit. I wondered what they fuck they was about to slide on my plate next . . . or was the money train coming to an end?

Dressed in my skinny jeans, heels, and a black silk tank, I walked down the long hall to the door with a white piece of paper with MAKE$ typed on it. I could already hear the music and the rumble of the voices of Make$'s entourage.

If that nigga was a friend and not just an associate I made money with, I woulda sat him down and told him he was straight throwing away money letting his ten-nigga crew ride for free. He wasn't nowhere near Drake, Weezy, or Birdman, so his ass ain't had money to burn.

I knocked. As soon as the door opened, weed smoke and liquor came through the door at me. Shit was so thick I coughed. I eyed about twelve niggas in the tiny-ass room before my eyes finally landed on Make$ laying on the couch.

This shit was mad dumb, but that's his shit to worry about.

"This the ho you was talkin' 'bout?" somebody asked behind him before a thick hand landed on my ass.

I whirled around, pissed off and ready to hurt somebody. The five niggas behind me ain't do shit but laugh. "Whoever said that shit and fuckin' put they hands on me better be glad I ain't got my motherfuckin' piece, 'cuz your family would be bringing pound cake and soda to your wake."

This fat, greasy-looking motherfucka in an orange T-shirt that I didn't recognize from the usual crew of wannabe niggas just looked smug as hell. I knew it was him. Nigga looked like his nuts stank. *Ole fat nasty bastard.*

"Whoa, whoa, whoa. Hell naw, Tank, don't handle Goldie like that."

Tank smiled. "My bad."

I just eyed him up and down like "fuck you" before I gave him my back. "What's up, Make$?"

"Y'all head to the VIP. I'm on my way," he said, sitting up on the couch as he pulled on a wife beater and then pulled his diamond chains on top of it.

No need having a quarter of a million in jewelry and your three-dollar T-shirt was covering it up. Ne-gro puh-leeze.

The fellas filed out the room. Make$ and Will eyed me. "So what's up? I really just want to get to the room."

"Make$'s shows been selling out and we just got word he's going back in the studio to start working on his second album," Will said, chinning and grinning.

I smiled like I was happy for him, but really I just wanted to know how this news affected me and only me. Flipping my champagne-soaked hair over my shoulder, I eyed Make$, who was looking happy as a crackhead who ran up on a cookie big as a spare tire.

"So . . . is Goldie's Girls in or out?" I asked, cutting to the chase.

"In," Make$ said, lifting a bottle of Cîroc vodka to his mouth.

"Might be time to renegotiate the terms," I said. "Like travel and per diem."

Will looked surprised, like he thought I wasn't shit but a dumb bitch who shook her ass. Do I have to say once again that I am young but so very far from dumb?

Make$ stood up. "It's time to head to VIP in this bitch and celebrate."

Since I loved when a plan came together, I actually agreed with this nigga. Rising up on my Enzo heels, I grabbed an unopened bottle of Grey Goose and popped the seal. "Let's celebrate."

* * *

It had to happen. At twenty-three years old, my ass ain't had many men in my life. Matter of fact, I was still on one hand and had three fingers left. Still, those two big-dick motherfuckas held it down.

Now this thin-dick motherfucka humping away between my thighs?

I rolled my eyes and fought like hell not to suck my teeth. "Yes, Make$, tear that pussy up," I whispered in his ear before I bit it and moaned in the back of my throat.

This dry-ass fuck wasn't worth sneaking around Luscious's back. Bunch of whack-ass bullshit. Ugh.

"Ride this dick."

I eyed this clown still wearing his fitted cap, his socks, and all his jewelry. I could slap myself for letting too much partying fuck with my good sense.

"Damn, ya pussy good. Let me take this condom off."

Nothing, motherfucka. "Hell no, I ain't on no birth control. I ain't tryna have nobody's baby."

"I'll pull out."

I pulled to the side to look up at this fool. "You better run that shit on them little girls or dumb bitches don't know no better."

Dyme got me pregnant the last time with that pull-out shit. I done learned my lesson. Plus, I wasn't fucking this nigga raw. Since we been doing shows I done seen this nigga take plenty of chicks back to his room. He probably was rawing they ass too. Fuck to the hell to the no.

Alcohol and being horny as fuck got me hemmed up with this nigga in this bullshit-ass jam, but I wasn't too fucked up not to make sure this nigga was strapped up.

Make$ pulled his dick out of me and I barely felt that shit. I felt like boxing his long-ass head when he shifted down to suck my nipples. Too hard. Too wet. Ugh.

Pushing him off me and onto his back, I smiled down at him while I squatted and eased down onto his hard dick, making sure that condom was in place. *Nigga, if I knew your dick was gone be this whack . . .*

"Let me see if you can work that pussy good as you dance."

Bitch, you fuck good as you rap. No wonder this motherfucka was a one-hit-wonder . . . and when it came to sex? Shit, I was still waiting on him to get *that* right.

True, I fucked Dyme's big-dick ass for six years, and then Rick stretched the pussy out a little more but damn, I knew my walls was straight. Wasn't no bottomless pit in this pussy. Fuck the dumb shit.

I just wanted this whack shit over.

His hands came up to rub my titties. I closed my eyes and tried my best to imagine being anywhere else with anybody else.

Maybe somewhere in the islands butt-naked on the beach with Has.

I bet Has got a big ole dick. Big old deep-stroking, thick dick. Uhmmmm. I shoulda went for that nigga when I had the chance.

"Damn, baby, this dick got your pussy getting wetter," Make$ said, finally tossing his hat from his head.

Nigga please. Just wanting this pure bullshit to be over, I leaned down low and rode him hard. My clit stroked the base of his thin dick and I actually felt a nut building. Suddenly things got a little more interesting.

"Lick my nipples," I whispered into his ear, my eyes closed while I pretended it was Has's tall black sexy ass beneath me and not this thin motherfucka who made me feel like all my thighs and ass was gonna squash him.

I leaned up just enough to grab the headboard, my titties swinging down as he licked and sucked at my nipples. Locking my legs underneath his, I worked my hips back and forth, not really giving a damn if it felt good for him. My mind was on Has. Rick. Shit, Dyme. Anybody but this whack bastard.

"Uhmmm," I moaned in the back of my throat when his hands came up to squeeze my hips.

It been months since I fucked something. Long-ass months since Rick worked me the fuck over. Over a year since Dyme fucked the shit out of me.

I pictured all three in the bed with me. Dyme working my pussy from the back. Rick laying under me while I rode his dick. And Has sucking and massaging my nipples.

The juices from my pussy drizzled. My clit swoll up. I felt that feeling from my toes on up that I was 'bout to get mine.

"Yes," I moaned, damn near snatching the headboard off while I let my head fall back as I circled my hips, easing my pussy up and down his dick.

Make$ hollered out, his fingers digging in my ass while he went stiff as hell just as my nut exploded deep inside me. I already felt his dick going slack but I kept shifting my hips pushing my clit against him as I screamed out myself.

"God damn."

I couldn't even look at the nigga as I rolled off his dick onto my side of the bed. I took just a second for my heartbeat to slow down and to catch my breath before I rolled out of bed. I wasn't even trying to spend the night with this nigga.

“Hey, shawtie, where you going?” he asked, peeling the condom off his dick to drop over the side of the bed to the floor.

“To my room.” I didn’t even take time to wash and just pulled back on the skinny jeans and silk sweater I had on earlier. My cell phone rang and I scooped it out of my pocketbook.

“It’s Luscious,” I told him.

“I don’t give a fuck.”

I held up my hand and flipped the phone open. “Whaddup, Luscious?”

“I hate to call you so late but I been calling my so-called man’s phone and that motherfucka ain’t answering.”

Cutting my eyes over at Make$, I watched him walking to the bathroom in his hotel suite with the used condom in his hand. “After the show, I left him and his crew at the venue. Maybe he in his suite wasted. They was drinking and smoking like crazy.”

Lying my ass off, I slid on my heels and grabbed my pocketbook before I booked it out his suite. “Would you go check his room for me? I don’t know why he ain’t let me go with him.”

’Cause he fucking like crazy. I didn’t say it out loud; my mind was busy on getting to my own room to wash my sex-funky ass and sleep off that nut before our flight back to Newark in the morning. It was time to throw up a deuce to Miami.

“Yo, Goldie, go check and see if he in his room . . . motherfuckin’ alone.”

I stepped on the elevator and looked down at my phone like “bitch, yo ass is crazy.” “Luscious, I’m in my bed. Just keep trying his phone.”

"I tried the other girls but they at some club."

Definite eye roll on this bitch tying up my line at two in the damn morning. Clubbing, plenty alcohol and sex meant bed for me, not fucking I Spy with some jealous girlfriend. "If I see him before we fly out I'll tell him you was looking for him. A'ight, then. Night."

Click.

I flipped the motherfucka closed on her. Luscious had every right to be watching Make$ like a hawk. These groupie bitches was throwing that nigga pussy left and right.

Blame it on the alcohol, but I just gave his ass a shot of this good pussy. Nigga wasn't shit. I wasn't either. But these days I was all about getting me. Fuck it. I didn't owe Luscious a motherfuckin' thing. I was still keeping her secret about her ass still stripping—and that's because that bitch was a moneymaker for me. So fuck it. If I had to keep my mouth shut to keep her ass on the pole, then my shit was zipped.

I stepped off the elevator and made my way to my own suite. I was trying not to trip off my first one-night stand, because Make$ wasn't getting no more of this here. Make$'s team only paid for one suite for me and the two girls, but fuck that, I paid for my own room. I wasn't sharing a motherfuckin' thing. Plus, they didn't need to be in my damn business. I was the boss.

In my room, I douched and took a super-hot shower that really made me want to climb between the sheets and sleep. But first I had to check on my business. My shit didn't come second to sleep. Money was to be made.

It took just about an hour to check my e-mails, book my dancers, and make a note to fire Hunni and Nanni for not showing to a bachelor party. Them bitches was outta here. Nobody was gonna make my shit look bad.

And I meant nobody and nothing.

I was excited about going on tour with Make$ for the rest of the summer, doing more shows and making more money. If this kept up, I'd be able to save up and buy my house cash. Fuck with me. I had plans to make, decisions to make . . . but that would have to wait for tomorrow.

I was just climbing into my bed when there was a knock at my door. Rolling out of bed naked, I grabbed my silk robe, tying it around my waist while I crossed plush carpeting to the door. Thinking it was Mink and Coko got they room across the hall mixed up with mine, I opened the door.

Make$ was standing there in nothing but his jeans and his jewelry. I eyed this nigga, thinking I fucked up. Fucked up big-time. Never mix business with pleasure. I didn't with Has's sexy ass. I tried it with Rick and I had to choose my heart or my hustle. Now this little nigga was hooked on my juicy, and that could fuck with Luscious working for me and me working for him on tour.

My ass was slipping.

He brushed past me into the room. I looked over my shoulder while his skinny ass dropped his pants, stepping out of them before he climbed into my bed butt-naked, his chains rattling against one another as he moved.

"Come sit on my face and let me eat that pussy, girl."

Licking my lips, letting out this sigh that was mad heavy with the problems I caused, I did the only thing I thought I could do. Closing the door, I dropped my robe and walked to my bed with his eyes all on me. Like he was sprung and couldn't get enough of me.

I closed my eyes and climbed on the bed, straddling his head with my thighs as his tongue split my pussy lips open and gave the first stroke to my clit. Seconds later his tongue flickered against it before he sucked it into his mouth.

It felt like my whole body tingled as I grabbed the headboard and arched my hips against his mouth with a moan.

Oh, I fucked up big-time . . . but at *least* this nigga knew how to eat pussy.

13

We don't buy no drinks at the bar
We pop champagne cuz we got that dough
Let me hear you say aah (aah, aah, aah, aah).

—Trey Songz, "Say Aah"

It was time to get rid of Dyme's influence in my life once and for all. I was working on building my credit and buying a house. First I'm selling the Lex and getting my ass into something I bought with my own dough. So doable. Watch me work.

My December birthday had come and gone, but I was 'bout to buy myself a sweet-ass gift and throw myself one helluva party. Fuck it. I worked hard. It was time to play even harder.

"I can't believe you're getting rid of your Lexus," Missy said, checking her hair and makeup in the mirror on the visor.

"Too many memories. I shoulda been got rid of it," I told her, steering with one hand. "Selling it might help my ex get it that's it over."

Missy glanced over at me. "That nigga still calling you?"

I shrugged, pulling the Lex to a stop at a red light on Route 22. "Ever so often, he'll call me or send me a gift or some shit. I didn't think I would ever really be over that fool . . . but I am."

And that's one hundred. I am so over Dyme to the point I wonder what the fuck I ever saw in him to make me sit around for six years waiting on his ass. Dick was good. Money was great. Six fucking years, though? Plus, he was a grown-ass man who shouldn't have found shit interesting in a teenage girl. Mama Bit was so right, but I was too hot in the ass and grown and greedy to listen. Fucking perv. Fuck him.

"You know, people talk shit about dancing but for a lot of chicks it's a way to get out some bad shit," Missy said, looking out the passenger window.

"For me it's a way to get into a bad Benz." I blew the horn twice on *that.*

Missy shook her head. "Not just that, Goldie. Shit like getting away from having your ass kicked for breathing too loud."

I side-eyed her. "Your boyfriend?" I asked her.

She shook her head. "My father."

Damn.

"I got my own apartment now, a little piece of car to get me from point A to point B, and I'm thinking about taking some classes at Essex County College."

"That's good, Missy."

"I ain't gone strip forever, but fuck that, it got me from a fucked place and gone help me get to an even better one, you know?"

I ain't say shit. I never really thought about other people's story. The bullshit that got them to the point they are now. The reasons why these chicks was on that pole. All I did was help get they ass up on it.

Sometimes taking on other people's shit could leave you all fucked up, like negative energy or some shit. I had enough drama in my own life.

I had to let Coko and Ming go. Them bitches was harder into drugs than I knew, and some of the other girls came back and told me them bitches was wilding out. Pouring candle wax on each other and some of the clients, whips and shit. I don't mind freaky, but that shit was on some other level . . . especially when the clients didn't ask for it and was shocked as a motherfucka by it.

That meant replacing them at Make$'s shows. I chose Missy and TipDrillz. That meant training them in time for the show in Atlanta next week.

Luscious was still expecting me to spy on Make$ . . . but her ass was lost in the sauce. I was 'bout sick of that nigga wanting to fuck soon as me and him got alone. His ass was sprung and I ain't want nothing but his tongue and his connections to the industry.

I made a right off Route 22 onto the car lot. I slid on my shades. The summer sun was beaming like crazy. I walked the Mercedez Benz lot with Missy looking for something to catch my eye. Not looking to drop eighty grand, I headed for the certified used vehicles on the side of the building.

"Good morning. Can I help you with something?"

I looked over my shoulder at the tall white dude standing behind me in a pin-striped suit. "I was looking at this used SLK500," I told him, circling the silver monster and thinking I'd look great behind it.

"This car retails for thirty-two thousand," he said, sounding all high up on his horse.

I eyed this motherfucka for a minute before I circled the car again. "What's your name, Mr. Car Salesman?"

"Victor Lathan."

I eyed him again. "Well, Mr. Victor Lathan, who really should be in a better mood when he's trying to sell a car. Tell me about the car."

"Let's go inside and fill out a credit application."

Oh yes, this motherfucka was pissing me off. I was young, black, and he assumed I was broke or my credit was jacked. I really hated people sometimes.

"I'll tell you what, Victor Lathan, why don't you kiss my black ass with your JCPenney suit on."

His whole neck got red and I knew I was right. Humph, Dyme and Rick? Them niggas wore nothing but the best, and I could spot bullshit one-hundred-dollar suits a mile away.

"Missy, I'll be right back," I hollered over my shoulder where she was circling this red convertible Benz. I gripped my Louis Vuitton tote tighter and strolled past this fool like he wasn't nothing but the wind.

I stepped in the building and looked around the showroom. Several salesmen stood up from their desks like vultures smelling death. Arching my threaded eyebrow, I cleared my throat. "Who wants to sell me a Benz . . . for cash?" I asked, loud as hell, my voice echoing to the roof.

The feet hitting the showroom floors as the salesmen dashed toward me was like horses during a race. I had to step back from they ass.

"What's your name?" I asked the first one to reach me. A tall, good-looking white dude who looked like he just graduated college.

"Hunt. Hunt Deitrich, ma'am," he said, holding out his hand to me.

"Let's go talk business, Hunt," I said over my shoulder as I walked to the desk I saw him sitting at.

Thirty minutes later, I strolled out with my new salesman, Hunt, walking beside me. "Missy, let's roll," I hollered over to her, climbing into my new Benz now sitting right outside the showroom waiting on me.

"Enjoy your car, Miss Dennis."

Missy climbed in, touching shit and "ooh aah-ing" like crazy. Truth? I was ready to rub this baby down like a new lover myself. "Thanks, Hunt."

I squealed off but came to a stop at Victor Lathan stepping out from between a row of cars with an elderly white couple. I lowered my driver's-side window. "Hunt thanks you for being such as asshole, Victor Lathan. Never judge a book by its cover."

Leaving Victor standing there with his mouth dropped open in shock, I left him, my Lex as a trade-in, and twelve grand behind as me and Missy sped up 22 in my Benz.

Life was sweet as hell.

Club 973 was packed to capacity. I knew they ass ain't had a set this big in years, but everybody was here to celebrate with me. I made sure mine was the hottest party going down that weekend. Club flyers. Ads on the radio. Word of mouth. It seemed like all of Newark and half of New York was trying to get into Club 973. Cars was lined up and down the street damn near four or five blocks back. The line at the door wrapped around the corner. Drinks flowed—especially the signature "Goldie" the bartender made up for me. The dance floor was packed. The music was thumping. Most of my dancers was performing topless on tabletops with sequined masks on. Then, to top it off, I had a party bus filled with VIP clients and four of my best dancers driving in from New York and then taking them straight to the VIP section upstairs.

I knew how to throw a fucking party. Holla at me.

I worked the floor making sure to meet and greet as many people as I could. I felt like a star. A lot of folks wanted to meet the chick crazy enough to run a strip club out her apartment and smart enough to grow that bitch into a business.

Was I rich? Hood rich, maybe, but I wasn't crazy enough to think I was ready to lunch with millionaires or even them six-figure-a-year folks. One day, though.

Even if I ain't had a million bucks I looked like a million bucks. Me and Missy scooped up one of my new dancers, TipDrillz, and we spent the day at all my beauty spots. I told all my girls I wanted them shining like diamonds tonight, and I made sure I did the same. My golden highlights were toned down and my hair was rod set and curled to perfection. Heavy, smoky eye makeup and mink lashes made my eyes pop, and a neutral lip emphasized my high cheekbones. There wasn't a hair anywhere on my body, and I felt silky smooth all over. The bustier I wore pushed my babies up high and made my waist smaller, making my hips, thighs, and ass look even bigger and better in the short-short ruffled ballerina skirt I wore with sequined booties.

"Congratulations, Goldie."

I was bending over at a booth talking to six of the girls dancing for me when I felt somebody bend over my back and whisper in my ear. I thought Make$'s ass was getting bold, coming at me in Newark. He was still fucking with Luscious, and we usually kept our shit popping on our road trips. Him and Luscious was in here somewhere. They just got back from they weekend trip to Antigua or some shit. Thank God, 'cause I was sick of him begging me for more of my pussy.

Turning, my heart damn near burst open at the sight of Has standing there. Everything on me thumped. My pulses. My heartbeat. My clit.

I threw my arms around his neck and hugged that nigga close while I closed my eye and took a deep inhale of his scent. The dreads was gone and he had just a low fade, but even that made this nigga just finer. Damn. "You out," I whispered to him, feeling like the music, the crowd, the noise all disappeared while I got lost in this nigga.

"Last week. My attorney got me off."

His words vibrated against my ear and his breath felt like everything sexy against my skin.

"Damn, I shoulda fucked you when I had the chance," I whispered, and it felt like a weight was lifted off my shoulders. The truth was the light and in that moment my ass was scared as hell of the dark.

Has stepped back from me and looked down at me under the dim lights of the club. The look on his face was surprised . . . and some other shit I couldn't name. This nigga wasn't feeling me no more? Did he have a girl—somebody that took time to visit, put money on his books, and take his collect calls? Did them months in jail bring out the homo in his ass? What the fuck?

"Let me holler at you real quick."

Humph. I thought so. I grabbed his hand, loving the feel of it in mine, as I led him through the crowd to the restrooms in the back. I knocked on the ladies' room door, waited, and then pulled Has in behind me. I did a quick check of the stalls before I locked the door and then I jumped right dead on this nigga. My fingers grabbed the back of his head as I pressed my mouth to his and grinded my body up against him.

The first feel of his tongue against mine and his hands easing from my back to my ass and I felt that same vibe. The time ain't did shit to wear it down. Nothing at all. My whole body felt so alive like nothing I ever felt before. I can't explain, but just being in this nigga's arms made me feel alive for the first time in a long-ass time.

"Fuck me, Has. I need you. Please fuck me," I whispered into his mouth, not giving a fuck how desperate I sounded. Not caring how much I exposed of myself and my feelings to him.

But instead of grabbing me up and sliding every inch of his dick in me, Has pulled my arms from around his neck and stepped back from me with that same surprised look on his fine face.

"What, Has? Whassup?" I asked, my heart still beating, my body still tingling, my head more confused than ever.

"Yo, Goldie, I really like you. I don't want to fuck you in no nasty-ass bathroom . . . and I thought the Goldie you was wouldn't get down like that either." Has wiped his mouth with his hand and looked down at me with them tiger eyes.

Embarrassed, I turned away from him and stood in front of the sink pretending that I was cleaning up my smudged lip gloss in my reflection over the mirror.

"Yo, I heard you stripping now and you some big pussy peddler on the East Coast. I'm like damn this all went down while I was locked up?!" Has walked over to stand behind me. His hands rested on my bare shoulders and his touch was hot, giving me goose bumps and making my nipples ache.

"I ain't peddling no pussy." I sounded all childish, pouting and defensive and shit.

He touched my chin and forced my head up to look in the mirror. "From what I hear, wild as the shows be, selling pussy ain't too far off, Goldie."

I looked at our reflection and on some real shit, me and this nigga looked good together. Like we'd have pretty babies. Like we'd be good together.

"So you judging me?" I asked him.

Has shook his head, his eyes on me in the mirror. "Never that . . . but every so often it's a'ight to check yourself in the mirror and see if you happy where you at in your life."

My gold eyes flashed. "So you the ghetto Dr. Phil now?" I snapped, moving away from him. "Fresh off your jail bid for selling counterfeit. Man, don't be a hypocrite."

"Man, whatever, Goldie. Do you a'ight."

I felt him come up behind me, and even though he was pissing me off, judging me and my grind, deep in my gut I hoped this nigga was about to hold me. He pushed something into my hand and I looked down at a wad of hundred-dollar bills before I turned and looked up at him.

"That's the money I owe you," he said, before turning to leave me with nothing but the scent of his cologne and the memory of that kiss. This nigga was walking out on me?

I hated like a motherfucka that I teared up. I hated that I gave a fuck what this nigga thought. Pissed off, I tossed the money wad at his back. "Keep this chump change. You probably need it more than I do," I snapped like a trife bitch as the hundred-dollar bills floated in the air before landing on the floor between us.

Has unlocked the door before he looked over his broad shoulder at me. Shoulders strong enough to have my back so I wasn't out in this motherfucka alone. He looked down at the money and then up at me with that fucking look, before he shook his head and walked out the bathroom.

Damn. I turned and swung and my fist landed against the mirror. The oversized onyx costume ring I wore cracked it but it still wasn't enough. I fought and scrounged like a bitch to make my life better. I was on my way to becoming a hood legend and just like that Has made me feel like I ain't had shit to be proud of? Just like that?

"What the fuck?" I swore, my voice filled with my rage and echoing against the bathroom walls.

The hinges on the bathroom door sounded off. I turned around, my chest still heaving, still thinking it was Has coming back to fucking validate me. Make$ stepped in the bathroom, closing and locking the door behind him as he looked down at the money on the floor.

"I saw you all up on that nigga. Then you gone bring him in here right in front of me. You selling that nigga my pussy?" Make$ asked me, shoving his tattooed hands in the front pocket of his jeans.

Has didn't want no stripper, huh? This nigga right here couldn't get enough of me.

I worked my thong bikini down my smooth shiny legs and hopped up on the counter in between sinks, pressing my back to the mirror as I opened my thick legs wide. "Come sniff and see if that nigga fucked."

I barely got the words out my mouth and that nigga was bending down to stick his thin face close to my pussy. "Fresh ain't it? Eat it," I ordered his ass, using my black-polished fingertips to open my lips and expose my fat wet clit to him.

Make$ squatted down between my legs, grabbing my knees before he licked from my asshole up to my clit to flicker the tip of his tongue against it. My hips lifted up off the wet counter as I bit my bottom lip.

Make$ moaned in the back of his throat before he sucked my whole pussy into his mouth. I grabbed the back of his head and worked my hips in small circles, pushing my clit against his tongue.

I didn't give a fuck we was in a bathroom in some club.

I didn't give a fuck Luscious was somewhere out there.

I didn't even give a fuck that some aggravating bitch needed to pee and was knocking on the locked door.

I just wanted Make$ to MakeMeCum.

I wanted to forget the memory of Has walking out that door.

"Oooh, I'm 'bout to cum," I moaned, biting my lip and reaching in my bustier to tease my own hard nipples while he sucked my clit harder and harder until I cried out as my nut shot into his mouth and the walls of my pussy spasmed.

"WHATTHEFUCK?"

I opened my eyes just in time to see Luscious pushing past the club manager to rush at me and Make$.

"Oh, shit," Make$ swore, jumping to his feet with his dick hard as jail time and pressing against his jeans, and his mouth and chin wet from my juices.

"You nasty, no-good bitch!" Luscious screamed.

With my pussy still tingling, I hopped to my feet just as that bitch reached past Make$'s short ass to swing. Her fist landed against my chin, knocking my head back. I refused to fall and squared up to straight beat this bitch ass. Wasn't no bitch gone hit me . . . and in my face? Fuck the dumb shit. It's on. "And you's a nasty *lying*-ass bitch," I screamed back, swinging out, not giving a fuck if Make$ caught some blows in the process.

WHAP. BAD-DHAP. POW.

That bitch caught a slap, a left-right combo, and an uppercut. Make$ grabbed her and pushed her away from me, looking all dazed and fucking amazed with a drizzle of blood coming from her bottom lip.

There was a crowd gathering outside the bathroom.

"You ain't shit, Goldie, I fucking trusted your ass. You knew I loved that nigga. You knew that shit and you steady fucking him behind my back. That's dirty. You dirty."

The two big bouncers from the door broke through the crowd. "This my party. I want her ass out of here."

The bouncers eyed the manager. "And the young lady threw the first punch."

Luscious was standing there posted up like she wasn't going nowhere. "This between me, the trick, and my no-good man. We got this. We don't need y'all."

"Come on, Luscious. Go on with that shit, man," Make$ said, looking bored as he called somebody on his BlackBerry.

One of the bouncers picked her up by her waist.

"Fuck you, Goldie. Fuck both y'all scandalous-ass trife-life bitches," she screamed over his shoulder. "The unjust don't prosper, bitch."

The club manager left behind them, being sure to close the door.

I was ready for the bullshit to end and my party to begin again. I couldn't stand embarrassing bullshit like this. "You leaving?" I asked him, turning to pick my thong up from the floor.

"Hell naw. I'll be in VIP." He reached over to rub my ass

and slap it just as his bodyguards squeezed in next and surrounded him to push him through the crowd and out of the drama.

That left me alone. I rinsed off with paper towels and hand soap before I pulled my thong back on. I felt like I was in a daze with all the shit that just went down.

I checked my appearance, making sure I was back just as fly as I was at the start of the night. I straightened my back and brushed the imaginary bullshit off my shoulder. I knew I was wrong for fucking Make$ behind Luscious's back. Hell, she could still have him and the title of being his girl. I wanted none of it.

I was about my grind, and nobody or no one was gonna fuck my shit up.

I meant that.

14

Everywhere that I be feel VIP baby
And everybody's cool but y'all just ain't me.
—Fabulous, "Everything, Everyday, Everywhere"

"Goldie, when you opening up the spot again?"

I was walking out my apartment, pulling my Ellen Tracy red crocodile carry-on behind me. One of my ex-regulars, a building maintenance worker, was leaning against a push broom in his dark green uniform. I couldn't remember his name but I recognized him right away. That nigga never missed one of my weekend strip shows in the crib.

I smiled at him even though I was nervous as hell I was running late and might make us all miss our flight to Atlanta. "Not for a while," I finally answered him. "I'm trying to save up to open my own club or something."

He nodded. "That's good, because somebody been complaining to my bosses about you."

I ain't surprised. "Thanks for letting me know," I told him, turning to head down the hall. The heels of my gray boots beat the tiles loud as hell while my carry-on rolled quiet as hell behind me. I looked over my shoulder. "You coming when it open, right?"

"No doubt. No doubt."

I just laughed as I pulled the door to the hot stairwell open. My steps echoed. Before I left the building, I had to wrap my silk wrap dress closer around my body. I left my Benz at a private parking facility 'cause there was no way in hell I was leaving my shit sitting like a duck for a whole week 'round this place. The devil is a liar.

Soon I'd be parking that pretty bitch in my own parking lot outside my house.

Watch me work.

The black Lincoln Town Car pulled up as soon as I stepped outside. Missy and TipDrillz was in the rear and waving at me as the tall white red-haired driver climbed out the car to take my suitcase from me to sit in the trunk.

"Ready, ladies?" I asked them, checking my vibrating cell phone. I rolled my eyes and deleted the animated text of some white chick riding *the* biggest dick backward. One of my dancers loved sending them things. A woman with a horse dick. Childhood cartoons getting it on. More freaky sex positions. Just dumb shit that was hit or miss on being funny—to me, anyway.

"It's gonna be nice to get a little mini vacation in Atlanta," Missy said, looking out the window as our driver sped us through the busted daytime streets of Newark. We were flying into Atlanta. Make$ and the rest of his crew were driving in on his pimped-out tour bus.

"That's what I'm talking about too . . . plus some shopping," I added, flipping my cell phone closed before I dropped it into the Gucci tote sitting between my feet.

TipDrillz ran her long neon green acrylic nails through the deep waves of her auburn weave. "I never been in a plane before. You, Goldie?"

I side-eyed her. TipDrillz was young, just nineteen, but she was really pretty in that innocent kind of way that men liked. In just the few weeks since she walked into my apartment looking to dance for me and I posted her professional photo shots on the Goldie's Girls website, she was booking events left and right. She had the look and the moves and no inhibitions.

She reminded me a lot of myself.

I picked her out of my girls to perform because of her look, and the way she wasn't afraid to stare a nigga in his eyes while she picked up a beer bottle with nothing but her pussy walls. Plus, TipDrillz was on point with her makeup skills, and I was glad to hand that shit over to her. She was way better than me, and I was a confident enough chick to give credit where credit was due.

"I been on planes whenever me and my ex went out of town," I told her, settling down in the leather seat with my head on the rest as I closed my eyes.

They must have known I wasn't in the mood to talk, because her and Missy started chitchatting about this and that, everything and nothing. I tried my best to tune they ass out. My mind was filled up with Has. I ain't seen him since the night of my party. Almost three weeks ago. There wasn't a night I didn't think of him. I lost count of how many times I woke up in a sweat, shivering like a fiend, my sheets moist because he was all up in my steamy, freaky, wet dream.

It's funny how I missed that nigga now more than when he was locked up. Way more than when he was locked up.

In another dream we was fucking like crazy on the rooftop of some hotel and suddenly Gunz's ghost popped up in the bed between us. I screamed like crazy while the spirit of crazy motherfuckas past told Has that it was my fault he was dead. That shit woke me right the fuck up and cooled any heat I felt between my thighs.

I didn't feel guilt over Gunz's death because in that moment—to me—it was him or me going to meet our Maker. But Has and Gunz was friends and I wondered what he would think if he knew what all went down the night Gunz's van crashed into that pole.

"I ran away from home when I was like twelve or thirteen," TipDrillz was saying, her foot shaking so damn hard that she was making my legs move. "Lived with boyfriends or friends from school and in a couple of group homes."

"Why you run away?" Missy asked as the driver steered us onto the New Jersey Turnpike.

"Got tired of my older brother fucking me all the time," TipDrillz said, all simple and plain like it was nothing that she was molested by her brother . . . when we all knew it was everything fucked up in the world.

I opened my eyes and looked over at her. She flipped open her cell phone and started texting with her thumbs.

Missy was leaning forward looking right at me with a look that said, "Told you we all got *some* kind of story."

I closed my eyes and turned my head to the window, pretending like I ain't heard shit, but knowing I wouldn't ever forget it. I just couldn't shoulder nobody else's drama. My own load was heavy enough.

"How we do, Goldie?" TipDrillz asked as we made our way down the long crowded hall of the Coliseum behind Make$ and his usual entourage to our dressing rooms.

"It was real good. We have some things we got to tighten up, but y'all did good."

Fellas was whistling and eyeing us in the sequined thong bikinis we wore. My eyes was on Make$ up ahead of our group and talking to Frederick King, an interviewer for one of those TV entertainment shows, whose cameraman walked backwards in front of them. My eyes were locked on them as we all moved.

"You're going into the studio to start working on your sophomore release," Frederick asked. "What can we expect?"

Make$ nodded, looking at the interviewer through his signature shades as his hands played with the diamond and platinum chains around his neck. "Just the same type of bangers from my first project, you know. I enjoy touring and doing shows and letting the people see me live, but I really am ready to do what I do best, and that's create good music."

One day those lights gone be on me.

I couldn't sing or rap so I didn't know what the fuck I was gone do to get them lights on me, but I knew I wanted to be the kind of person that was in the spotlight and not part of the crew walking behind the person in the spotlight.

All eyes on *me.* Fuck the dumb shit.

"Goldie, I need to holla at you," Make$ said before he walked through the door his bodyguard held open for him. I eased through the crowd to follow him into the dressing room.

"You did good out there," I told him, kicking off the stilettos I wore as he popped a bottle of champagne and poured a glass to hand to me.

He unscrewed the diamond-encrusted replica of the world

hanging off one of his chains. I sipped my champagne, wishing it was Nuvo or a mixed drink. Champagne wasn't really my thang. When Make$ lowered his head and sniffed the back of his hand, I can't lie and say I was shocked like a motherfucka. Make$ got high. I wondered if it was cocaine or dope or crushed OxyContin. I took another sip to keep from frowning.

He sniffed and pinched his nose before he turned and offered the world to me. I just shook my head. "My mama got caught up with it, didn't know how to just have fun, you know. She loved it . . . loved it more than me. So I don't fuck with it."

He just shrugged his thin tattooed shoulders and screwed the world back together. "I don't love it," was all that he said.

What the fuck ever. I didn't even fuck with weed too hard no more. I was all about staying focused on my grind. Drugs was a no-no. There was no way I could pass all them cracked-out, doped-out people just surviving and not living and choose to fuck with that shit. Big nothing.

"I wanted to show you what ya girl been up to," Make$ said, his chains hitting against each other as he picked up his iPhone and tossed it on my lap where I sat on the end of the black leather sofa.

I sat my plastic champagne flute down and picked it up. The web page was already opened to MediaTakeOut.com. My mouth fell the fuck open. "Platinum-Selling Hip-Hop Artist Caught in Club Bathroom with One of His Strippers/Dancers!" I scrolled down while my heart was beating like crazy. There was a picture of me, sweaty, golden highlighted head soaked to my face as I squatted in front of Make$ with the mic in his hand with all my ass on display in the thong I wore. Another picture of us in some VIP at some party. Another one of me straddling his hips while he sat in a chair onstage. And then a picture of Luscious looking sad and brokenhearted.

"And I was thinkin' 'bout taking that begging bitch back too," he said, taking a liter bottle of Cîroc to the head.

Truth? I was scrolling back through the pictures peeping out how I looked in each one. "Dumb bitch," I said, meaning it, but not because Luscious's cornball ass was looking for vindication on a tabloid site. She was a dumb bitch, period, who deserved to be on the sidelines watching and worrying about me. Luscious was all over Newark talking shit 'bout me. Now this. Just dumb as hell. DUMB. AS. HELL.

In fact, she helped me. If her and Make$ got back together, she mighta pressured him to get rid of me; now her stupidity for some shine put a kibosh on her ass.

"She ain't to be trusted, that's for sure. A move like this makes me think of sudden pregnancies and child support for eighteen years." Yeah, I was putting the nail in the bitch's coffin. Fuck her.

I still didn't snitch on the bitch stripping behind his back because I didn't want him looking at me sideways for keeping her secret from him.

"I'm going to get changed," I said, the leather sticking to my bare ass as I got up to my bare feet. I bent over to grab my stilettos, my hair swinging down to cover my face.

"We might need to chill out for a little bit," he said.

I flipped my hair back as I stood up to watch him. "You firing us?" I asked, eyeing him as he snatched off the black beater he performed in.

"Hell no. Just uhm . . . you know . . . the little thing we had going on."

Thank God. "So the rumors 'bout you and the new singer

chick, what's her name, Chaunci, it's true, right?" I asked him, looking over my shoulder at him with my hand on the door. I had to pretend to give a fuck and not jump for joy 'cause his whack-ass dick was no longer a part of my life. Shit, I felt like going to church and catching the Holy Spirit in that piece. "She getting all on you 'bout this, ain't she?" I handed him the iPhone back.

Make$ laughed. "You don't miss shit, do you?"

"Not much." I walked out the door and the wall of black broke in half when his two bodyguards separated to let me out.

A few of Make$'s entourage was outside the door to our small-ass dressing room. They snickered and giggled when I pressed through them to reach the door. "What the fuck is so funny? Why y'all acting like a bunch of damn kids?" I snapped, fighting the urge to straight knock one of them motherfuckas out.

I opened the door. TipDrillz was squatting in front of Tank, one of Make$'s entourage. His jeans was down around his ashy knees and she was humming loud as hell while she sucked his dick. The sounds of her slobber echoed in the little-ass room.

"Suck that motherfucka," Tank said, reaching down to grab a fistful of her hair and thrust his ashy-ass hips forward.

"She a fuckin' pro, yo. Fucking Supahead Part II and shit," one of them clowns said from behind me.

I turned and pushed the chest of the one right behind me hard as hell, sending all they ass toppling back like bowling pins before I slammed the door closed.

TipDrillz still ain't stop sucking him like a fuckin' Hoover vacuum. Pissed, I walked over and mushed the side of that bitch's head hard as hell. She fell over off her heels.

"Ow!!" Tank hollered out, grabbing his freed dick. "She bit me."

I eyed his short, fat dick and just shook my damn head. The round tip was barely peeking out of his fist. Damn shame. *No wonder she went to town, ain't like she had to deep-throat that mess.*

I threw up a deuce and opened the door wide for that nigga and his short dick to bounce. "'Bye Tank," TipDrillz called out to him from behind me.

"Shut the fuck up," I snapped on that dumb bitch, eyeing her while she wiped some of the spit and God knows what else from her mouth and chin.

"What's wrong, Goldie?" she asked, looking innocent as ever.

Tank pulled up his pants and finally strolled his big ass to the door, looking at me like he wished he had big enough balls to slap me. I just saw firsthand that he sure 'nough didn't.

I slammed the door as soon as the big bitch crossed the threshold. "Where in between you meeting Tank today and now did you decide to suck his dick?" I asked her, hating that I was just four years older than this cracky bitch but she made me feel like her mama or some shit.

"He cute, Goldie."

That's all the bitch said in that same simple and plain way as she told us that her brother used to fuck her. *This bitch ain't bright worth a fuck.*

"Look, I brought you out here to perform on the stage, not give out tricks to second-string fools offstage. You pull some hooker-type shit like this again and your ass is outta here. You feel me?"

TipDrills gave me a thumbs-up and a big old smile.

The door to the adjoining bathroom opened and Missy stepped out in a towel. She eyed me and TipDrillz. My face was still tight as hell with anger. "What I miss?" she asked.

I straight ignored that bitch.

Boom-boom-boom-boom.

I peeled back my lavender-scented silk sleep mask and opened just one eye, still trying to figure out what was fucking with my sleep . . . and my dreams of that house in South Orange, shopping sprees, Caribbean vacations, and freaky sex with Has. All good things. Damn good things. Shit.

Boom-boom-boom-boom.

The door. Someone was at the door. I threw the covers back and pushed my mask up atop my scarf-covered head, yawning as I sat up. I grabbed my black silk robe, throwing it on while I stumbled my half-awake ass to the door.

Boom-boom-boom-boom.

Closing my robe with one hand, I put the chain lock on the door and opened it to peek out. Missy was standing there . . . with blood smeared on her oversized T-shirt. She looked up and her eyes locked with mine. "Come quick, it's Tip," she said, turning to head back across the hall to their room.

I slammed the door and snatched off the chain lock with trembling hands. My mind was racing, like "What the fuck happened?" as I zipped across the room and pushed through the open door of their room. The three of us went out to eat after we left the Coliseum and then we all went to our rooms. I saw them walk in their room.

TipDrillz was laying on her bed, clutching one of the pillows to her so tight. Her bottom lip was busted and bleeding, already swelling and turning colors and shit. Her eyes was staring off into the distance and I couldn't help but wonder what she was seeing.

"What the fuck happened?" I asked them, my voice cold and hard.

"I woke up about a hour ago and her bed was empty. I felt like she was grown and I went back to sleep. She came back like this just now."

I moved over to the bed and squatted down beside it. "Tip—"

It felt so dumb and childish to call her TipDrillz in that moment but I honestly couldn't remember her real name. They were too many stage names to keep up with to remember all the real names too.

"What happened?" I asked her, shaking her a little bit.

Her eyes shifted to me and that shit almost made me jump out my skin. "Tank . . . Tank—"

"What did he do?"

"I told him you said I couldn't do that to him no more and . . . and . . . he made me. With a gun to my head . . . he made me . . . in front of all those boys . . . he . . . he . . . made me do it."

Damn, that nigga wanted his dick sucked that bad? Fucking oversized-body, undersized-dick self. Ugh.

"I'll be right back." I hopped to my feet and walked fast as hell out the room, my robe flying open and up in the air behind me like a fucking cape or some shit. I wasn't a superhero but I was a super-mad Negro.

Boom-boom-boom.

My knock on Make$'s room door sounded like I had a battering ram, but that wasn't shit but my fist and anger.

Boom-boom-boom.

The door to his junior suite finally opened. He was still awake and dressed in his jeans. The silver haze of weed smoke flew out the room above his head. I always thought he looked different without his "costume" of that fitted shirt, his diamond jewelry, and those shades. Sometimes I felt like I didn't even know who this nigga was without all that bullshit on.

I closed my robe when he eyed my nakedness. "Tank's crazy ass put a gun to one of my dancers' heads to suck his short-ass dick."

Fuck it. I was getting straight to the point. No time for the niceties and shit.

He grabbed my arm and yanked me inside his suite. I turned in the lit foyer to watch this nigga look up and down the hall before he closed the door behind me.

"Yo, you need to check your boys. It ain't even nowhere near that serious to get blown, dude."

"This bullshit could fuck up my tour," Make$ said, all low in his throat like he was talking to himself. Like I wasn't even standing there in front of him.

"What?" I asked him, my face scrunched up in confusion.

He looked over at me and rubbed his head with his tattooed hand. "Was it the same one in the dressing room with Tank earlier?"

A vision of TipDrillz squatting in front of that nigga flashed. I knew what the fuck he was getting at and it was fucked up. "There's a difference between wanting to suck a dick and some fool making you suck it with a gun to your head."

"This went down in her room?"

"No, she left the room. I . . . I . . . didn't ask her where."

"So he kidnapped her out her room?" Make$ eyed me,

and beneath the ceiling light of the foyer, I felt like I was in an interrogation room with the police.

I crossed my arms over my chest and rolled my eyes. "No."

"Did he rape her?"

This nigga was straight trippin'. "Make$—"

"Did he?"

"No, but—"

"Did he?" he asked again, his voice all hard.

"No . . . she didn't mention nothing about no rape."

Make$ shook his head and shrugged before he smiled. "So take away the gun and you got the same fuckin' scenario that went down in that dressing room."

True, but a gun to her head was major. Real major.

"Look, we both need this drama to go away, a'ight. Tank probably got a little too freaky for her and I'll tell him to chill on that shit." Make$ reached out and stroked my chin. "And you tell your girl to stop sucking dicks like they lollipops and going to niggas' room late night."

Truth? TipDrillz played a dangerous game and I thought I told her ass to chill with groupie shit. Still, that nigga straight violated with a gun to her head. One thing I knew for sure, that was some crazy shit going down.

Make$ walked past me into the darkness of the suite. Behind me a door opened. A few minutes later it closed. I just stood there waiting, not knowing what in the hell I was waiting on. I didn't know what reaction I expected that nigga to have, but this laid-back blasé-blasé bullshit was nothing I woulda ever guessed.

Make$ stepped back in front of me in the circle of light shining down from the ceiling. He stretched his tattooed hand out with a thick stack of hundred-dollar bills in the center of his thin palm. "This here ten thousand dollars, Goldie. Go back to her room, calm her ass down, and make sure the police ain't got shit to do with it. Send her home, put her ass back on the pole, and get me a new bitch out here to dance and not cause no trouble . . . for *us*."

All of a sudden that ceiling light felt like a spotlight down on us, showing everything wrong with this moment . . . this conversation . . . this dirty deal.

My eyes shifted to the stack.

I had money of my own, but the emphasis that nigga put on "for us" let me know that I could walk out here and do what I please but my days of dancing for him was over. One, because he would fire me and second, because the bad press would hurt his bookings.

I wasn't no dumb bitch. I got the picture clear as hell.

Or I could take the money, talk to TipDrillz, and make this shit go away. Back to business as usual. Grind on.

I licked my lips again and reached out my hand to take the money. My eyes looked up and locked with his. It's funny as hell that I could see my reflection in his eyes . . . just like a mirror.

"Every so often it's a'ight to check yourself in the mirror and see if you happy where you at in your life."

Has's words came to me and sent a chill down my spine. I let out his shaky breath while my hand closed around the money and I moved to the door.

"Don't let me down, Goldie. Don't let *us* down."

He hit the switch to turn off the light and for the few seconds before I got myself together and headed back to Missy and TipDrillz's room I was glad for the darkness.

15

We bang, bang, bang, bang, bang, bang
I said we load it, cock it, aim and shoot.
—Raheem DeVaughn ft. Ludacris, "Bulletproof"

I used to believe in C.R.E.A.M. I used to consider that one of my anthems. Now I ain't so sure that cash rules everything around me. Cash can buy you all those material things that I wasn't ashamed to admit I loved. There was nothing better than the feel of designer gear on my back and my feet or swinging on my arm.

But after that shit went down with Kerri (aka TipDrillz) last week, my ass found out that money can't buy away a guilty conscience. The shit that really kept fucking with me was the memory of Kerri saying, "Got tired of my older brother fucking me all the time."

Damn. I couldn't get that shit out my head for nothing in this world. Nothing.

Not when I walked back to that room.

Not when I explained to TipDrillz how her actions earlier made Tank look innocent.

Not when I lied and said that nigga apologized and wanted to pay her five thousand dollars for his disrespect.

And especially not when Missy looked at me like I was in bed with the devil and not to be trusted worth a motherfucka.

I let TipDrillz go and Missy quit. I called two more chicks to replace them. Later that morning I put TipDrillz and Missy on a plane back home to Newark and picked up Destiny and Dyamond—the twenty-five-year-old twins who done seen and done it all. I could only hope TipDrillz took my advice and went to school to get her license to do people's makeup. And Missy? The choice was hers to leave, so I didn't wish her well or bad. I didn't wish her anything.

"Got tired of my older brother fucking me all the time."

Truth? That girl done been through enough in her life, but what was I supposed to do? Lose my business. Chance my own livelihood? Then I'd be around somewhere numb as hell, sucking dicks at random, selling ass or back at Dino's serving up tables?

Nothing.

I focused my eyes out the window of my hotel room looking out at Philadelphia at night. Me and the twins got in a few hours ago. We would perform tonight, head to Atlantic City in the morning, and then some birthday party in Connecticut this weekend.

Make$ was finally headed into the studio to record, and after that he wasn't booked for any shows for the next month or so.

My ass was glad for the break.

I was gassing up my Benz and heading to some town called Cottageville in South Carolina to see Yummy. Fuck cruising to the Caribbean to lay on the beach. I was going to spend time with my best friend and check out some down-south living for a hot minute.

Knock-knock.

"*Gol*-die."

I looked over my shoulder at the door to my room. The sound of them twins calling my name like that—in unison—through the door irked my nerves. Humph, I was regretting working with they ass. They picked up the routine real quick, but these birds stayed sucking Blow Pops and popping they gum. They was putting my *last* nerve on overtime duty.

In the fluffy slippers I put on as soon as I got to my room, I crossed the floor and opened my door. No one stood there. I stepped out, fighting the urge to get pissed. The hall was empty. I stepped back, making a mental note to check them bitches that I *never* was the one to play with. I wasn't never in the mood.

"No, Tank, stop playing."

"Yeah, Fiyah, quit."

Even though I heard the twins laughing, I headed out my room and down the hall in the direction of their voices. I was not in the mood for a repeat of that shit that went down with TipDrillz . . . Kerri . . . whateva.

I turned the corner and saw Tank and Fiyah carrying the twins into Make$'s suite at the end of the hall. I strutted down the hall and banged on the door like the police looking for fugitives.

The door opened and I looked Fiyah dead in the eye. The nigga wasn't but five feet tall but he was built like his ass lived in the gym pumping weights. His eyes were red and glassy. "Look who came to join the party," Fiyah said, stepping back to open the door wide. "Get your fine yella ass in here. We got plenty money."

Music was playing and the sounds of the twins' hyena kind

of laughing came out into the hall. I could smell weed thick as hell. All of this shit was a motherfuckin' recipe for disaster. I stepped in the room past him. *What the fuck?*

Cocaine was on top of the desk. Bottles of liquor was everywhere. Dyamond and Destiny was dancing butt-naked on a pile of money scattered on the floor. Tank was sitting on the sofa videotaping the twins, with the camera so close up on them like he never been nowhere near pussy before.

All these chicks was gone make me old before my time. "Can I holla at Make$ real quick?" I asked, my eyes going to the bedroom of the suite.

"He ain't here. He's with his new bitch."

I turned to eye Fiyah and caught a wad of singles flung at me.

"Dance, bitch!" he said, and then laughed loud as hell and started dancing close on me.

You can always remember the moment—the exact moment—when you made a vic-ass move. Always. This was mine.

"Dyamond and Destiny, we gotta go practice. Make$ wanna add some new shit to the show." I was lying my ass off but I just wanted the easiest damn way to get the fuck outta that suite.

Fiyah slapped my ass hard as hell. It stung but I ain't say shit. Nada. "You too good to fuckin' party?" he asked, bending over to snort a line of 'caine from the table.

Dyamond and Destiny bent down to start scooping up the money.

Tank leaned back against the sofa and eyed me. "How TipDrillz doing?" he asked, the smile at his mouth looking more like the sneer of a dog about to attack.

My first instinct was tell this short-dick motherfucka how much of a loser he was, but I would feel much better coming at him like that with my gun or Taser—neither of which woulda made it through airport security.

Instead I ain't say shit.

Dyamond and Destiny grabbed their clothes from the floor and made it toward the door. "'Bye Tank. 'Bye Fiyah," they said in unison.

These bitches had no clue the shit they almost got into. No clue at all.

I turned and followed them out the door.

"I asked you how TipDrillz doing. Now *that* bitch suck a mean dick."

Fiyah stepped in front of me and licked the cocaine from his finger. "My boy talking to you."

My eyes met his and straight the fuck up, I thought, *I ain't see shit but crazy in them motherfuckas.*

"They say you teach all them bitches of yours everything, so you suck dick good as TipDrillz? Huh? You taught that bitch how to suck dick like that?'

Click.

I closed my eyes at the feel of the cold metal barrel pressed to the back of my head.

"Make$ not gone go for this," I said, keeping my voice soft.

They laughed at me.

"Bitch, please. Make$ said the dancers was up for grabs . . . including you. He done with your ass," Tank said, nudging my head with the gun.

Fiyah reached and yanked the black silk shirt I was wearing apart. The buttons flew and hit the walls and objects in the room. "We love his leftovers."

I slapped his hand away when he squeezed my titties.

WHAP.

My head swung to the left and my cheek stung from that nigga backhanding me. I grabbed my cheek. My eyes flashed. I knew if I had my gun I woulda blew his dick off and handed it to him.

"Ow!" I cried out when Tank grabbed a fistful of my hair so hard that I felt sharp pains in my scalp. Tears filled my eyes but I refused to let them fall.

He pushed me down to my knees by my hair, jerking my head around like I was a doll or some shit. Hate for that nigga burned in my guts.

Fiyah rubbed his hands over my face. "Now it's time to party."

My face tingled. I knew that nigga put coke on me.

He bent down and licked my face.

Tank jerked my head back. I opened my eyes just in time to see him hold his short dick with his fist and tap the tip against my mouth.

I gagged from the scent of that nigga's nuts hitting against the side of my face. I squeezed my mouth shut as he tried to press his dick through my lips. The devil is a liar.

"With a gun to my head . . . he made me . . . in front of all those boys . . . he . . . he . . . made me do it."

I couldn't stop the tears. I couldn't override my fears. I felt so fucking helpless. So fucking afraid. So out of control.

I felt the gun pressed to my face.

"Suck my dick."

The gun dug deeper into my cheek.

"Fuck it. Suck mine too."

My back went weak at the feel and smell of another damn dick on my mouth.

I watched enough *First 48* and *Crime 360* to be afraid these niggas would kill me to keep me from reporting they ass for the shit they doing to me. I was scared as hell and could feel my fear damn near choking me worse than their dicks. I honestly didn't know if they gave a fuck about living or dying . . . for me or themselves.

That scared the shit out of me.

Sometimes things happen to you in life and you feel like you'd rather be dead. My whole body was sore as I lay on that floor and tried to forget the hell these niggas put me through. At some point them niggas had slapped or punched every part of me from my head to my toes.

I didn't know how long they assaulted me.

I didn't know why the twins didn't come back to check on me.

I didn't know why Make$ never came back to his suite.

All I knew was I needed to get out of there. I needed to run for my life.

I opened my eyes and spotted them niggas sitting at the table.

"I don't know why he gave up all that good pussy. I damn near bust off soon as I put my dick in."

I winced at the memory of them taking turns on me.

"He said he was done with that bitch. They wasn't serious anyway."

The skirt I had on was up around my waist. The lower half of my body felt numb. Between my legs I was sticky.

"With a gun to my head . . . he made me . . . in front of all those boys . . . he . . . he . . . made me do it."

I closed my eyes and swallowed. The pain in my throat made me shiver and I felt like I would throw up.

We all got stories to tell.

So now, if I made it out alive, this would be my story. Would I feel numb and disconnected like TipDrillz? "They raped me," I would say, all simple, like it was nothing when it was everything.

"What we gone do with that bitch?" one of them said.

"Nothing. Make$'ll take care of it. Tricks like her love money," the other one said.

"Send her home, put her ass back on the pole, and get me a new bitch out here to dance and not cause no trouble . . . for us."

"I'm gonna piss."

I opened my eyes enough to see Fiyah's cocky ass walking toward me to the bathroom.

"Hey, ho," he said, his voice slurred so thick from all the coke he snorted. He laughed and kicked me on my thigh as he passed me.

Everything on my body ached. I fought like hell not to cry out in pain. Let them think I was unconscious.

"Get like me . . . I'm who you wanna be . . . get like me . . ."

Tank took his cell phone from his hip. "Whaddup, dawg," he said, rising to his feet. Blood was smeared across the zipper of his jeans.

I knew it was *my* blood.

"Naw. He ain't answering 'cause he with his new piece of pussy."

I watched that nigga close. He raised his shirt to scratch his wide-ass back. I didn't see the gun on him.

That nigga turned his back to walk over to the window

laughing at something like a big dumb-ass gorilla. I took a deep breath and sat up. I spotted the gun sitting on the table.

"Man, that powder make my dick hard," Fiyah said from behind me.

Now or never.

I got up, ignoring the pain, and jumped. I came down on the table.

"Yo, Tank, watch out."

I cried out when one of them punched me in the back of my head but I rolled over and aimed the gun I grabbed into my hands.

CLICK.

Them niggas' eyes got big as hell and they both jumped back from me. I aimed the gun from one heart to the other, forcing my hand to stay steady. Not giving a fuck if I shot both they ass.

"Yo, Goldie, you better know what you doing," Tank said.

"I know what you motherfuckas did to me." My voice was cold, but the hate I felt for these niggas burned like fire.

I eased off the table, kicking the chair out my way as I stood on my feet before them. I ached. My body and my soul was tired and in pain. I wanted to crawl under a bed and sleep . . . but fuck the dumb shit. Payback was a no-good bitch. I reached out and knocked the cell from Tank's hand. It dropped to the floor with a thud.

Fiyah lunged toward me. I held my ground, turning and pointing the gun at him but ready to swing that bitch back in Tank's face if he even *thought* about making a move.

"Take another step and I will burn your ass, motherfucka. Fuckin' try me and see."

I had to do what I was gone do. I didn't know when somebody else was gone walk through that door. “Strip, motherfuckas,” I told them, my bottom lip feeling like it was swelling by the second until it weighed my mouth down.

“Goldie, you gone regret this shit—”

“STRIP!” I yelled, my face hurting in a thousand different places.

I kept the gun and my eyes on them niggas while they peeled they clothes. I snatched up Tank’s T-shirt and tore it into strips using my teeth and one of my hands. When I realized my skirt was still up around my waist, I pulled it down. “Get on your knees.”

My heart was racing. I was scared and excited all at once. Mostly I was glad to be alive.

And I was gonna make these niggas wish they was dead.

“See, niggas like you think it’s funny to grab a gun and make women do shit they wouldn’t do unless they had a gun to they head.” I stepped forward to first backhand Tank across the cheek with it.

“Ow!” he fell back to the floor, his jaw twisted at an odd angle.

I hoped I broke that bitch. Fuck him.

Then I brought the gun down on the back of Fiyah’s head. Blood gushed as he cried.

“Shut the fuck up!” I yelled.

I threw some of the strips of shirt at Fiyah. “Tie that nigga’s wrists,” I ordered him, trying to ignore the flashes of every bit of their violation of me. Hands. Fists. Dicks. All on me. Inside me.

I watched that short, muscular motherfucka tie Tank’s hands behind his back. “Tighter.”

He looked up at me.

WHAP!

I slapped the shit out of him with my free hand and my eyes dared him to complain. He just tightened the straps until they cut into Tank's wrists. I ain't give a fuck it they lost circulation, dried up, and fell the fuck off.

Just like he ain't care about raping me.

These niggas was mad, but they was scared, and I loved that shit. I put the gun to Fiyah's head, standing behind him so he couldn't rush me.

CLICK.

"Now, you short son of a dumb bitch. Suck *his* dick."

Both of them looked up at me. "What?"

I pressed the gun deeper into his cheek. "Do it!"

"Fuck you."

I came around to kick that stocky and cocky motherfucka in his side with all the energy I could muster. I didn't give a fuck that pain shot from my between my thighs on down.

He hollered out and I just elbowed him in the forehead, knocking his head back hard as hell and hoping I cracked his neck.

I walked around them and grabbed a handful of the coke, dashing it on Tank's dick and thighs. "You like licking coke so much. Suck it off his dick."

I pointed the gun so that it was aimed directly between his eyes. Dyme taking me to the shooting range was paying off. "Do it or I will make your head explode like a watermelon and then call the police myself. After the shit you two did to me. It's justifiable homicide, bitches!"

POW!

I fired a round into the sofa. The stuffing flew out. "NOW!"

Both them bitches was crying like babies as Fiyah lowered his head and took Tank's dick in his mouth. The sight of it made me sick, but I thought of what they put me through and laughed hysterically even as tears streamed out my eyes. The sound of Fiyah slurping on Tank's dick was awful, but fuck them.

"Put your hands around his back, bitch," I told him, wiping away my tears with the back of my hand.

Tank was crying like a baby, his big shoulders shaking while Fiyah sucked away with tears and slobber dribbling down Tank's ashy thighs.

I stooped down and tied Fiyah's hands behind Tank's waist, setting the gun down just long enough to make sure the knot was tight. Next I took the long ends of the cord and wrapped it around to tie at the back of Fiyah's neck. That locked that motherfucka's head to Tank's groin.

Fuck them. I picked up the gun as I backed away from them. My hand shook so bad from wanting to put a bullet through each of they hearts.

"Y'all punk bitches ain't worth the jail time."

I turned and rushed into the bedroom, snatching a pillowcase from a pillow. I spotted some of Make$'s jewelry laid out on the dresser and I politely rushed over to drop all of it into the pillowcase. *Done with me? No, bitch, I'm done with you.*

I rushed back into the living room of the suite, ignoring them motherfuckas as I scooped all the cash from the table into *my* pillowcase. I backed away to the door with the gun steady on them. Trust and believe I would shoot if one got loose and rushed at me. "Be glad I'm letting you motherfuckas live," I told them, almost to the door.

I spotted the video camera. I remembered the light of the camera beaming down into my eyes while one of them pushed his dick down my throat, gagging me. Them bastards recorded the shit they did to me? I rushed forward to snatch that bitch up too.

I stepped on something and looked down to spot Tank's cell phone open on the floor. My eyes cut over to them and back to the phone. My body was aching everywhere, but it still couldn't fuck with how fucked up I was emotionally. I couldn't believe the shit these niggas just put me through. "Let's see how the fuck y'all feel," I said, easing my aching body down to snatch up his phone. I found the button to turn on the camera and aimed it straight dead at the duck-asses. "Say cheese, bitches."

SNAP!

Tank's eyes got big as hell. "Goldie, stop play—"

"SHUTDAFUCKUP!" I screamed, raising the gun at them. "Trust and believe, that little picture is going to everybody in your contacts, you short-dick bitch."

I turned and walked to the door. Everything on me ached.

I knew everything that went down in this suite had changed me forever. I wasn't gone ever be the same.

I left the suite, running down the hall for my life.

Bzzzzzz.

Sitting behind the wheel of the rental car, I looked down at my cell phone vibrating on my lap. The caller ID said Make$. It wasn't his first call in the last hour.

I hit Ignore.

I pushed my oversized shades up on my face, hoping to hide my bruises. I zipped up the black tracksuit I wore, hoping to not feel so exposed. I clutched the gun sitting on the middle console, hoping to feel safe.

None of that shit worked.

All of my clothes and shit was still at the hotel. I took just enough time to change, grab my purse, tell Dyamond and Destiny to pack ASAP and get to another hotel to wait for me, and then hopped my bruised and battered ass in a taxi to the nearest car-rental place.

Bzzzzzz.

I looked down at the phone. Something flashed on the screen:

NEW VOICEMAIL MESSAGE.

I hit Listen.

"Yo, Goldie, that's fucked up you stole my jewelry and shit when I put you on, yo. I mean that's cruddy, dirty-bird shit. I didn't know you got down like that."

I rolled my eyes. This nigga think he slick leaving a message putting shit on me. I eyed the plastic bag holding my bloody clothes and the video camera. *Humph, well I got proof to put the shit back on them.*

"Call me back, yo. I really want my shit. . . . I can even offer a reward or something for everything *ya heard me?"*

I flipped my phone closed.

Humph. Slick bitch just offered me money to bring him the evidence. Playing innocent like he don't know his boys raped me. Like he ain't find they ass strapped together in his suite. Negro, puh-leeze.

"Well, what's the price for your boys' freedom, bitch?" I asked aloud, flipping the phone back open to call that nigga. As the phone rang, I shifted my eyes up to look through the windshield at the local police station. The navigation system in the car had led me right to it.

"So you a bad bitch, Goldie, huh?"

"No, I'm a raped bitch. You know about it."

The line went quiet. I wondered if them two bastards,

Tank and Fiyah, was there with him. Was they kicked back smoking blunts, snortin' powder, and reminiscing on the turns they took on me?

My gut clenched. I closed my eyes tight like I was a child trying not to see the boogey monster late at night.

"Look, Goldie, I want my shit—including my video camera."

I looked out at the police station as a tear raced down my cheek. "I want my life back. Them niggas took a lot from me. *Your* niggas took a lot from me."

"The way you left them tied up? Look like you got some payback to me."

"They lucky I didn't I make 'em fuck each other," I spat.

"Look, Ma, I don't need no details. I saw enough."

"Just like Kerri."

"Who?"

No, he didn't know her real name. Probably been forgot her stage name. He gave her the choice to take the money or fight for her rights by pressing charges. She chose the money. He paid for her to disappear . . . and I helped him.

"Look, Goldie, hundred grand, a'ight."

"A lot of money to keep my mouth shut, right? Just like TipDrillz?"

That bitch got quiet. Maybe he did remember her. I wasn't gone ever forget her.

"Whaddup, Goldie?"

Hundred grand was a lot of money and a big chunk toward buying my house or getting a club open . . . or whatever business I put my grind to.

Do I take the money, or walk into that police station and use the power I hold in my hand to demand my respect?

And so the choice was mine . . . like it was hers.

Karma's a bitch.

Epilogue

It's the key to life.
Money, power, and respect.
Whatchu' need in life."
—The Lox ft. Lil' Kim, "Money, Power & Respect"

One Year Later

> Today in entertainment news, platinum recording artist Terrence Gardner, better known as Make$, was spotted leaving the Fulton County Courthouse in Atlanta in the case against him for aiding and abetting and also trying to bribe the unidentified victim of a sexual assault by two members of his entourage who have already been found guilty of the assault and are awaiting sentencing. It is rumored that Gardner will accept a plea deal from the district attorney's office, but a minimum jail time of one year is expected. . . .

Click.

I never got tired of knowing that those bastards were paying for what they did to me. Never.

And I didn't regret my decision to turn down the money

Make$ offered and turn the tape and the gun over to the police. It wasn't easy but it was worth it, because *I* was worth it.

Plus, well, I kept the money and jewelry I stole from them, and it came in real handy when I took a step back and decided it was time for some *upgrades* in my life.

No more Goldie's Girls strip shows.

No more King Court.

Tacking an eviction notice on my door and putting my shit on the curb was the best thing the Housing Authority ever did for me. They booted my ass out for running the strip club in my apartment. Fuck it. Fuck them. I had outgrew that motherfucka a long time ago anyway. It had been past time for me to spread my mink wings and fly.

I swiveled in the chair in behind my oversized glass desk. Through the floor-to-ceiling windows of my upper Manhattan apartment, the New York landscape was laid out before me. Life was *damn* good.

Humph, I had a brand-new hustle . . . but the same old grind.

Acknowledgments

After eleven years of having my books published, I feel like I'm thanking the same people over and over, but then that feels right because many of these people never stop helping me get through each and every book. So even though it sounds like a rewind, a remix, or version 11.0, I would like to give much thanks to:

It was a simple conversation with my moms that put the idea for this book into my head. She's my angel in heaven now, but I will never forget how much she has done to help me get published. She believed in my dreams, and I know she is so proud of me now.

Tony, you are my heart and my backbone. I could not do all this without you. Lots and lots of love.

Caleb, I love you, big brother. Thanks for understanding when I am deep in a deadline and not able to call like I should. Kiss Kal-El and Hajah for me.

My cousin, Felecia A., I prayed so much that you were out there and well and I thank God to know that my prayers were answered. I love you, big cuz.

Rest in peace: my father, Ernest Bryant; Bertha "Granny" Bryant; Clarence & Sally Johnson; Marion Bryant; Lil Marion; and Cheryl Johnson.

Thanks to my agent, Claudia Menza, for keeping me straight in the publishing biz. I appreciate you always.

Big thanks to Sulay Hernandez, Stacy Lasner, Justin Mitchell, and the rest of the Simon & Schuster/Touchstone team. Thank you for always being on point with what you do and for being fully behind this series. I appreciate y'all.

Thank you to the continued support of the African American BookClubs, especially Tasha Martin and the SistahFriend Book Club out of Columbia, SC, and the AAMBC (African Americans on the Move Book Club).

Thank you, thank you, thank you to Carol Taylor and the Black Expressions Book Club team and members for all the support you gave the Hoodwives series and *Message from a Mistress.* Last year you celebrated ten years, and here's to ten more.

Lastly, but most importantly, the readers. I cannot thank you enough for helping this ghetto girl from Newark, NJ, realize her big dreams.

To those I forgot, please know you are in my heart.

Best,

Meesha Mink

About the Author

Meesha Mink is the coauthor of the popular and bestselling Hoodwives series (*Desperate Hoodwives, Shameless Hoodwives*, and *The Hood Life*). *On the Grind* is her first solo work of fiction—but not her last. Mink is also the acclaimed and bestselling author of both romance fiction and commercial mainstream fiction as Niobia Bryant. She writes full-time and lives in both New Jersey and South Carolina. She is busy at work on book two in the Real Wifeys series.

CONNECT WITH MEESHA

Websites:	www.meeshamink.com, www.niobiabryant.com
E-mails:	meeshamink@yahoo.com, niobia_bryant@yahoo.com
Twitter:	InfiniteInk
MySpace:	meeshamink, niobiawrites
Facebook:	InfiniteInk (Meesha Mink & Niobia Bryant)
Shelfari:	Unlimited_Ink (Meesha Mink & Niobia Bryant)

For more on the bestselling Hoodwives series, please visit: www.hoodwives.com